NOTHING SPECIAL

Geoff Herbach

sourcebooks
fire

Copyright © 2012 by Geoff Herbach

Cover and internal design © 2012 by Sourcebooks, Inc.

Cover design by William Riley/Sourcebooks

Cover images © Steve Weinrebe/Getty Images, © Phartisan/Dreamstime.com, © Willeecole/Dreamstime.com, © Yuri Arcurs/Dreamstime.com, © Steven Cukrov/Dreamstime.com, © Olga Semicheva/Dreamstime.com

Published by Sourcebooks Fire, an imprint of Sourcebooks, Inc.

P.O. Box 4410, Naperville, Illinois 60567-4410

(630) 961-3900

Fax: (630) 961-2168

teenfire.sourcebooks.com

Library of Congress Cataloging-in-Publication data is on file with the publisher.

Printed and bound in the United States of America.

BG 10 9 8 7 6 5 4 3 2 1

Praise for *Stupid Fast*

ALA Best Fiction for Young Adults Selection
YALSA Best Fiction for Young Adults
2011 Cybils Award Winner, Young Adult Fiction
Junior Library Guild Selection
ABA Best Books

"Whip-smart and painfully self-aware, *Stupid Fast* is a funny and agonizing glimpse into the teenage brain."

—*Minneapolis Star Tribune*

"Funny and compelling."

—*Bulletin of the Center for Children's Books*

"Wonderfully funny and touching…it made me laugh out loud, many, many times. Don't be a poop stinker. Read it."

—Christina Mandelski, author of *The Sweetest Thing*

"*Stupid Fast* is Stupid Good. Felton Reinstein is one of my favorite male protagonists of the year."

—*The Happy Nappy Bookseller*

"This is one of the best books I've read this year…even if you're not a fan of boy books or sports books or books with numbers on the cover…*Whatever*. Give this one a try. If you don't like it, I'll eat my shoe."

"Felton's manic, repetitive voice and naïve, trusting personality stand out in a field of dude lit populated with posturing tough guys and cynical know-it-alls."

—*Kirkus*

"I was blown away by the multilayered, quirky characters. The observations told from Felton's eyes are so hilarious and heartbreaking. Great, great voice!"

—Julie Cross, author of *Tempest*

"If you want to read something fantastically funny, pick up *Stupid Fast*. If you want to read something honest and refreshing, pick up *Stupid Fast*. I can't recommend this debut novel enough."

—*YA Love*

"In this struggling and often clueless teen, Herbach has created an endearing character coming to terms with his past and present in a small, well-defined Wisconsin town."

—*Booklist*

"A rare mix of raw honesty and hilarity. *Stupid Fast* is Stupid Good!"
—Peter Bognanni, author of *The House of Tomorrow*

"You know when you read a book in like two days because it's so good? It kind of feels like speed reading, but really you're devouring the story every second that you can. That's what I did with *Stupid Fast*…Please read this book. It is really good."

—*Desirous of Everything*

"A real and raw protagonist with great humor."

—*The Book Pixie*

"This story isn't just about high school and puberty and sports. It has a dark side…Geoff weaves drama, comedy, and tragedy together seamlessly. The story is heartrending, yet hilarious, evocative, yet poignant."

—Megan Bostic, author of *Never Eighteen*

"I read Geoff Herbach's YA novel *Stupid Fast*—er, pretty darn fast…it has a great character voice, Pete Hautman–esque storytelling, and a deft recognition of human complexity."

—*Daughter Number Three*

"It's a great book for guys who don't like to read…there's enough adrenaline in this book to keep a guy powering through to the end."

—*The Librarianista*

"I devoured this book in one complete sitting. The mixture of serious emotions, life changing discoveries, and all-out humor made *Stupid Fast* a book that I simply couldn't set down…Trust me, you need a copy."

—*Hopelessly Devoted Bibliophile*

"This is a masterfully written book that perfectly captures the vibrating energy some teenage boys have. You can *feel* the hormones coursing through Felton's veins and completely understand his need to run, run, run."

—*Ms. Yingling Reads*

What Readers Are Saying

"*Stupid Fast* is stupid awesome. I am amazed by the author. Seriously amazed. He got into the head of a teenaged boy and made it possible for me to imagine what it might be like to be stupid fast like Felton."

—Bridgid, 5 stars

"This book is funny and real and heartbreaking and hopeful, and more than that, unique and genuine. Trust me. *This* book."

—Gail, 5 stars

"*Stupid Fast* is honestly one of the top three books I have ever read. It seriously made me laugh out loud. I would get dirty looks from old ladies at Borders because I would constantly chuckle and start to annoy them. I also liked that it wasn't only funny. The serious emotions and the suspense of uncovering the mystery kept me turning the pages, even when I had more important things to do like homework."

—Adam, 5 stars

"I'm pretty sure that anyone who has ever been a teenager will have no problem identifying with Felton and loving every bit of this book as much as I did."

—Alissa, 5 stars

"Geoff Herbach's characters totally come alive on the page…I totally recommend this book to anyone who likes a great sports story with heart."

—Kerry, 5 stars

"Throughout the book, there were things I could laugh at because they were funny, things I could laugh at because I related to them, and things I probably shouldn't have laughed at, but did anyway because I'd been there myself. It's a *really* compelling novel and I've seriously recommended it to everyone I know."

—Random Theater Kid, 5 stars

"Full of heart and soul, this is one of the best realistic YA novels I've read in a long time."

—Diana, 5 stars

For Leo and Mira

August 20th, 1:33 a.m.
BLUFFTON, WI

Hey, Aleah, I just thought I'd drop this in, because it's sort of interesting to know what Andrew was thinking back in January, before he got messed up. From his blog at felton reistein.com:

Felton is Number 2!

"Reinstein is the rarest of athletes, a freak of nature with great size and speed combined with crazy-quick animal reflexes. That Reinstein has played just one season of organized football should strike fear in the hearts of coming opponents and has already caused seismic recruiting efforts among collegiate programs across the nation."—*Wisconsin State Journal*

You probably already know this, but Felton has been deemed the #2 sports story in the state of Wisconsin for the year (right behind the Green Bay Packers' mid-season resurgence—I had no idea they had gone downhill ever—I pay no attention to professional athletics).

We had six *State Journal* newspapers jammed in our door, and Felton had approximately ten million voice mail messages from people wanting to congratulate him.

Did Felton celebrate this coverage? Not at all. He went running for about ten minutes. Then he came back because he kept falling down in the snow. (Snow hasn't stopped him before, I promise you.) He watched TV for ten minutes and groaned about how he'd seen every *COPS* episode ever made. Then he went to bed. It's not even dinnertime yet.

Jerri is concerned for him. I suppose he is feeling pressure. Why, though? He likes playing football. He just has to do what he likes. That is easy.

Jerri is making him some hamburgers for dinner. She's a terrible cook. Maybe he'll sleep through it? I won't, unfortunately.

Happy New Year!

—Andrew

Air Travel

Monday, August 15th, 12:06 p.m.
DANE COUNTY REGIONAL AIRPORT

Hi, Aleah. Did you kick piano ass? I bet you did! You're coming home Friday?

I just tried calling your cell for the first time in a few months. Apparently it doesn't work in Germany? My call went to voice mail. I just left the greatest message of all time: "Uhhh. Hi?" *Pause. End call.*

Then I texted, *Sorry.* Then I figured you probably aren't getting texts if your phone doesn't work.

Then I thought about emailing you, but you don't respond to my emails. (At least you didn't last time I tried, plus I have to pay somehow to get Internet access in this airport.)

So…here I am! Hi!

I'm just writing on my computer. I want to say, *Sorry.*

Oh. People are lining up at my gate. I can't understand a dang word the lady at the desk is saying on her microphone. This is what she sounds like: *We're now going boinging those pigeonholes in the rows twenty-two gloves.* I guess she's saying I should get on the plane.

I didn't really write anything, did I?

Sorry. Things went wrong.

Oh, man. Flying.

August 15th, 12:45 p.m.

AIRPLANE TO CHICAGO

Holy Balzac. I'm a tremendous dork. When the plane took off, I totally whooped. Like, "Wooo-hoo! Yeah!" Everybody turned and looked at me.

Planes are very, very fast. Exciting.

Embarrassing.

I wish I could act like I look. I'm a big-looking man, Aleah—I know that from seeing pictures of me—but I feel like a dumb little kid a lot (and act like one). It was awesome taking off. Am I a dumb little kid?

No. I turned seventeen a couple weeks ago. Remember last year when you played piano for me, and your dad cooked me chocolate-chip pancakes for my birthday? That was before I became the best high-school football player in the state of Wisconsin. (I'm not trying to brag, just tell the truth.) That was right when I figured out I look and act like my dad (loaded situation, you know?). Big year.

Whoa. We're above the dang clouds. This is awesome. (At least I'll write it if I can't shout it without everyone giving me the crazy eyeball. Woo.)

Okay, so here's why I'm writing. It all went wrong.

Even though I was totally freaked this spring, worried about football recruiters and defeating my enemies, etc., I had no inkling that things had gone wrong until Gus got really mad at me on March 24. (The next week was our bad week, if you'll recall.)

Later—when we were talking again—Gus told me about Narcissus. He actually called me a narcissist, which is a medical term for somebody whose head is stuck in his own ass.

Ha-ha. Gus. Funny guy.

On March 24th, Gus called me about a hundred times. I didn't call him back, which makes me a donkey, apparently. I was in Madison at the State Indoor Track Meet. How could I call?

I could've called him later.

Gus left messages that I didn't hear until the bus ride home. *"Felton, I have to know today. Prom? Limo? Maddie will pay for a third. Aleah's coming up, right? Call me, you rank taco dip!"*

(You didn't come up for prom, did you?)

When I heard his message, I thought, *Jesus. Prom? It's only freaking March. Give me a break. I have bigger stuff to worry about.*

I had stuff to worry about, I guess.

Here's what you don't know because you stopped talking to me. There was a huge crowd at the track meet. All these college coaches from all over the country were there to see me race Roy Ngelale, that Nigerian kid I told you about who plays football too. (Game against us this coming Friday.) Roy "The Nigerian Nightmare" Ngelale. I actually didn't notice all the coaches at first, which is good for me because I don't run well when I'm thinking about scholarships and coaches and my future.

Both Roy and me breezed into the 60-meter final. And I felt

good. Loose. Powerful. Generally, nothing bothers me when I run (other than recruiters).

Right before the final, Roy and I shook hands. We were in Lanes 3 and 4. He sort of looked nervous. I hadn't seen the college coaches, so I wasn't.

When the starter started his business, supercharged nitroid kangaroo power inflated my body. *Take your marks…*exhale…*set…* drink rocket fuel…*BAM!*

I exploded and the red track blurred. I saw nothing but color, no other runner near me, just waves of red and the color of fans blending in the stands.

Whizzzz (the sound of me running…sort of sounds gross, huh?).

At the string I'd run the fastest high-school 60 in state history. I killed Roy Ngelale and the whole stadium went totally nuts. The loudspeaker dude blurted, "That's a new state record!" Karpinski and those guys fell all over, crashing over the railing high-fiving each other and screaming.

Aleah. I know you sort of know…but seriously. I am very fast. That's a given, I guess.

Unfortunately, after the race, all these college coaches waved at me, gave me thumbs up and crap, although they couldn't speak to me due to NCAA rules. I was all like, *uhhh*…because after that, I knew they were there.

Back in the stands, Cody said, "Dude, if there was any doubt before, there's none left. You're the top recruit in the state."

I nodded but thought, *Don't screw it up…don't screw it up…*

Listen, I have a serious problem performing in front of dudes who hold my future in their hands. They start my head monkey-talking. And, in the next race, the 200 final, they caused me to seriously run weird.

In the blocks, I was totally aware of the guy in the gold and blue standing at the railing. I thought: *Michigan*. He stood next to another guy in a red and white shirt, with a little tree on his boob. I thought: *Stanford*. I should've been thinking, *Explosion*. I should've been filling with Jamaican Kangaroo Juice. Instead, I felt weak pools of tar in my legs and my heart pumped funny.

When the gun popped, I struggled out of the blocks. My brain said, *Run fast. Jerri won't have to pay for college. This is your future!* My legs said, *We are made of elephant turds.* Because I was out front of Ngelale on the stagger, I still led the race for most of the way (me sort of odd-running, sort of stumbling down the track). He was not bumbling, though. He flat-out flew and he caught me on the final curve. (Indoor track curves are tight.) Then we were stride for stride down the straightaway (lots of crowd screaming) and right together when we crossed the line.

Because I ran funny (not my normal easy stride), something weird happened in the last few meters. It felt like a tiny man had a wrench cranked on one of the tendons in my hamstring. I actually slowed a little, I'm sure. And I was thinking, *Huh? What is that little pain?* Turns out short hamstrings are a genetic Reinstein disorder. I didn't know that then. I thought, *Huh???*

At the line, Ngelale threw his arms over his head and screamed like he was the king of the whole world, because he thought he got me. He turned back to me and hugged me, and I hugged him back and said good job, but I wasn't even worried about whether I'd won or not. I worried that I'd forgotten how to run. I worried that I had a little man in my hamstring, and I bent over and thought, *What in the hell is that?* and started massaging the little man, trying to get him to go away.

Unfortunately, just as I bent over, a photographer for the *State Journal* snapped a picture (me bent over, rubbing my leg in front of Roy Ngelale's groin…he standing above me screaming, his arms in the air).

The crazy thing is this: even with my terrible race, the electronic clocks had me beating Roy by like a hundredth of a second, which made him throw a pretty bad temper tantrum and threaten to kill me in our football game (coming this Friday!), which doesn't really scare me (not like football scholarships scare me).

Still, it was a terrible day.

What did I get for winning two indoor track titles? A hamstring strain, an intensifying complex about running in front of college coaches, and a vaguely pornographic news photo, which was distributed all over the state of Wisconsin in the newspaper the next day (and was used against me the following week).

And, I got this: while I was still at the meet, my hamstring man hurting, Gus called and called and called, and I didn't return his calls so his messages got bitchier.

"*What part of* call me now *don't you understand? Come on, Felton.* CHOP-CHOP!"

And then, I think, he started going super crazy, which seemed wrong at the time but, in retrospect, makes perfect sense.

After the team got home, I went over to Cody's house to eat some burgers and brats with everyone. (I did not enjoy this, as I'd stopped enjoying everything.) While we were all sitting outside Cody's on those white plastic lawn chairs (fifty-five degrees, warm for March) and shooting the crap, my phone kept buzzing and buzzing and buzzing and buzzing, which is crazy. Gus called every minute for like twenty minutes—until I turned off my phone.

"Who is blowing you up, man? Your mom?" Reese asked.

"Nobody," I said. I didn't worry about Gus at all.

Later that night, when I turned my phone on to call you, I had twenty-five new messages from Gus (all of them crazy—"You're a butt munch, man!" etc.). While I was calling you, he called again, which sort of freaked me out, you know?

And he called again while I was leaving you a message and again while I texted you to call me, which you didn't, which began to seriously freak me out, because why weren't you returning my texts or calls?

Turns out, while Gus was calling to curse me out, you were talking over Germany with Ronald, right? You couldn't call me because you were in "Serious Discussions about Your Future."

What happened to *our* future?

I know. We're just kids. Children…

Gus didn't stop calling until like eleven that night (when I turned off my phone again).

I woke up Sunday morning thinking about him, feeling bad about him. He's been my best friend my whole life. I called him to say sorry for not answering, sure he'd understand that I'd had a rough day.

He answered and said, "You are dead to me, Felton Reinstein."
Then he hung up.

I called back. He didn't answer.

I called again. Nothing.

For some reason, right then, I remembered this time, this sunny day, when Gus and I were both in diapers, running through a sprinkler, our dads laughing so hard because our diapers got so huge and loaded with water that we looked like we had elephant privates and butts. Squish, squish. I can still feel how heavy that diaper was on me.

"*You are dead to me, Felton Reinstein.*"

I did feel sort of bad, but remember my head was in my ass, so I forgot about it.

Holy crap. We're already going down. That's because Madison and Chicago are really close (in the air—doesn't feel so close in the car, does it?).

I have to find the gate for the Fort Myers flight at O'Hare when we land. O'Hare is supposedly the busiest airport on the planet. Nice. My ears hurt. Jerri told me to chew gum, but I forgot to get gum. My ears! Feels like my brain is trying to suck air through my dang ears.

• • •

You flew out of O'Hare on your way to Germany, I bet.

This is what I want to say: I was a really messed-up person when you broke the news that you were going to Germany for the summer. Narcissus, head in butt. Gus called me dead. Hamstring man. Weird newspaper picture. It got worse too.

Ow. Ears.

I'm not making any excuses, Aleah. Okay?

August 15th, 1:48 p.m.
O'HARE AIRPORT

Yes, O'Hare is pretty big. I had to walk like six freaking miles, dragging my *muy gordo* backpack too. (Like my Spanish? I learned that in school!) It has a Hickory Farms Sausage and Cheese Gift Platter inside it, which is extremely heavy.

A few minutes ago, I got lost and asked this bagel-selling lady for directions (she was all like, "What did you say?" and I was all like, "Uh, um, I'm looking for, uh, Terminal 2…uh…") and she sent me down this escalator and through a long tunnel with neon lights all over the place and I sort of thought she was jerking me around, but when I got to the end of the tunnel, I was at the right terminal. Then I found the concourse right away because the signs made sense.

Now I wish I would've bought a bagel from her because I'm hungry and the food smells are killing me softly with their delicious aromas and I had already established a speaking relationship with her, so it would have been easy to order a bagel. ("Uh…I would…uh…like one of those…uh…round things with the hole thing in the…uh…middle.")

I've got two hundred bucks in cash from Jerri. I'm rich! I could buy like twenty-two airport bagels!

There are long lines everywhere. There are a million people and they're all talking really loudly.

I hate talking to people.

Remember when you had to order for me when we biked to Country Kitchen that one time last summer because the waitress said I mumble?

Oh God, I'm hungry.

No. I will not eat this Hickory Farms Sausage and Cheese Gift Platter. It's a gift.

Oh God, three-hour "layover." Can I run sprints in the airport?

Back in Bluffton, my teammates are about to practice, for crap's sake. Cody and Karpinski were pissed when I told them I was leaving, but I'll be back for the game Friday. I need to be there so Roy Ngelale can kill me. Ha-ha.

Look at all of these people. Are they looking at me? Do they know I'm Felton Reinstein, Ass-Whupping Prep Football Player?

Jesus, I hope not. I have to stop thinking like that. It drives me crazy. Shh. I'm a little jumpy.

• • •

Okay, Aleah, when you called that Sunday, I was already down. My hamstring hurt. I'd just seen that porny Ngelale picture on like ten thousand laughing Facebook pages. Gus had already told me I was dead to him. You hadn't returned my calls the day before. *Things are coming apart…things are breaking…*

When your number popped up on my phone, I was relieved. I wanted to tell you about the meet. I wanted to tell you about my leg. I wanted to make stupid jokes that you'd laugh at.

Instead, you breathed really deep, then said you had some great news (but sounded all breathless and hesitant).

"I've been asked to join this incredible youth orchestra in Berlin, Germany."

I can hear your voice saying it, Aleah. I can hear you, still.

And for a second I felt proud and then I said, *When?*

And you said, *For the summer.*

And then I thought, *It's all coming apart.*

But I couldn't say anything, couldn't respond, because I was suddenly super mad because we'd been planning our summer in Bluffton the entire year, because exactly what I feared would happen was happening (everything breaks), and it felt like someone (you) had taken a sledgehammer high in the air and dropped it onto my gut.

I shouldn't have hung up on you. I shouldn't have thrown my phone across the room and into my clothes hamper. Did I worry about how you felt while you were texting and calling and I wasn't answering?

No. I worried about me because my head was in my own rear (and also my heart hurt).

Instead of talking to you, I called Karpinski and he picked me up and we went out to Walmart and got a sandwich—and that's where I saw the actual newspaper with a huge picture of me bent over in Ngelale's groinal area while he celebrated.

"Whoa-ho-ho!" Karpinski said, because Taylor Olson, who works at Walmart, held it up in the air.

"Oh crap, no!" I shouted.

"Tasty." Taylor nodded and smiled.

Taylor is a douche sack.

Then I got so mad at you, Aleah, for choosing Germany over me that I wanted to kick over the newspaper rack and punch Taylor, so Karpinski took me home.

I don't know why I blamed you. Probably my mental illness (narcissism).

The rest of Sunday was filled with more Facebook posts about that picture and someone posting on a blog a Photoshopped re-do of the piece-of-crap picture that made it look like I was really doing something porny to Ngelale.

It drove me into silence. That night I just lay in my bed, in the dark, with no phone, laptop, or TV on anywhere. I stared at the ceiling and thought, *It's breaking*...I couldn't speak to you and I couldn't speak to Andrew who kept knocking on my door to ask me if I was okay.

The reason I couldn't call you back the next day? Someone blew up that stupid picture (the real porny one) to poster size, with the headline "Squirrel Nuts Blows" at the top.

I should have known before I left home that something terrible was coming. After Jerri made us breakfast, Andrew said, "Hang in there today, Felton."

"Hang in where?" I asked, stuffing some burned scrambled eggs in my mouth.

"You know, with Aleah..."

"How do you know about Aleah?" I snapped at him.

"She called me because you won't talk to her."

"Great."

"And there's a lot of chatter on the Internet."

"Chatter?" I said. "About what? Aleah?"

"Uh...no. It'll be okay, though," he said, looking over his nerd glasses, acting all sad. "See you at the concert tonight, right?"

"Okay. Gotcha. Don't be such a freak, Andrew," I said. I had no idea what he was talking about.

He left the table without another word.

Because my hamstring man was stiff and I was upset about you, I rode my bike to school instead of getting a ride with Cody like I usually do. The ride was meant to calm me down and loosen my leg. Didn't work. And, when I got to school, I knew what Andrew was talking about. Someone had gotten there super early that Monday morning, and they'd plastered the blown-up porny picture all over the commons and up and down the halls. I'm serious. It was terrible, Aleah.

"Oh. Shit," I whispered, walking in.

Like a hundred of my stupid jackassed classmates sat in the commons, whispering, covering their mouths, totally laughing. Gus was one of them. He sat there giggling with freaking Maddie O'Neill, who he'd just started going out with.

I went over to them.

"Did you guys see who did this?" I asked.

Gus wouldn't look at me.

Maddie sort of sang, "Somebody doesn't like you."

"Somebody?" I asked. My face got hot. I got dizzy. I thought: I'm going home, which is what I would've done when I was a little squirrel-nut kid who everybody picked on. (*Run away! Run away!*)

Hmm. Actually, I ran away just this summer, last time I was in Florida.

My second response: I will figure out who made these freaking pictures. I will hunt them down. I will beat them into a red mist. (*Kill! Kill!*)

Maddie said, "It's okay that you're gay, Felton."

"Somebody is going to pay," I said, and walked away.

By second hour, the janitor had gone through and taken all the posters down, but I could still hear the laughing in the halls and in class, and my hands were trembling with rage (bombed a calc test). Then Reese and Karpinski both made stupid gay sex cracks when I got to chemistry. (*Kill! Kill!*) But, Karpinski also said, "Dude, let's go to Steve's and plan how you're gonna get your revenge, man."

"Okay," I said. "Yes."

"Freaking punk kids," Reese said.

"Punk kids?" I asked.

"Gus and those guys."

"Gus?"

"Of course, man," Karpinski said. "Who else would do that shit to you? Dude calls me a honky (Gus still calls townie kids that, Aleah) and crap. He's the only one of those dicks who isn't afraid of me."

"Gus?" I said again.

Gus. Gus…for a moment I wanted to wrap up in blankets and lie down in a corner somewhere. Gus.

After school, while I was heading into the locker room for track practice, I saw Gus and Maddie laughing in the commons. Maddie waved at me and said, "Hi, Felton!" really sarcastically and then my

19

guts just tightened up so much I thought I'd get sick and I sort of scuttled away. He and Maddie totally laughed behind me.

Gus. Poor guy.

I didn't stay after track practice to do extra running and stretching like I usually do. My hamstring hurt. Plus, during track practice I moved from wanting to wrap in a blanket to very big anger. It wasn't about the poster anymore. It was about Gus, who betrayed me! *You've betrayed me!* I hissed inside my monkey head.

I will throw you in the Mississippi and watch you float away.

After practice, I threw my bike in the back of Cody's pickup truck and went to Steve's Pizza with Karpinski, Cody, and Reese.

We ordered pizza at 6:25 or so. (Something important was happening at 6:30, of course. Andrew's concert. Crap.)

While we waited for the pizza to come, Karpinski went over options for getting revenge on Gus for putting up the porny pic, even though there was no confirmation that Gus had done it.

Karpinski suggested the following: slash Gus's car tires, beat Gus up in the bathroom, break Gus's car windows, kidnap Gus and throw him in a wet ditch, piss on Gus's locker, tie Gus to a tree, etc.

Reese nodded thoughtfully.

I stared at Karpinski's forehead, occasionally wincing (but still very, very angry at Gus and ready for some kind of action).

Cody, who is a better human being, shook his head, *no*.

The pizza came and we ate in silence for a while. Then Karpinski said, "Toilet paper, dudes. We'll cover his whole house."

Reese said, "Yeah. That way no one gets hurt, but we send a message not to screw with Felton."

I liked the idea. *Gus should know that I travel with a posse.* "That actually makes sense," I said.

Then I thought: *Gus's house? My best friend's house? The house where Aleah lived last summer when Gus was out of the country? The house my dad hung out in when he was alive? Trash it?* Then I pictured Gus's mom, Teresa, out there pulling wads of wet toilet paper out of her bushes, wondering why the world is such a terrible place.

"Wait, I don't know…" I said.

"Of course you don't," Cody said.

"I know," Karpinski said. "I completely know."

"No. It probably wasn't Gus. Felton and Gus have been buddies forever. Just relax." Cody shook his head.

"That's bullshit," Karpinski said, stuffing more pizza in his mouth. "He's the only one, man." Pizza popped out of his mouth.

"Isn't that Maddie chick one of Andrew's friends?" Reese asked. "Would she really be mean to Felton?"

It's true, Aleah, Maddie, Gus's girlfriend, and Andrew are friends.

"You are so dang wussy," Karpinski said, shaking his head at Reese, pizza bits firing onto the table.

Maddie was a percussionist in Andrew's middle-school orchestra last year, when she was in eighth grade. I pictured her whacking a kettledrum with her buzzed-up, bleached punk hair. I pictured Andrew whacking a drum next to Maddie, his hair flopping around. Then I remembered Andrew saying to me at breakfast, "See you at the concert tonight, right?"

Andrew had been practicing for months to do a piano solo at his spring concert.

"Holy shit. Andrew!" I shouted.

"What?" Cody asked.

I looked at my phone. 7:10. There was a text from Jerri. *Where are you?*

My throat clenched. "Oh no. I have to go."

"You need a ride?" Cody asked.

I shook my head and jumped out of my seat. Karpinski called after me, "You still owe for pizza!"

I ran out the door, grabbed my bike out of Cody's truck and, angry hammy and all, pumped it like a mother all the way to the middle school (going the wrong way up Second Street for half the trip—dumbass cars honking at me).

I was way late. I missed the whole crappy concert. Jesus, I still feel sick about this. Andrew spent half his free time last year writing feltonreinstein.com for me, and what do I do? Forget his whole concert.

• • •

Crap. I have to take a whiz. Someone is going to take my seat (I can see an old man eyeballing it, I swear) and I have to take my carry-on bag into the bathroom where it will absorb weenus germs. Gross.

Okay. Going to do this.

August 15th, 2:50 p.m.
O'HARE AIRPORT, PART II

I did not die in the bathroom. That's good, huh? They have these crazy hand dryers in there. It's like sticking your hands into a tiny, wicked tornado. Awesome. Your skin blows into crazy ridges.

Some plane to Philadelphia is boarding, so there are plenty of seats for me at the gate. Woo!

Okay. Back to the tragedy of the missed concert.

• • •

Andrew's concert was getting out right when I got to the middle school. Parents were flowing out. Dorky kids in their high-water black pants and neck-choking white shirts carried violin cases and cello cases. I saw Bony Emily, Andrew's best friend, walking next to her mom.

"Andrew still here?" I asked.

"No. He left right away. Nice going, Felton," she said.

"Crap."

Mr. Burkholz, the middle-school gym teacher, shouted to me while I rolled past: "Nice picture in the paper! Ha-ha!"

My stomach twisted. *Jerk.* Mr. Burkholz is one of those teachers who could give a shit if jocks are beating up other kids. He treated Cody and Karpinski like they were his best friends when they were like thirteen. I remember him asking them what they did for fun.

Seriously. "What do you dudes do for fun?" They were thirteen. What a chump, Aleah.

I took off on my bike, then slowed down because I didn't want to actually get home and have to encounter the disappointment of Andrew and the sadness of Jerri. As you know, though, it only takes a few minutes to get from BMS (Bluffton Middle School) to our house, even if you're going super slow (which you often did on your Walmart bike last summer). I rolled down the main road hill, saw Jerri's Hyundai parked out on the driveway, swallowed hard, and thought: *I have an excuse, right? Aleah…and my hamstring hurts and someone put posters of me up in school.*

Jerri and Andrew were up in the living room, having the post-event ice cream. (This is a long tradition, as you know.) Usually Andrew is fairly chattery. Usually he is talking a lot, going over the highlights, talking about who screwed up where, how he could've improved his performance, etc. When I climbed up the stairs from the garage and basement, though, there was no talking at all. Andrew and Jerri sat in silence.

Jerri shook her head at me.

Andrew said, "You missed it."

"I…I had a bad day."

"Andrew has been talking about this concert for months, Felton," Jerri said.

"I know," I said.

"It hurts my feelings…" Andrew said.

"I didn't mean…" I said. "Listen. I'm just…I'm just having a tough few days, okay?"

"Because you set a state record in track and got your picture in the newspaper?" Andrew asked.

"Somebody made copies of that picture and put it all over the school today," I said. "It's terrible."

"As of this morning, seventy-three people have left comments on feltonreinstein.com congratulating you on your 60-meter record. Forty-three people have left comments saying that picture is terrible. Why are you having a bad week?" Andrew asked.

"Oh...That's awesome." I nodded. "Thanks for telling me," I said. "But you know that picture is really..."

"I didn't play very well. I was looking for you in the audience before and then when you weren't there I..."

"Oh crap, Andrew. I'm really, really—"

"It's fine. I don't want to...I'm not like you. I don't need stupid fans who want to kiss my nuts."

"Jesus," I said.

"Andrew," Jerri gasped.

"I'm sorry for the language, Jerri." Then Andrew put down his pint of Ben and Jerry's Chubby Hubby, stood up, and walked to his bedroom.

Jerri's face went totally red.

"Jerri. I didn't mean to miss—"

"Here's the problem," Jerri whispered. "Your intentions don't matter, Felton."

"I'm seriously having a bad—"

"You're not the only person in this family."

"Someone put up a poster—"

"This was Andrew's time to shine, Felton. When does he get that?"

"I don't know."

"How could you?"

"I don't know."

Jerri stood up. She shook her head at me. Then she said something pretty bad, Aleah. She said, "Your dad always claimed ignorance too, Felton. He couldn't be bothered to remember anything important to me."

"Oh shit," I said. Then I turned and walked back down the stairs to my room. I expected Jerri to follow me, but she didn't.

I still maintain that it's a low blow to say I'm like my dad. He did have affairs and he did commit suicide. That's a pretty big thing to just throw around, you know?

• • •

Whoa. What time is it? Okay, I'm fine.

Okay. The airline finally posted Fort Myers on the gate. At least I'm not lost, Aleah.

I'm hungry.

August 15th, 3:12 p.m.
O'HARE AIRPORT, PART III

I have eaten a fettuccine Alfredo with some cold and chewy chicken. What did it taste like? The kind of paste I ate in first grade (pretty delicious).

Can you believe Jerri said I am like Dad? That's pretty mean. She did apologize a few days later.

Am I like my dad, Aleah? I'm wearing his Stan Smith shoes right now. They fit me perfectly.

Do I sort of want to be like my dad?

I can't begin to even address that, because saying to me I'm like my dad is like saying twenty-eight thousand things at one time.

I don't know how much like him I really am (which is a good reason for me to be going to Florida again, I suppose).

Am I just a little bit selfish and deluded (Narcissus), or am I possibly a cheater, a self-hater, a home-wrecker, etc.?

He was a great athlete. I am too.

He was also seriously smart (PhD). I'm not, I don't think.

I look like him completely.

I act like my dad in how many ways? I don't know, because he's dead.

If I won the NCAA Championship in tennis, wouldn't I smile? Wouldn't I be happy? There's this picture of him right after he won his championship where he's out the on the court with a medal around his neck, and he's not smiling. He's sort of staring vacantly into space with this sort of sad look on his face. Maybe I wouldn't be happy. Maybe I walk around looking sad too.

Because of my hamstring injury, I haven't really won anything big, yet. We lost the semifinal in football. Hamstring killed the outdoor track season.

Would I be happy if I really won the big one like he did? I don't know.

You were happy when you got invited to Germany, right?

Are we through? I mean, is our relationship done?

Oh, I'm having a great time writing this!

Screw it. No more writing. I'm going to play Skee-Ball on my phone.

Holy nuts. I've written a crapload of pages.

August 15th, 3:31 p.m.
O'HARE AIRPORT, PART IV

S kee-Ball?

I freaking hate Skee-Ball! Yet I insist on playing it over and over and over. My finger is kind of sweaty and it keeps getting stuck on my screen, so the ball won't roll right. I got my high score like three weeks ago, and I can't get close to it anymore for some reason (I lost my Skee-Skills!), but I keep rolling the freaking phone balls anyway.

While I was playing, this little like five-year-old kid came over and sat on the chair next to me and watched. I asked if he wanted to play, but he shook his head, no (really slow, with his mouth open like, "Nuh-uh," which was pretty funny). Then after I bounced a ball off the 100 hole, I shouted, "Dick Butkus!" really loud and the kid ran away and his dad glared at me.

Why must I screw up all the time?

At one time, I thought I'd be a great Skee-Ball champion...

No more Skee-Ball.

How about this?

Let's just get this over, okay?

When we finally talked on Wednesday night that week, the reason I sounded distant is because I felt distant. Andrew wasn't talking to me. Jerri wasn't talking to me. Gus wasn't talking to me. Karpinski had called me a wuss for not throwing toilet paper on Gus's yard. Reese does whatever Karpinski does, so he called me a wuss too. At lunch on Tuesday, because I was totally stewing in my own meatballs, Cody told me I better shake off this stupid crap because I'll soon be facing a lot worse stress than just a faked porn picture of me.

"You think Ohio State fans are gonna be all 'Welcome to the Horseshoe, Rein Stone' when you go in there to play football in college?"

"What?" Apparently the Horseshoe is the Ohio Stadium's nickname. I had no idea.

"People aren't nice. They don't like success. Shake it off, man," Cody said.

Yeah, but it wasn't just the porn pic, was it? I hadn't told anyone about my hamstring. I didn't tell anyone about you or Andrew.

Shake it off? Not so easy.

The reason I didn't react at all when you said, "Should we take a break this summer?" is because I was a total basket case, Aleah. No, I didn't want to take a break. I don't know what a break is. But my mouth didn't work and my chest hurt so I couldn't breathe and I was mad at you for even saying that.

(You know I tried calling you in May. You know I texted you a lot. You didn't ever respond. You were already on a break. I didn't want the break.)

When does it end?

Man! What a sad story!

Shake it off, Rein Stone!

If it makes you feel any better, you weren't the only person I treated badly during those twenty-four hours. The next morning, Thursday morning of that bullshit week, Andrew came into the living room while I was putting on my shoes and said, "Felton. It's okay. I forgive you for missing my concert."

Before you hate me for what I did to Andrew, you should know I hate me for it worse. Okay? Also, I hadn't slept for three days and I was constantly on the edge of barfing and I hadn't been able to run all out in track and there was a track meet that night and I was so upset about you…I just sort of went illogically mean.

There is no excuse.

He said, "I forgive you."

I said, "Great, Andrew. Thanks. You're a bigger human than me. Happy?"

Andrew paused and stared at me. He peered over his nerdly glasses. "I'm not trying to be a bigger human being. I would like to be nice."

"Stick it, Andrew."

He said, "What do you mean?"

"Stick. It."

"Stick what?"

I said, "Jesus. It's no big deal. Okay?"

"What isn't a big deal?"

"You. Your concert. You're not that great at piano. You're not like Aleah. You should probably be a pharmacist." I stared up at Andrew. I nodded at him.

"I was trying to be forgiving, Felton," Andrew whispered.

"I am trying to be truthful. Pharmacist," I said.

"God, Felton," he whispered. "Why are you so mean?"

"Shake it off," I said. Then I got up and left the house.

You can begin to understand why Andrew might want to run away without telling me, huh?

• • •

Wait.

What's going on? There are a whole bunch of people standing at the desk talking to the lady back there. Something's going on, Aleah. We're supposed to take off in like forty minutes, but there's not even a plane here yet. I'm going to go stand in that line like a donkey because everyone else is.

August 15th, 4:50 p.m.
O'HARE AIRPORT, PART V

Oh shit.

My flight was canceled because of extreme heat in Little Rock. A runway buckled? I am not exactly sure where Little Rock is. Arkansas, right? I don't understand how a runway in Arkansas can make me not fly in Chicago, but that's what happened, Aleah.

Stranded. Sort of.

I'm sort of freaking out.

Eyeballs hurt.

Me. I have to make a choice: stay in Chicago overnight to get the next direct flight into Fort Myers or fly to Atlanta, which might get me to Atlanta with enough time to connect to Fort Myers—or it might not, because I'd have about three minutes to get off the plane and run to the other plane, which I would be happy to do, except I know it took me forever to get the sausages to ask a bagel lady for directions to find my gate here and I'm sort of not feeling that great right now, Aleah.

Stay overnight in Chicago?

There's a hotel right here, but I only have that money from Jerri. If pasty fettuccine Alfredo costs like twenty bucks (that's what it cost!), won't a hotel room cost like $500 or something? I could ask. I should ask. Maybe I'll ask.

I'll call Jerri and ask her.

Jerri isn't answering the phone. You know why, Aleah? She's probably off in the woods some place making out with your freaking dad. Why won't she carry a damn cell phone?

Okay…I just have to ask somebody about something because I don't really want to stay here, but I don't want to go to Atlanta. I've been to Atlanta, with Gus, and it is too hot there for anyone to survive.

Why am I writing you when I should be gathering pertinent information?

Because I don't know who to ask.

August 15th, 6:28 p.m.

O'HARE AIRPORT, PART VI (HOTEL)

Jerri gave me a credit card to use in case of emergency. I'm beginning to suspect I have a good mother, Aleah, which means I can't blame her for my lack of humanity or my narcissism.

Not Jerri's fault.

After I wandered around for a half hour, staring at knickknack shops that sell magazines and little metal models of Chicago skyscrapers and these neck pillows that look like they would strangle me in my sleep and other assorted crap, the whole time wondering what in the whole wheat world I should do, Jerri called me (because I'd left her a message freaking out about how I was stranded and didn't know what to do). She told me to go to Atlanta, except by that time there was no space left on the flight to Atlanta. I called Jerri back, and she said that this constituted an emergency and that I could use the credit card she'd stuck in my backpack, in the very back pocket, zipped in a pocket inside another pocket.

Oh yes. It terrified me to have to book a room. Mumbled and stumbled and I'm sure the clerk person thought I was mentally ill. But...

Now I'm on the biggest bed in the entire world! In a room with a big wood desk and serious air-conditioning!

Emergency!

I've taken an excellent shower and I'm wearing a robe, Aleah! It is the whitest, fluffiest robe on the entire planet!

There are also white slippers that say "Chicago Hilton O'Hare Airport" on them! My feet are too big to fit in them, but that's okay. I don't like slippers very much!

There's a giant TV in here!

Emergency!

I like credit cards.

What else, Aleah?

Here's something totally weird that just happened: There I was on my giant bed, minding my own business, resting with my thoughts and a little Tosh on the TV, when this reporter called me from the *Milwaukee Journal Sentinel*. I don't answer the phone if I don't know the number, so I just watched it go to voice mail. In the message, the reporter said there was a rumor going around that I am committing to play football for Wisconsin, because I haven't made any other visits and I skipped the Michigan camp.

Uh, no. I told colleges I'd make official visits this fall. (I didn't want to last year because I'm new to football—okay, I just didn't want to make visits.)

I skipped the Michigan camp for personal reasons (my brother disappeared and I don't like people!), not because I was committing to any other school...

No! I haven't committed to anything. I don't want to commit yet!

You and I were going to try to go to school in the same area, remember? Maybe New York somewhere?

You were supposed to come to Bluffton for the summer too. But you didn't....

I don't want to commit. Should I call the reporter back?

No.

I like my little hotel room without anyone to talk to in it (except you, and you're not really here).

Let me just tell you how my week of terror came to a close: We had a track meet against Lancaster that Thursday. Even though I sort of knew I was injured, I wanted to run because I hate Casey Steinhoff from Lancaster (John Spencer's cousin—John dumped all that trash on my lawn last year, if you'll recall). Like John Spencer, Casey calls me Squirrel Nut and Squee-Tard. So, I wanted to run against him and make him look like the jerk he is.

Revenge.

Unfortunately, I had a tiny man in my hamstring.

And right out of the blocks, the little man in my hamstring set off a napalm bomb that blew out my leg big-time (this was no ordinary strain—it was a Reinstein explosion), which led me to miss the rest of the track season. I fell over in a puddle screaming. Casey Steinhoff squealed with joy.

Picture me lying in a spring puddle, Aleah.

It was a huge deal that I got injured. I think Coach Knautz cried. I might have cried, except I was in a state of shock and could feel nothing at all.

Gus, you, Andrew, hamstring...

By Friday night, Aleah, I wasn't sure who the hell I was. Seriously. The doctor in Dubuque told me I'd be fine to run normally by June but would miss going to Outdoor State in track…I just nodded. *(It did all fall apart!)*

Want to know a secret?

Here's the dirtiest little secret I've got.

Although I moped and acted sad and depressed and told Cody I couldn't take it…I was actually relieved not to have to race Roy Ngelale again. I was relieved I couldn't run for coaches who came on evaluation visits in May. I was secretly hopeful I wouldn't be able to go to the Michigan technique camp in late June, because I didn't want anybody watching me run, asking me to sign any letter of intent. I liked the idea of disappearing.

I sort of still do.

After Jerri and I came back in the house that Friday after the doctor, I fell onto the couch without thoughts of you or Andrew or Gus or anyone, and I watched six of the best hours of TV I've ever watched. (Don't even remember what I watched.) Around midnight, Jerri came down to tell me she was so sorry about my leg.

I whispered, "It's okay."

Then I slept like a baby.

Do you remember at Christmas when Andrew and I were in Chicago visiting and your dad gave me that poem by John Updike about the former high-school basketball star who never made it big and just ended up bouncing inner tubes around in a gas station? I think about that sometimes. I think, *That could be me.* I think, *When I get old, I'll sprint back and forth between pallet and shelf out at Walmart. I'll be the fastest stock boy who ever lived.*

It doesn't make me sad, Aleah. I think I'd like being just a stock boy. Just a nobody.

I'll serve the fastest slushy at Kwik Trip!

My dad was a collegiate national champion in tennis. He killed himself in the garage when I was five.

• • •

Do you think it's cool if I order room service on Jerri's credit card?

It's kind of an emergency.

Donkey real hungry!

August 15th, 8:15 p.m.

O'HARE AIRPORT, PART VII (HOTEL)

Dear Aleah, I have eaten an amazing chicken quesadilla. I ordered it.

A man delivered it.

I tipped the man because I'd looked up tipping on Google and I knew how to do it.

I am a man.

(Who can order room service with his mom's credit card.)

Here's something pretty funny I was just thinking about: in eighth grade, whenever I was having a lot of trouble (and, holy ballz, I had trouble in eighth grade), Mr. Faherty, my language arts teacher, would pull me aside and say, "Journal it, Felton. Make some sense," and I would start journaling in my brain. *Abby Sauter shoved me. Karpinski told me I smell like shit. Kirk Johnson knocked me off my bike. My elbow hurts for no reason.* I'd just start listing crap in my brain and then I'd repeat it over and over, but I didn't do the main thing: write it down, make any sense. I just listed the shit.

Not now. Feels like I'm journaling for you. Am I not a good enough person to journal for myself?

"Journal it!"

Okay, Mr. Faherty. I will.

• • •

Saturday, March 31st was the first day of the rest of Andrew's life. Overnight, something big happened to him and he will never be the same, I'm sure. I think. Makes me miss the old Andrew a little. He was a wonderful, innocent boy!

Me? That morning?

I comfortably watched beach volleyball on ESPN2 while icing my blown-out hamstring. It was the first day of what I assumed was going to be total isolation and relaxation for several months, and I was in no mood for interaction.

Andrew has a habit of getting in my business at exactly the moment I crave his attention least. He sort of stumbled down the stairs wearing ratty boxer shorts and his Mozart T-shirt, which he's had for about ten years (one of the few pieces of clothing he didn't torch last summer when he decided to dress like a pirate), so it is gross. He said, "Felton?"

"I can't talk to you, Andrew."

"What if our dad…"

"I can't talk to you."

"…contacted you from beyond the grave?"

"*What?*" I sat up and turned to him. "What the hell are you talking about?"

Upstairs, out of no place, Jerri sang, *This is the dawning of the Age of Aquarius…*

Andrew flinched at the sound of our mother's voice.

"What, Andrew?"

"Why can't you talk to me?" he asked. He had big bags under his eyes.

"Because I'm in recovery. Did you have a bad dream?"

"I didn't sleep last night."

"Join the club, man. You're a Reinstein. We don't sleep. Shake it off."

Jerri called from upstairs, "Felton, do you want a grilled cheese?"

"Yes! Yes, I do, Jerri!" I called back. I smiled. This felt like the good life to me, Aleah. "Andrew," I said, "take a nap, okay? Enjoy your Saturday. Dad didn't contact you from beyond the grave."

"Okay. He didn't," Andrew said. He turned and slowly loafed back up the stairs.

I felt great. A few minutes later, Jerri brought me down a glass of milk and two grilled cheese sandwiches on wheat. (Fine—I prefer white, but I can't push Jerri too far off her whole-grain, granola base.) While she was downstairs, she asked, "Did Andrew tell you what's bothering him?"

"No."

"He's really behaving strangely."

"Oh?"

"I hope this isn't the start of something."

Suddenly I pictured Jerri last summer when she was going crazy—her hair all snaggly and gross, her skin so pale. I pictured Andrew with his shaved head and pirate outfit, which he wore because he was crazy. I thought about what Andrew had just said: *What if Dad contacted you from beyond the grave?* My heart accelerated. My forehead got sweaty. A chill wind blew… "He had a bad night's sleep," I said.

"Poor guy," Jerri said. "Maybe I'll get him some peach yogurt at the store."

"He'd like that," I nodded.

• • •

It was the start of something new, Aleah.

Man. I think I should stop now and watch some TV.

August 15th, 10:55 p.m.

O'HARE AIRPORT, PART VIII (HOTEL)

Journal it!

TV is boring.

Have you ever received an email from Randy Stone, Aleah? Maybe? He smokes cigarettes.

Do you know what I'm talking about?

Because I have been on the news and stuff, and Andrew had a link to email me from feltonreinstein.com, I sometimes got weird emails (mostly from like ten-year-old boys). I opened them, because they always made me feel good about myself.

(Stuff like this: Dear Felton, That run you had against Richland Center was awesome. I just watched it on YouTube. You are very fast. You are awesome. Keep kickin' butt!!! Sincerely, Jared)

So when, during the evening of that same Saturday that Jerri made me grilled cheeses, the same Saturday Andrew said that weird thing about Dad, something arrived from det.randystone@gmail.com, I clicked it without thinking twice, even though I didn't recognize the name. This is what it said (cut and pasted from the actual email):

The very brilliant child detective Randy Stone lit a cigarette.

It flamed up and scared him. Then he smoked and coughed, because he doesn't smoke and thinks cigarettes are stupid. He threw the cigarette into Felton Reinstein's closet and the closet went up in flames, because Felton smells like a big sack of cow manure and cow manure is highly flammable. There were big manure flames that burned the detective's eyes.

Good work, detective.

This was the break in the case Randy Stone needed. "This Felton character has serious problems. This Felton Reinstein cannot be trusted."

Randy Stone left the basement bedroom, turned to the garage door, and walked into the garage and out onto the country drive.

Where is he? Where should he be?

Our boy must go.

That was it. Detective Randy Stone?

My heart pounded. I read it again. It seemed sort of threatening. Before that moment, I'd sort of recovered my sense of ease (which I'd momentarily lost after Andrew's weird question). I was just lounging in bed. But after that email? I sat upright and braced myself against the wall. My feet got cold. My sweat went cold. I had to breathe deep to not hyperventilate.

I emailed back: *Who is this?*

I waited—staring at the laptop screen like a hypnotized rabbit—but received no reply.

Then I considered calling the cops. *I smell like cow manure? I can't be trusted. Our boy must go?*

I printed out the email and crawled upstairs to talk to Jerri. (Blown-out hamstring hurt.) At the top of the stairs, I pulled myself up on the railing and limped over to her in the living room, where she sat reading by the light of a single lamp. She looked up. "What's going on, Felton?" she asked.

"Jerri, let me read you this email."

"Okay. Something interesting?"

"No. Well, yeah, I guess." I nodded. "Check this out...this is a personal email, Jerri. To me, okay?" I switched on the overhead light and read her the email.

"Hmm. Wow. Pretty goofy," she said.

"Goofy? I don't know who Randy Stone is."

"Really? You don't?"

"I don't. Seriously, Jerri."

She paused. She smiled. "Sure you do. One of your friends, don't you think? They know the layout of the house."

"A friend?"

"Gus, probably."

I imagined the dwarf mouth of Gus, anger and ridicule pasted there underneath the chronic hair wad that always hides his face. "Maybe," I said.

"Of course."

Gus. Gus who would not look at me. Gus who I suspected made porn pictures of me and hung them around the school. Gus.

I stood balanced on my poor left leg for a moment longer. Jerri looked at me and shrugged. She smiled bigger, trying to be comforting.

"But what if it isn't Gus?" I asked. "What if it's a crazy person who saw my picture in the paper? Do you think I should call the cops? Just in case?"

"No."

"Better safe than sorry, Jerri."

"I don't know, Felton."

I stared at her, images of her craziness from last summer dancing through my memory. Then I said, "Jerri. Is it reasonable? After what we've been through? To not take strange behavior seriously?"

She squinted back at me. The smile left her face. She said, "Okay. Seems like paranoia, but sure. Why don't you call Cody's dad, if it will make you feel better?"

Yeah. Cody's dad. That made my desire to call a cop a little less attractive.

"I'm being harassed by a child detective, Officer Frederick! Help! He thinks I smell like manure! Help!"

If I called the cops, Aleah, I'd be notifying Cody's dad.

I stayed down in my room the rest of the night, my hamstring throbbing and awful. At a certain point, I figured, "Why not?" and called Gus to accuse him of being Randy Stone. He didn't pick up.

I left a message:

"Screw you, Randy Stone."

He texted back: *?*

I texted: *Screw you, Randy Stone.*

I waited for a reply but received none.

Late that night, because I couldn't sleep at all, like around 2 a.m., I got fearful for Andrew and how if Randy Stone wasn't

Gus, maybe somebody was coming to get all of us. I rolled out of bed and crawled my way up to Andrew's room. Even though it was so ridiculously late, he was awake. A little light flowed out from under his door. I pushed it open, which caused Andrew to turn away from his desk where he was working on his computer.

He stared down at me on the floor.

"Can I help you, Felton?" he whispered (so as not to wake Jerri).

I whispered back, "Hey, Andrew, will you keep your eyes peeled for weirdos? I'm a little worried that someone is stalking me. Like maybe a psycho fan or someone."

Without a pause he whispered, "Shake it off."

"Come on, Andrew. Don't be a jerk."

"Me?" he asked.

I nodded.

"Felton, I don't have time for you."

"I'm trying to protect you."

"No need."

I glared. Clenched my jaw. "What, are you some kind of super ninja now? You can take care of everything?" I asked, my voice rising.

"Shh."

"Ninja?" I whispered.

"Necessity is the mother of all invention," he said.

"Fine. Whatever," I said.

I crawled back down the stairs (backward) and went to bed, not even thinking for a second about what the crap Andrew was doing working on his computer during the wee hours of the morning.

I didn't sleep a damn wink, Aleah. I heard Andrew walk around a little. At one point, I heard him go out the front door then come back in. Apparently he couldn't sleep either.

I was seriously spooked by that email, and my monkey brain totally took off with it. *Our boy must go…Our boy must gooooo… What is Andrew's problem?* Do you know how I regulate my monkey brain in times of unease? Running. But I couldn't run. Hamstring.

Early the next morning (April Fools' Day! Appropriate), me all dizzy and gross and totally mummified by the freaking sweaty sheets that were wrapped all around me, I opened my email to find another dispatch from Detective Randy Stone.

Oh shit!

Detective Randy Stone, the most brilliant child sleuth in America, hunts through the Yellow Pages of Fiddlesticks, Florida. He finds a business. The perfect business. A carpet-cleaning business that specializes in parrot poop, because he knows the dirt has been building up for too long.

In Fiddlesticks, there's a cleaning business, Happy Halpen Cleaners, that can restore this carpet to its most gigantic beauty, and maybe one day it will carpet the floor next to presidents or great tennis stars or old men sitting alone in their dens listening to music because they think there is nothing else left, but maybe a good, reasonable carpet can help. That's what carpet does!

The poor boy Randy Stone lights another cigarette, which flames up very high, and he totally chokes, because cigarettes are so dumb. After he is done hacking up his tender lungs and dousing the flames, he nods and says, "Mmm. Sweetie. Oh lord, yes. That's good cigarette flavor."

What the hell?

I read it twice. Heat rose in my face. My hands started to shake. Oh, yeah, I got incredibly mad. I knew exactly who was behind this crappy writing. I recognized the freakiness. No doubt Jerri was right. *Gus.* He was hell-bent on torturing me. Even though it was like 6:30 a.m., I called him five times. He didn't answer.

I waited ten minutes, then called again.

He didn't answer.

I lay in bed staring at my ceiling, anger bolting like Jamaican Kangaroo Juice through my body.

I called him again.

He didn't answer.

I called again, then again.

On my tenth or fifteenth call, he answered.

"You must stop buzzing my phone immediately."

"*Randy Stone!*" I shouted.

"Cease and desist."

"*Randy Stone!*"

"Felton, Jesus. Somebody better be dead."

"Whatever, Randy Stone."

"Is this how you wish me a happy birthday a day late?"

"What?" I asked.

"My birthday," he said.

"Randy Stone?" I asked.

"Are you on drugs, Felton?"

"Randy Stone might be."

"What?"

"Dirty carpets, Randy Stone."

"Shut the hell up, Felton."

"It was your birthday yesterday," I said.

"I went to Steve's with Maddie and Peter Yang."

"What about Randy Stone?" I asked.

"Who?" he asked.

"Sorry," I said.

"Is there an emergency of some kind, Felton?"

"No."

"Worst April Fools' joke ever?"

"No."

"What the hell are you doing?"

"Um…"

"It's like dawn on Sunday, man. It's not enough that we're not friends? You want to torture me too?"

"That's not what I…"

"Screw off."

Gus hung up the phone. He clearly hated me, which seemed reasonable since I'd just missed his birthday for the first time in our lives. But still, there was no doubt in my mind that he was Randy Stone, Aleah. I just didn't know how to deal with it, so I tossed and turned in that stupid bed.

Then what? I marked the Randy Stone email as spam. *Take that, Randy Stone!*

Then, because I can't calm myself without running, I tried running even though I could barely walk. I limped into my shorts and shoes. I limped out on the driveway. I zombie-walked down the hill to the main road. Then I turned and attempted to bolt up the hill toward the house. But, holy crap, in about three steps the little man ripped me up, Aleah. I ended up lying on the lawn crying. (Oh, I am not proud.) Jerri had to come out in the yard, help me up, and half drag my ass back into the house.

"I can't believe you tried to run," she said. "The doctor said not even light jogging for a month."

"Oh crap," I cried.

Who am I if I can't run?

Squirrel Nut.

• • •

Jesus. I have to go to sleep. I have to be at the gate by like nine.

August 16th, 12:05 a.m.
O'HARE AIRPORT, PART IX (HOTEL)

Are you in love with some Amadeus Vienna Weiner musician, Aleah?

Sorry. We're on break.

I shouldn't care if you're in love with some German sausage.

Crap.

When I finally got my driver's license in February, I figured we'd drive out in the country and go to the Mississippi and drive into the bottoms around Bluffton and see everything, but that never happened. Not once. We never even parked at the big M to make out.

Maybe *you* were with Wolfgang Amadeus Schlong during the break, but I have not been with another girl. I stayed alone, and the rest of the school year went okay. Jerri and I watched a lot of TV. (I told Cody and Karpinski I had to rest for therapeutic reasons, which Cody accepted. Karpinski kept asking me to do stuff, but I wouldn't.)

It was weird to have no sport to play. It was totally, painfully, depressingly, completely awful not to be able to run. (Except when coaches visited me in May and Jerri cooked them bad dinners—I liked not running then. Unfortunately I had no doctor excuse to keep me from talking, so I had to talk, which made me sound like an idiot.)

During track practice, while my friends all ran, I lifted weights like a crazy man, and for a month or two I sort of looked like a dude who takes steroids to model tight underpants in some gross magazine. I got so bulky that I felt kind of embarrassed. (Thankfully, when I started running again in June, I dropped a little bit of the bulky-underpants-model weight. Now I look like me but just a little bigger).

Maybe the best thing about April and May is that I received no more email from Randy Stone. (Turned out to be the *spam* filter at work.) Gus didn't want anything to do with me. I didn't want anything to do with him. I began to think his Randy Stone stunt had sealed the end of our friendship.

Andrew was the only weird part. He didn't hang with Jerri and me at all. He stayed in his bedroom all the time. He read this fat book constantly (Spinoza's *The Ethics*—Spinoza is some old philosopher). He stopped talking. He stopped eating with us (ate only crackers and cheese). He got sent home from school for fighting one day (crazy). And, what's worse, he did what he always does when something is filling his little, obsessive walnut brain: he stopped showering (*gross*).

Weirdo. You probably haven't seen his eighth-grade yearbook picture, huh? Everyone else is smiling in the yearbook, but he took off his glasses and rested his hand on his chin and stared at the camera flat, like he was some kind of old man artist or something. Freak boy. But I guess Andrew looks sort of cool in that photo.

Finally, in mid-May, while we were watching a seriously horrifying episode of *Hoarders* (lots of dead cats buried in piles of junk), Jerri said, "Oh crap. Does that lady remind you of Andrew or what?"

"Yeah," I nodded. The hoarder lady had plastic nerd glasses. She was tiny and frail. She had giant stacks of fat books. She fought with the people who were trying to help her. And she obviously hadn't showered in months.

"Has Andrew said anything to you, Felton? I asked his teachers if he was acting strangely or writing strange stuff. Other than his weird fight, nothing seems to be up. He's doing fine in school. What is going on?" Jerri asked.

"I don't know." The truth is that I hoped his weirdness would go away. I didn't want to open another worm can. Ten months earlier, Andrew had practically lived in the garden, you know. I wanted normalcy.

"Shit. Do we need an intervention?" Jerri asked.

"Should we call Grandma Berba?" I asked.

"Why would we do that?"

"Because…" I pictured Jerri in her bathrobe, depressed out of her freaking nut. "Because, you know?"

"I'm fine. I'm great. Don't worry about me," Jerri said. "Let's have an intervention right now."

"Uh…" This didn't seem like a great idea, Aleah. I did not want to go into Andrew's room. I did think this, though: *When Jerri went nuts, I tried to ignore it. That did not work.* "I guess we should," I said.

Jerri stood fast and walked across the living room. Our new TV blared *Hoarders* in the background. I stood and followed her. We entered the dark hall, where just a little light was emanating from around Andrew's cracked door. She knocked.

Andrew said, "Who is it?"

"Jerri. Jerri and Felton," she said.

"*Entrez vous*," Andrew said.

"That's French." Jerri nodded at me. She opened the door.

Andrew lay on his belly on the floor. He had the big book cracked open in front of him. His glasses hung off his nose. Pamphlets with cellos and pianos and harps were scattered around him. The room smelled vaguely of maple syrup. Why? I do not know.

He looked up. "Can I help you?" he asked.

"This is an intervention," Jerri said.

"Yes," Andrew said. "An inconvenience."

"Felton and I are worried about your behavior. You're isolating yourself—"

"And reading big books. What is that?" I asked, pointing to the fat thing in front of him.

"Spinoza. He's a mystical Jewish philosopher…I think," Andrew said. "I don't really get it all, but I'm trying."

"Reading doesn't worry me," Jerri said.

"Thank heavens," Andrew said.

"You're not playing piano, and your isolation—"

"And not showering!" I barked.

"I shower," Andrew said.

"You won't talk to us," Jerri said.

"Sure I will," Andrew said. "What do you want to know?"

"What on earth are you doing in here all the time?" Jerri asked.

"Lots of things."

"Like what?" Jerri asked.

"Tonight I've called Grandma Berba and asked her for money so I can go to an orchestra camp in Door County this summer. Most of the time I'm studying or reading Spinoza, which isn't easy, Jerri."

"Wait. *What?*"

"The philosopher."

"Andrew, you called Grandma Berba for money?"

"Yes."

"For a camp? What camp?"

"Orchestra camp. Door County is beautiful." Andrew nodded. "The camp is right on Lake Michigan."

"Why wouldn't you ask me for money?" Jerri barked.

"Grandma Berba has more money than God," Andrew said. "I don't want to be a burden to you, Jerri."

"That's ridiculous. You need my permission."

"Andrew makes a good point, Jerri," I said. "You're starting a new career—"

"Shut up, Felton," Jerri said. Her face had turned dark red.

"Jerri, can I go to orchestra camp this summer? It's eight weeks. Very intensive. I'm trying to avoid my fate," Andrew said.

"What fate?" Jerri asked.

"Felton thinks I should be a pharmacist," Andrew said.

"Oh crap, Andrew. I was in a bad mood when I said that. Don't take everything—"

"Yes," Jerri said. "You can go, Andrew. I'm glad you're being constructive. How long is it again?"

"Eight weeks," Andrew said.

"Fine. Good. Show me the information and if it seems legit…just tell me where to sign," Jerri said.

"I'll have the paperwork filled out by morning," Andrew told her.

We stood there staring at each other for a few seconds. Then Jerri said, "Thus ends the intervention." She turned and pushed past me. I followed her. In the hall, she whispered, "Why do you have to be such a jerk, Felton? A *pharmacist?*"

"I didn't mean it," I whispered back.

"Is there no space between your brain and your mouth?"

"Sometimes," I said. "If I'm supposed to talk…then there's a big space."

"Backward," Jerri said. She didn't go into the living room. She went into her bedroom, so I had to watch the end of *Hoarders* by myself.

Apparently, the camp was legit, Aleah. Jerri signed the papers.

• • •

Whoops. I'm blowing up here. Karpinski text.

August 16th, 2:17 a.m.

O'HARE AIRPORT, PART X (HOTEL)

Karpinski texted to tell me that practice is stupid without me and I better get the hell back to Bluffton or he'll quit.

He won't quit.

We texted back and forth for a while. He totally doesn't understand what the hell I'm doing right now. I'm not exactly sure either. What's with me and my commitment to football, Aleah? Do I even care about it?

Yes. Yes, I totally do, but…there's definitely something going on.

In February, I committed to go to the Michigan technique camp because your dad told me that Michigan might be a really good fit (good sports and really good academics).

As soon as I told the offensive coordinator there that I was coming (he was too psyched—he wooed), I began having nightmares of giant asswipe dudes, other football players, trying to push me around. I dreamed of coaches screaming with crazy idiot voices, like *South Park* cartoon-freak coaches might scream. I dreamed of running through dorm hallways trying to get the hell away from dudes chasing me.

Seriously, I got all whacked out and sleepless, until Jerri asked me what the hell my problem was one winter morning. (I totally fell asleep while eating a flaxseed frozen waffle.) Because I was weak and half asleep, I told her that visions of this stupid camp were driving me crazy.

Jerri sat back in her chair and squinted at me. She said, "You don't have to go if you don't want to."

I sat straight up in my chair, all filled with monkey juice. I spat at her, "You don't want me to go! You hate football!"

She folded her arms and smirked at me. "Felton, I'm trying to comfort you. Do whatever you want. No matter what, I'm firmly committed to being the mother of a dumb jock."

"That's not nice!"

"I'm making a joke."

Jerri has gotten in the habit of making sort of mean jokes, if you haven't noticed. (Gus totally noticed this summer.)

But here's the truth: as soon as Jerri said I didn't have to go, the dreams went away. Pressure release. I never cancelled the camp, never called to tell them I wasn't going, but in the back of my head I sort of thought I wouldn't go.

I didn't go, but not exactly because I was scared of my dreams—Andrew gave me an excuse.

Is Andrew turning into my way out of football? Here I am, chasing him instead of playing the game.

Karpinski texted at one point tonight: *You think peyton manning would miss practice week of first game???*

I've been thinking about that. Do you know who Peyton Manning is? He's like the Yo-Yo Ma of football. I don't really know if Yo-Yo Ma is that great a musician. He is, right? Peyton is like a super great, one of the best quarterbacks ever.

So, here's a good question: Would Peyton Manning drop everything—drills, fitness, training camp—to go find his little brother, Eli, if little Eli were lost on the Florida Gulf Coast?

That's what I'm doing.

I don't know how to answer the question. Would Peyton leave practice the week of a game?

He's a serious professional football player, and that means he's had to make serious sacrifices, like maybe not helping Eli out when he was in trouble in the past. Maybe? "Can't save you from those bullies, little buddy. I've got passes to throw…"

But, really, I don't know. Peyton seems nice.

Actually, my guess is that Peyton Manning would go find Eli if he were lost. My guess is that part of the reason Peyton's such an awesome leader is that he puts people ahead of his own personal gain. That's why everybody thinks, "Thank Gawd we got us a little Peyton in our lives…"

He's also not crazy like I'm crazy.

I think I've got good reason to be crazy.

Maybe I really would be like Peyton Manning, except my tennis dad killed himself and didn't play football, like Peyton's did, and didn't raise me in a giant mansion with this perfect Manning-style family, so my problems are a lot bigger, much, *much* bigger than Peyton Manning ever had to deal with, and so I'm not crazy but actually just doing the best a totally broken dude like myself can expect to do.

• • •

Jesus. No way. No way I can freaking sleep.

61

You know, Aleah, I've already been gone from Bluffton for like twenty hours and I'm still in Chicago. I could've driven almost to freaking Georgia by now. Haysoos Christmoos.

I don't want to be a football slacker. I'm going to do some freaking running. Maybe run stairs? I'm going to donkey-run my ass up some stairs.

August 16th, 3:17 a.m.

O'HARE AIRPORT, PART XI (HOTEL)

I just got yelled at by a man in a white bathrobe, which was sort of dangling open. "Stop your goddamn running around the halls right now, you drunk!"

I'm not drunk. I'm weird. I said, "Sorry."

He squinted at me, nodded, and said, "Just go to bed."

"I'm not tired," I told him.

"Go to bed," he said, sort of mean, so I came back to the room.

I ran a good bit on the stairs but had only gotten in like ten hallway wind sprints before robe man put the kibosh on my training.

Man. I want to go home, Aleah. I want to be back in Bluffton. I want to be asleep. This is happening, though. I'm in.

Andrew.

In June, like five days after school ended, Jerri and I drove Andrew to Madison to catch a bus for his orchestra camp. Jerri wanted to drive him all the way to Green Bay, where he was supposed to meet up with the other mighty dork campers, but he said no.

For about a week before this trip, Jerri and Andrew argued about it. "That's ridiculous, Andrew. Absolutely not. You're not taking the bus. I *want* to drive you."

"It's not ridiculous at all," he said, "I'm fourteen and I need to learn to take care of myself. This will be a very safe adventure, Jerri."

"Andrew, no! I want to meet your counselors. I want to see the other campers."

"Jerri, please. Don't be such a mother, okay? This isn't about you."

Aha, Aleah. He played the self-reliance card perfectly. It's one that works well on Jerri, because she's watched a lot of the Oprah Winfrey Network. He made her believe somehow that the adventure of traveling alone part of the trip would benefit his quest to become an excellent adult. Well played.

So we put his bag filled with many mallets and drumsticks of multiple kinds, his giant-ass book, and like one change of underpants in the back of the Hyundai that Monday, and off we all went.

Andrew barely said a word the entire drive. Jerri kept looking back at him in the rearview mirror. I turned around a couple of times and saw him staring out the window. His face was a little red, which might have been a clue. But if I were heading off to a scary camp among perfect strangers, I'd be freaked, for sure. (Michigan technique camp drove me crazy, for instance.)

Of course, Andrew is not me.

At the bus station—this place is really like a strip mall with a giant garage attached in the back—Jerri said, "Call me every day, Andrew."

Andrew said, "Um. Maybe. I'll probably call you every few days."

Then I said, "Have a good time, Andrew. I really hope it's great."

Andrew stared at me through his nerd glasses for a moment. Then he dropped his suitcase and hugged me extremely hard around my stomach (because that's how tall he is). He said, "Here I go, Felton. This is it."

I nodded at him. "Good luck, man."

He backed up a step and squinted.

Then he turned and threw his suitcase into the luggage compartment of the fugly Greyhound bus. Then he climbed aboard the fugly Greyhound bus. Then he sat at the window and stared out at us as other sad and tired passengers piled on behind him. A hugely fat dude with a ponytail and a pink T-shirt that didn't cover his belly completely cried like a baby next to Jerri. He'd just put his very tiny, extremely pierced girlfriend on the bus. Then the bus honked, backed up, and was gone.

Jerri sort of sniffled as we climbed into her Hyundai.

"Going to miss the boy?" I asked.

"Miss what? Your brother is a ghost."

"I know."

"He's a complete mystery to me," Jerri said.

"No kidding," I nodded.

The house felt extremely empty without him there. Jerri and I did what Jerri and I do: watch dumb TV together. Even though he didn't talk to us, Andrew was action. He was always really busy: computer, whispering on the phone, writing crap down, digging around in his room while classical music blared. Sort of ridiculous…what would an eighth grader have to be so busy about?

Actually, he's always been that way. Andrew is no vegetable.

If I'm not running, I am a vegetable. Jerri is a vegetable unless she's with your dad.

Thank God I got to start seriously running the same week Andrew left or I might seriously have missed him. (Plus I was porny-underpants-model bulky at that point and needed aerobic activity.)

And, after all the rest, my hamstring man felt good and I went from light jogging to doing some pretty intense running over the next few days (800s and 400s at the college track). I mean, really, the hammy man was gone. I could run hard without feeling any pain, which was a huge, huge, huge relief. I began to meet up with Cody and Karpinski to catch passes—I hadn't cancelled Michigan, so I sort of thought I should get ready for it (which caused palpitations in my squirrel heart).

And, things were good…

• • •

Somebody is pounding on my door.

August 16th, 3:34 a.m.

O'HARE AIRPORT, PART XII (HOTEL)

I've been officially warned by the hotel: No Exercising In The Halls. Okay! How did they know it was me? Video?

I am sort of stressed out, Aleah…

Journal it!

Where was I? Here.

The first real indication that seriously weird stuff was afoot with Andrew came a week after he left.

I spent that cloudy afternoon at the track running ten sets of 400s and playing catch with Cody and Karpinski on the infield. (Karpinski was late because he'd been pulled over by the cops for shooting popcorn seeds out of a straw at kids on Main Street. Nice, huh?) It was a good time. I felt seriously good. Catching a ball is like breathing to me, Aleah.

After, while I was riding my bike toward home, up that huge freaking hill on Hickory Street and feeling the power coming back to my legs, a car pulled up behind me and drove slow, way too close.

Sometimes people in small towns can act like this. I know you think Bluffton is all sweet views and nice people, but that's not really the case. People just mess with you in Bluffton. We don't have enough to do here, Aleah.

Maybe you figured that out so you went to Germany?

When this car started tailing me, I figured I'd just keep biking. I'd maintain my dignity. I wouldn't do what I wanted to do, which was throw my bike down and freak out.

Generally, if you don't pay attention to them, the person who is messing with you will just get bored and leave.

But it kept going and going, this car on my tail. My heart started pounding hard, not just from pedaling up the giant hill. The car followed me closer and closer all the way up. I was thinking, "What if this is a real psycho who really wants to kill me? Need to be ready…"

When we got to the top, I had gorilla adrenaline pumping through every part of my body.

I turned to shout, and who was it?

Gus. He laughed.

I did not find this funny. I hadn't spoken a word to him since the Randy Stone call two months earlier. He wouldn't acknowledge my existence at school.

"*You ass*," I shouted.

He smiled like an evil monkey from under his hair wad. (It took a full ten months to grow back after his grandma made him cut it off last summer.) "Get off the road, you bike hippie," he shouted out his window.

I pulled over. He pulled alongside me and rolled down the passenger-side window.

"Why would you do that?" I asked.

"I don't know. I really hate bikers, I guess. Why didn't you turn around earlier?"

"Because I wanted to get to flat ground so that I could more easily punch your face in."

"Nice. Good thinking. You're a jock strategerist, aren't you?"

"No."

"How've you been?" he asked.

"Why would you care?"

"Good point," he said.

"Are we done here?" I asked.

"Could be. I have a question, though."

I got ready for something mean. "Okay…"

"Where's your little brother?" Gus climbed out of his car and looked at me over the top.

"Orchestra camp."

"No, seriously. Put your bike in the trunk, Felton. I've been calling you for like three hours. Where's your freaky little brother?"

"What are you talking about?" I hadn't taken my phone with me to run routes.

Gus popped the trunk. I climbed off my bike and watched him jam it into the small trunk of his tiny Celica, which I didn't like because the front wheel dangled out and the trunk door was unsecured and was thus free to bounce up and down on the frame.

"I don't think that's safe, man."

"We have to talk to Bony Emily," he said.

"Emily Cook?"

"You know any other Bony Emilys?"

Here's where Bluffton becomes multigenerationally incestuous and gross, because it is so tiny. We climbed in the car.

As we drove off, he said, "Get this. Emily told Maddie that Andrew ran away."

"You're talking about Andrew's Bony Emily?"

"Yeah, man."

If you'll recall, Aleah, Emily Cook, the very skinny and dorky girl I call Bony Emily, is Andrew's best friend. Maddie, who likes to smoke cigarettes and wants a tattoo, is Gus's girlfriend. Andrew and Emily seem like little kids. Maddie, even though she acts like a burned-out twenty-five-year-old, is only a year older. Maddie was in their orchestra last year. And Emily and Maddie share a love of some weird music, I guess, so even though Maddie is a townie and Emily's parents are professors, they're friends, which, since Gus started hanging with Maddie, makes me think of Gus as a cradle-robbing pervert. This is all confusing to me, but whatever.

"She's full of crap, man. Bony's gone haywire. Andrew is at orchestra camp in Door County."

"Yeah, that's what he told you. Do you know for sure?"

"He calls Jerri every freaking day. He even said he wouldn't call her that much, but he can't help himself because he's a little kid. Run away? I don't think so."

"I'm not buying it, man. Andrew's one crafty little bitch."

"He is not. Jerri put him on speakerphone last night, and I could totally hear orchestra people warming up in the background. He is really, totally at orchestra camp."

"Emily says he's on an adventure."

"Bony is weirder than I thought."

"Psycho Emily?" Gus asked.

"She is more than just skin and bones?" I said.

"She's a freaky psycho," he said.

"A crazy psycho killer?" I asked.

It was weird how fast we fell into our old way of speaking.

"Okay. Well. If she lies, then let us drive to Bony Emily's house and give her a piece of the business," Gus said.

"I'm down."

Gus turned up the music, Bad Brains ("Classic punk, my man"), which sort of gave me a headache (Dad liked this music), and we rolled on over to Bony Emily's.

Thankfully, we caught her mowing the lawn in front of her big house and didn't have to knock on the door and potentially deal with her weird professor parents. She was wearing a pink and sparkly unicorn T-shirt, I kid you not. When we pulled up, she blinked at us, then let go of the handle of the mower, turned, and started walking really fast toward the side yard.

"Hey," Gus shouted. "Are you trying to run away?"

"Like my brother!" I shouted, getting out of the car.

Emily turned back slowly. She was red in the face. She pointed at Gus. "Your stupid girlfriend gave me lemonade with alcohol in it."

"She's very bad," Gus nodded.

"My mom says I can't be friends with her anymore."

"Your mom can't pick your friends. That's not right," said Gus.

"Hey," I said. "I'm not interested in your mom troubles."

"You're an ass, Felton," Emily said.

"Whoa. Bad mood, huh?" Gus said.

"Is my brother on an adventure or is he at orchestra camp?"

"He's on an adventure *at* orchestra camp." Bony Emily glowered. "Go away."

"Why would you tell Maddie that Andrew ran away? That's pretty psycho, don't you think?" Gus said.

"Maddie made me drunk. Now I'm grounded."

"So you lied?" I asked.

"I don't know what I said. Andrew's at orchestra camp, okay?"

I turned to Gus. "I already knew that."

"Yes. Of course. Thought we better check."

"I appreciate your concern." I actually really did appreciate his concern. "Let's go."

"Stay off the juice!" Gus shouted back at her.

"You can both screw off," Emily shouted back.

I stopped, turned, and stared at Bony Emily. "What did I do?" I asked. "Why do I have to screw off?"

"You're mean to Andrew, and that sucks."

"I am not."

"Go to hell."

Ouch. I told Andrew he should be a pharmacist.

As we drove away, Gus said, "She's sort of hot, isn't she?"

"If you like ten-year-olds," I mumbled.

"Dude, she turns fifteen in September. Andrew and his friends aren't going to stay little kids forever. She's *la high school chica* now. And, totally *en fuego*."

"No, Mr. Pervis, she is not remotely *en fuego*."

"Bet she trades that unicorn-wear for some tight black jeans and eyeliner in like a day. *La chica's* angry!" Gus said.

"Yeah, that's true…" I said. I was drifting off. Andrew on an adventure? I couldn't help but think about that word, *adventure*. Emily told Maddie that Andrew was on an adventure. Andrew told Jerri he wanted to go on an adventure by taking the bus to Green Bay alone.

Adventure.

Gus peeled around a corner. I heard my bike slide in the trunk.

"Jesus, Gus. Please slow down. Your crap driving is killing my bike."

"Crap driving?"

"Yes."

"How about this? How about you get out of my car? Our business is done."

Gus pulled over.

"Seriously?" I said.

"Seriously."

I got out and pulled my bike out of the trunk. When I closed it, Gus peeled away without saying good-bye. I watched his Celica go up Fourth Street and turn right at the next corner. I decided I'd never speak to him again.

Then, a few days later, Friday, June 21st, Andrew called while we ate a dinner of organic chicken breast and bitter artichokes. (I remember this dinner well—right before we sat down, Jerri had made plans for us to meet up with your dad in Chicago on the way to the Michigan camp, which I hadn't yet cancelled, and which I was beginning to seriously worry about.) As Andrew spoke, there was that sound of an orchestra warming up in the background, lots of sawing on strings and tuning. There were kids talking too.

Jerri asked a lot of questions about what the orchestra was doing. "Lots of practice? Trips to the Door County coast?"

"What? Coast?" Andrew asked.

"I saw your pelican picture."

"Oh. I didn't know you looked at my website…Yes, we went to the beach last week," Andrew said.

"What website?" I piped in.

"Well, your website," said Andrew.

He was referring to feltonreinstein.com, which he—very sweetly, I might add—had made for me to track all the articles and crap people wrote about me, which I never looked at because it made my stomach tie up in knots. My laptop was on the table, so I pulled it out and opened the site while Andrew described his work at the camp (in *great* detail), learning timpani from a music major named Rami (lie) who was about to be a senior at Oberlin College in Ohio (lie). "He is a wonderful teacher. A true percussion genius." (Andrew is so crafty, just like Gus said).

Here's what I saw on feltonreinstein.com: a picture of a terrifying pelican (a little scratched lens fleck in the picture, which marked it as Andrew's because he'd dropped his phone while hanging upside down from the bleachers during one of my football games in the fall). It was the first entry on the website in months. He'd abandoned posting otherwise in the middle of April.

A freaking pelican?

Andrew had written underneath it. *These birds have terrifying rubber beaks. More power to them.*

"Pelican?" I shouted.

"What?" asked Andrew.

"Pelicans in Wisconsin?" I shouted.

"Sure," Jerri said. "Pelicans migrate."

"Right," Andrew said. He sounded nervous.

"Are you meeting interesting students?" Jerri asked.

I put my ear close to the speaker. There was something artificial sounding about the background sounds. Have you ever listened to sound-effect tracks on iMovie? Gus has a really nice Apple computer and he's always made these dumb little movies (this summer starring Maddie smoking cigarettes like she's some kind of weird French girl) and he's always put lots of background sound in them.

I thought: *That noise is "Orchestra Warms Up" on a Mac computer.* Hum, hum, hum…It just kept going and going while Andrew talked about his new friends.

I kept my ear close, listening as hard as I could. Jerri swatted at my Jewfro a couple of times, but I wouldn't move away from the phone. And, suddenly, I was sure the loop started over and the same tapping and conversations were going on again.

"Holy crap!" I shouted.

"What is your problem, Felton?" Jerri hissed at me.

"Shh." I pointed at her. "Andrew," I shouted at the speaker. "Can we talk to one of your friends?"

There was a long pause.

Then Andrew asked, "Um. What?"

"Your new orchestra friends. Let's have a chat!"

"What are you doing, Felton?" Jerri asked, her face all scrunched up, her neck popped at a weird angle.

"Why would you want to talk to my friends?" Andrew asked.

"I don't know. Just for fun. Who's talking in the background?"

"Um. Tovi," Andrew said.

"Who?"

"My new friend, Tovi. She's really cream of the crop. Another really great percussionist."

"Where's she from?"

"Well. Milwaukee. Right, Tovi?"

A girl's voice sounded from the back. "Yeah," she said tentatively. "Milwaukee?"

"Really? What school?" I asked. I knew schools in Milwaukee from track and football.

"South!" this Tovi shouted.

"South?" I'd never heard of Milwaukee South High School. "South? Milwaukee South?" So many schools are south, west, north, east. *Right, good bet, fake friend!* But I had never heard of such a school in Milwaukee!

Andrew jumped in. "South Milwaukee. South Division High School."

"Right," the girl said. "South Milwaukee. South Division."

Then Jerri said, "Great! Sounds like you're having a good time. When's the performance?"

"Uh. Five weeks from Saturday, I think," Andrew said.

"Mind if Felton and I come?" Jerri asked.

"I don't know. We'll find out. I'll ask," Andrew said.

"South Division High School?" I asked.

"The brochure said the final performance is open to the public!" Jerri sang.

"Okay, well, we have to get going. Night rehearsals are pretty serious."

"I know people in Milwaukee, Tovi!" I shouted.

"Okay. Bye?" the girl replied.

"Right. Talk to you soon," Andrew said and hung up.

"She sounds nice," Jerri said.

"Oh my God! They just looked up a Milwaukee school on the Internet while we were talking. Something's going on, Jerri. He's not at orchestra camp. No way."

"*What?*" Jerri shouted.

"I'm serious!"

"What?" Jerri laughed.

"Really, Jerri. He's somewhere. He's not there."

"Felton." Jerri shook her head.

"What?"

"Crazy," Jerri nodded.

"No!"

"Really, really crazy," Jerri nodded.

"Why would you trust Andrew? There is mounting evidence!"

"Evidence? Of what?"

"I don't know. Of him not really being at the camp?"

"Uh-huh. Really?" Jerri was totally sarcastic.

"Yes," I said. I didn't want to mention drunken Emily.

"Good Lord, Felton. Chill, kid. I signed the camp permission slip. I received confirmation of payment from this camp. Where would he be, if not…"

"Grandma Berba paid for the camp!"

"So?"

"Did she send the camp the money, or did she send it to Andrew?"

"The camp sent a paid-in-full receipt here."

"Oh."

"And I received detailed instructions about where, when, how this whole thing would happen. Wouldn't the camp call me if Andrew didn't show up?"

I paused for a moment on that. Uh-huh. Logic. "Good point," I said.

"Andrew's at camp, Felton. I don't get this at all. You're crazy. Are you weirded out about Michigan? You'll be fine."

"No, I'm not worried about Michigan." (Lie.)

"Well, you're clearly the one with the problem."

"Hmm…That's possible." I thought about my problem. Give Emily away? I thought I better. "It's not from nowhere, Jerri. Bony Emily got drunk and told Gus's girlfriend that Andrew ran away."

"She *what*?" Jerri barked. "She got drunk?"

"Oh Christ." I knew I'd just blown a hole in some code of teen conduct. *Dear teen fellow…Do not tell your parent about a minorly misbehaving acquaintance, as you do not know the repercussions.* "I don't know what she did. I'm crazy."

"I'm calling Emily's mother."

"I believe she knows. Emily's grounded."

"Emily loves unicorns!" Jerri shouted.

"I know," I said. "But Gus thinks she's hot. So she's growing up."

"Emily Cook?" Jerri shouted.

"I'm a little crazy. Think I'll go for a jog."

"Andrew can't be friends with Emily if she's going to be a drunk party girl."

"Right, Jerri. You're going to tell Andrew what he can or can't do?"

"Stupid Andrew." Jerri shook her head.

"I really don't know anything, Jerri. I highly doubt Bony Emily is a partyer."

"Stupid Emily."

"Very dumb." I stood up and stretched.

"Don't run too fast, Felton," Jerri said, clearly not thinking about my running.

"Um…okay?" I said. I stared at Jerri.

Jerri shook her head at me, mouth hanging open, eyes wide. "Emily Cook."

"I know," I said, and clapped my hands and went for a jog up and down the main road, where I tried to make sense of this whole business. I was actually worried for Andrew. Could he possibly be alone some place other than camp?

No. Jerri has receipts. Brochures. Jerri's right…

Wrong.

The next couple of days I worked out a ton and did what I was supposed to do, but I couldn't concentrate for crap. (Cody actually hit me in the face with a pass once because I wasn't paying attention.) I could only think about Andrew, and my fear about him grew and grew. I felt pains in my chest, Aleah.

The following is a mantra I repeated in my brain for like seventy-two hours straight: *This is a well-known and reputable camp! They wouldn't just forget a kid is supposed to be there! They'd get sued!*

Then, in the middle of the week, I couldn't take it anymore. I was supposed to meet Cody and Karpinski to run routes, but I hadn't slept the night before and was seriously obsessing on Andrew's whereabouts, so I called Andrew's phone.

He didn't answer. His voice mail message sang (Andrew's crazy-high canary voice singing "Leave a Message!" instead of "Hallelujah!").

I left a voice mail. *Andrew, I have a weird feeling. I have a weird, weird feeling that you're not where you say you are. Please call me. Jerri needs to know if you're doing something weird or unsafe, okay? Are you at camp? If so, prove it. God damn it, Andrew. I don't need this crap! I have things to do!*

Yes, I got angry while I spoke to his stupid phone.

Andrew didn't call me back. I could barely run routes. Cody shouted at me, "What the hell, Rein Stone? Do you have a brain disorder?"

"Maybe," I said.

After Andrew didn't respond for like ten hours, I sent him a few angry texts and left one more message: *You are messing with me!*

Then, finally, Thursday morning of that week, things began to come into focus.

I woke after not sleeping again. I checked for messages on my phone. There were none. I called Andrew. He didn't answer. I opened my email and here is what I found: A message from Randy Stone, but from a different email: FtMyersStone@gmail.com.

Dear Sir,

The underestimated child detective, Randy Stone, knows a few things all too well. First, those who assume tiny Andrew Reinstein to be somebody other than what he purports to be are correct. He is not a percussionist. Second, those who find Andrew's older brother to be remotely intelligent have been utterly fooled and are obviously not terribly intelligent themselves. Felton has refused to figure out that which is directly in front of his face, though he has been prompted. He has refused to listen to that which has been placed directly in his ears and eyeballs again and again so that he might figure the world out by himself. He learned nothing. Now, when it is too late, the dull Felton Reinstein has an inkling something is off. He should not be proud.

I stopped reading. My mouth, I'm sure, was hanging open, my eyeballs likely popped out of my head. Wait…Wait…Who is *Randy Stone*?

I read on…

In his second missive, the detective mentioned Fiddlesticks, Florida. In his third missive, the detective alluded to three non-Felton "Reinstein" hits on the Internet provided by his Google

Alert. Felton failed to follow up on either clue and is thus a complete dunderhead with no brain to speak of.

I stopped. I hadn't received a third missive. Then I thought and realized that—holy balls, Aleah—I'd marked Randy Stone email as spam because I didn't want to get bad stuff from Gus, but this wasn't Gus and I didn't receive the third email at all. I went back into my trash folder and—holy balls—I found it.

It was dated April 15th. I'd never, never read it. I didn't see it. This is it:

The brilliant child detective Randy Stone has pursued Felton Reinstein in the following ways: He has established a Google Alert on the word "Reinstein," which returns each day a list of places on the Internet where Felton Reinstein has been mentioned. These sites describe Mr. Reinstein's prowess on both field and track. They herald his "motor" and his "competitive spirit." They detail his future prospects as a collegiate athlete and suggest collegiate athletic programs where Mr. Reinstein's particular and peculiar skills would best be put to use. The good detective then compiled these articles on a website, feltonreinstein.com, in order for all fans of Mr. Reinstein to find the news they want in one place. Along with the web links, Randy Stone uploaded pictures and nice biographical information regarding Felton Reinstein and his family.

Let it be known: Randy Stone enjoyed doing so.

Here is a bit that may not be known:

By placing a Google Alert on "Reinstein" without attaching the name Felton, Randy Stone hoped to capture any other information about the worldwide Reinstein clan that might shed light on the detective's inability to smoke cigarettes adequately. Only three times did other information show up on the Net.

1. Once when Andrew Reinstein made the honor roll in February.

2. Once when the combination of Robert Rein was pressed accidentally against Stein, Gertrude in a bibliographic catalog. It looked like this: "…authored by Robert Rein; Stein, Gertrude, *Collected Works*…"

3. And, finally, two weeks ago, when there was one other very significant non-Felton mention.

The talented child detective tried to speak with Felton Reinstein about this third mention. But, Felton would not talk and told the detective he should "shake it off."

That is it. That is the end. No more feltonreinstein.

The detective is on his own.

"Holy shit!" I shouted. It was only at that moment that the full truth of the matter came into my brain. Andrew. Andrew was Randy Stone. Andrew had warned me about what he was doing, but I'd paid no attention. Andrew had closed himself in his bedroom to get away from me and to plan…whatever the hell he was up to.

I went back to look at the second email Randy Stone had sent. It was totally whacked out and talked about Florida, but was mostly about a special carpet and delicious cigarettes. I'm supposed to follow any of that? I'm supposed to think someone with some kind of superior intelligence is leading me through a series of clues?

Seriously, Randy Stone did not help communicate anything for Andrew. He just made me mad and what he said was pretty much unintelligible. For instance, that Fiddlesticks clue would be totally meaningless to anybody (not just dumb me). Fiddlesticks? A real place? How would I know?

Then I read his third email again.

I focused on this:

> 3. And, finally, two weeks ago, when there was one other very significant non-Felton mention.

What the hell did that mean?

So, I did it myself. I Googled Reinstein, which I hate doing because there's so much crap about me. And, yes, up popped a giant wad about me. A tremendous, ridiculous, confusing wad. Also, up popped a tiny little bit about my dad, which detailed how Steven Reinstein was an All-American tennis player at Northwestern University in the 1980s. But, really, mostly all of it was about me. There were like 75,000 hits. Was I really supposed to wade through these to figure out the tiny few that weren't about me or my dad (or maybe Andrew on the honor roll)?

Then I became very, very mad. Picture me shaking my fist in the air, crying out, *"Andrewwwww!"*

He spent all his time gathering Google crap. When whatever website went up that had the non-Felton info on it, he received that alert that day. For me, finding that odd Reinstein mention was like searching for an ant with a weird-shaped thorax, but still just a single ant, in a giant freaking Mexican ant hill. Impossible!

I almost called Jerri at her job. She was already gone for the day. She was at the Edward Jones office, where she works part-time. I wanted to yell at her for having created the terrible monster Andrew. I wanted to tell her that she'd been duped, and, according to Randy Stone, Andrew wasn't even a percussionist (whatever that means). I picked up the phone, then stopped myself, because freaking out on Jerri did not appeal to me in the slightest. *Repercussions? Crazy Jerri?*

I went back to Randy Stone's new message.

The outlook is not "rosy." A rose of another name would not be named "Rose" Reinstein.

With this, the child detective Randy Stone lights another cigarette, which catches fire and nearly burns his hands off. He hacks out his totally sick lungs, watches the smoke trail up into the tropical sky, and wonders if Andrew and Felton could even possibly be related, because Felton is so sadly dumb.

That Felton figured out the lack of percussion instruction in Andrew's present is a near-on miracle that should be taken to the Pope.

Good day.

P.S. Randy Stone knows not to tell Jerri because she might go crazy like last summer.

Jerk, Andrew!

What about his P.S.?

Here's me: *Can't tell. Can't tell. Whatever Andrew is into might be bad enough to knock Jerri off her solid rock. What if Andrew is part of an apocalypse cult? What if he's wearing long burlap robes and is taking hallucinogenic magical mushrooms that make him think his name is Randy Stone? What if he's decided to grow roses in Florida? Wouldn't that freak Jerri out, because he refuses to help in the garden ever? What does a rose of another name would not be named "Rose" Reinstein mean?*

ANDREW!

I stood up. I looked toward the door, toward the freedom of the road where I might run…

But, instead of just running around Bluffton and jumping up and down like a monkey and cursing Andrew's name, I paused, breathed, sat back down, and Googled "Rose" Reinstein.

Every result that came up on the Google page referred to me, except for the very first one. I stared at this result. It was an obituary from the *Fort Myers News-Press* dated March 29 (the same week when everything went bad for me—and you, I guess, Aleah). I took a deep breath and then clicked on the link. Here's what I saw:

Rose Reinstein, 71, of Fort Myers died the morning of Wednesday, March 28, surrounded by family. Survived by her beloved husband, Stan; daughter, Evith (David Halpen); granddaughter, Tovi; and two grandsons, Felton and Andrew. Preceded in death by son, Steven. Born in Prague (the Czech Republic);

an accomplished tennis player and track athlete in her youth. Rose played golf at Fiddlesticks with the same group for fifteen years and volunteered for numerous local organizations. She was a beautiful light to all who knew her. Services will be at the Centennial Cemetery on Monday. In lieu of flowers, please send gifts to the American Cancer Society.

Holy God, Aleah.

Do you have any idea? I mean, what the holy freaking…what?

Rose. Stan. Steven.

Tovi?

Andrew. (Poor Andrew.)

Felton.

Rose and Stan. My grandparents. I met them when I was a little kid (tiny). A couple times. In Florida too. (That other time I flew.) I could picture a skinny woman with big hands and a giant smile that took up the bottom half of her face. She had black, curly hair like mine. This is what I knew too: these grandparents, they did not like Jerri. They did not like Grandma Berba. They stayed away from Andrew and me entirely: no cards, no phone calls, no anything.

(I didn't know anything.)

They lost their son because he killed himself in our garage (Dad). And, Rose, my grandmother, died of cancer.

• • •

Jesus, Aleah. It's like five in the morning.

August 16th, 9:15 a.m.
O'HARE AIRPORT, PART XIII

I was just going to leave it at that, Aleah. I finally (like three hours ago) fell asleep thinking: that's all she needs to know, that Andrew disappeared because of something to do with my dad's parents (one of whom is totally dead, like Dad). Aleah's not my family. Ronald has probably told her everything anyway and she never bothered to contact me, which is terrible.

Aleah? You've really made me feel bad. Do you know that? What am I suppose to do?

Forget it.

Want to know something funny? There's a heat wave in the South. One airport is having delays because of pavement issues. One airport just shut down completely because of some kind of power outage. Fort Myers is fine, apparently, but they're having problems with planes getting where they need to be everywhere in the system. I am very confused.

I actually said to the gate agent, without stuttering or stumbling, because I was pissed: "The South doesn't know how to handle hot weather? That's ridiculous."

"Not this kind of hot, sir. This is unprecedented."

Sir? Unprecedented? Like in the world? Makes me worry about the future.

Now they won't tell me if my flight's going to get the crap out of here on time.

I am angry. *Angry! Monkey chest pound.*

I do not enjoy air travel, for it puts me in prison.

• • •

My legs feel like Jell-O. Donkey needs to run.

What if I'm stuck in Chicago forever?

Jerri would come get me.

Your dad is still in Bluffton, so he can't just drive over to O'Hare and take me for breakfast.

Maybe I'll still be here when you get back from Germany on Friday morning. Then you can spit on my shoes in person.

Or maybe we'd make up?

No. Maybe.

Gus and I sort of made up after I received that unbelievable email from Randy Stone. Who could I call? Who could I talk to? Not Jerri, you know? After falling on the floor for like three hours, I decided no, no, no Jerri.

I called Gus.

(After I left Andrew several hysterical voice mails, by the way.)

Gus didn't pick up when I called, of course. But in my message I pretty much shouted: "Check your email immediately!" Then I forwarded him the child detective Randy Stone dispatch.

Gus called me back about thirty seconds after I hit *Send*.

"Holy shit!"

"Yeah," I said.

"Randy Freaking Stone! Andrew!"

"Uh-huh," I said. "I'm sorry I blamed you for that crap."

"I wish I did it because Randy Stone's awesome, but I didn't," Gus said.

"Uh-huh."

"Jesus. That drunken, bony unicorn girl told the truth, didn't she?"

"Looks that way," I said.

"Whoa, man. So weird."

Gus knowing about this made me feel better.

"Where do you think he went? Is he smoking cigarettes, that sly devil? What the hell is going on? What's all that 'rosy' babble about at the end?"

"I think he's probably in Florida. I think maybe with our cousin, Tovi. I don't know for sure, though."

"Evidence?"

"He posted a picture of a pelican on feltonreinstein.com."

"Solid."

"Couple days ago he claimed his new friend at orchestra camp is named Tovi."

"So?"

"The Rose babble at the bottom led me to my grandma's obituary where a girl named Tovi is listed as our cousin."

"Grandma? Grandma Berba? What do you mean? Grandma who?"

"Grandma Rose Reinstein."

"Wow." Gus's voice lost its normal edge. No one else in the world other than Andrew and Jerri would know exactly what that meant. (Long. Lost. Grandparent.) "No shit, Felton."

"Yeah. Yeah. Seriously."

"What are you going to do? Tell Jerri?"

"I don't know. I don't know…No."

"Whoa," he said.

"I don't know," I said.

"Aw, Jesus Christ, Felton."

"What?"

"Do you want to hang out or something?" he asked, clearly not totally convinced he should.

"Yeah," I said. "Please."

"Okay," he sort of whispered.

• • •

Announcement on loudspeaker…

Oh, god-dang dog crap.

My flight is now officially delayed.

I'm in prison, Aleah.

August 16th, 9:43 a.m.

O'HARE AIRPORT, PART XIV

At least another two hours…

Just talked to Jerri. She says she'll drive down to Chicago right now to pick me up and take me home. I'm only supposed to be in Florida until Thursday at the ass cracker of dawn (to get Andrew).

"Is it really worth this?" she asked me. "You could go to football practice the rest of the week so you'll be ready for your game, and you know Andrew is fully capable of taking care of himself. He's fine."

"No," I told her. "I want to go to Florida."

Now I'm not exactly sure I'm making the right choice. I mean, in a lot of ways, I really don't want to go to the Dangling Sack (Florida). Most ways, really. *Okay…Okay…Calm, boy.* I can't just run away.

Do not be reactionary, young Felton. You want to be there for your poor brother, Andrew.

Reactionary. Monkeys fling their own poop, Aleah. Why? Because it's there.

• • •

Gus and I spent that afternoon driving around trying to figure out what Andrew, aka Detective Randy Stone, was up to.

"Is there any way the little dude is actually at camp and is pulling stuff just to mess with you? You know, asking Emily to spread rumors and then sending weird emails and grandparent links?" Gus asked.

"No. I don't think he's into random torment. I think he has a real agenda. He always seems to, anyway."

"Such a weird kid, man. And you're not telling Jerri because…? What? Her crazy breakdown last summer?"

"Yeah."

Gus smoked cigarettes, which I don't appreciate very much, but what was I going to say: "Please don't smoke in your car while you try to help me even though you don't like me anymore?" Then, when he ran out of cigarettes, we drove over to Maddie's house to pick her up, because apparently she's his supplier.

"I don't want Maddie to know about this."

"Uh. She already does. I called her before I picked you up," Gus said.

"Everyone's going to find out!" I shouted at him.

"Maddie is far more loyal and dependable than the people you know," Gus said.

Maddie smoked many, many cigarettes, especially after we purchased two more packs at this decrepit gas station out in Stitzer that didn't even question her status as an eighteen-year-old. (She is fifteen.) I rode in the backseat. They cranked music. I thought about how I should be running, packing, getting ready for Michigan instead of sitting there gulping poison. Gus smoked even more cigarettes. I hacked and hacked in the gross Toyota backseat, while they smoked those freaking cigarettes and sang along to loud songs. Everything in the world smelled like their smoke.

I like Gus, though. I do. He's good. Maddie's good too.

We drove out to Belmont Mound Woods and climbed the old fire tower out there. Maddie talked a million miles a minute, even as we climbed up, which impressed me because how could Missy Smokes-so-much get enough air in her tarred and feathered lungs?

"Let him live his life, Felton," she said. "Andrew's finding out the truth about your whole thing, right? Figuring out the family. It's amazing. Let him do it, man."

"Yeah, but I don't know what he's doing, and he could totally get killed or something."

"By who? His old grandpa?" she asked. "His grandpa's going to kill him?"

"No. By gangs, maybe. He's alone and tiny. I don't know that he's with our grandfather. I'm pretty sure our grandpa hates us."

Gus piped in. "You should call your grandfather, man. He might be in on this, don't you think? Where's the money coming from? Trips to Florida aren't free. He probably paid to get Andrew down there, but he really has to know that Andrew's a slippery little bitch," Gus said.

"Please." My chest ached when Gus said that. "Please. Stop calling him 'bitch.'"

"Sorry. He is slippery like a mossy rock."

"He's awesome beautiful," Maddie said. "Andrew's like a French film."

"He's crazy like a French film," said Gus.

I thought about calling my grandfather, and my stomach knotted up and I pretty much dry-heaved. I had no idea really who he was, and anything I knew was bad. (Grandma Berba said terrible things about him.)

From up on top of Belmont Tower you can see a ton of rolling southwest Wisconsin. You can see the backside of the big mound with the M on it where you and me hung out, where I used to run, and where my dad used to run before me. *You should be running, not hanging out with skinny jean smokers…*

Then Gus said, "We should go to Fort Myers."

Maddie said, "*Yeah!*"

Gus said, "Just me and Felton, probably. We don't want kidnapping charges, Mads. Your mom would totally press charges. Let me think."

I said, "What? What? Jesus. *How?*"

"Let me think," Gus said.

• • •

Damn it. They're announcing something over the loudspeaker, but I can't freaking understand a word of it. What a damn joke.

August 16th, 10:25 a.m.

O'HARE AIRPORT, PART XV

The airline is offering vouchers for people not to fly. That means if I choose not to take this flight to Fort Myers I could get a later flight and then get a free ticket any place in the U.S. Great news, except I have no place else to fly. They aren't even certain there will be a plane available to go to Fort Myers for this flight, Aleah. I really wish I were driving.

Maybe I should call Jerri? Shit…

• • •

Okay. Jerri was sitting in the living room when Gus and Maddie dropped me off that night. It was 10 p.m., so she was pretty sleepy, because 10 p.m. is what she calls her "witching hour" (which I don't understand because why would "witching" make you sleepy?). When I climbed the stairs she said, "Who were you with?"

"Gus."

"I can smell that."

"Oh?"

"I hope you don't do things that Gus does."

"Of course I don't."

"Well…your dad, you know genetics…You should tell Gus to

cut it out. I saw him smoking in front of the Piggly Wiggly the other day. He's going to get himself addicted."

"Dad?"

"Nothing, okay?" Jerri said. She was a little pale.

"Are you okay?"

"Just Andrew didn't call tonight," she said. "I'm worried."

"He's probably busy."

"I know. He said he wouldn't call every night."

"Right," I nodded.

"Wish you hadn't accused him of running away," Jerri said.

"Ha, ha, ha...I'm crazy," I said.

"I almost called the camp today to..."

"No need to do that! I talked to Andrew. He's fine. He's doing great. I'm paranoid."

"You talked to him?"

"Yeah!"

"Good. Good. I'm actually glad you care about him, Felton. It's not always clear."

"Really?"

"Yeah, really. I'm going to bed," Jerri said.

That hurt. Shouldn't have shocked me that she'd say that, of course.

Later, I sat awake imagining Andrew alone in Florida, a little homeless boy panhandling on a beach.

Here's what's weird: I couldn't really be sure he was in Fort Myers, not from the freaking Randy Stone emails, you know? It could all be a smoke screen...But, actually, I knew. I knew it. I knew he was there. I also knew this: there was no way in hell I wanted to go to Florida.

Possibly meet my dad's dad?

No way.

But...I knew I could go. I knew I could work it out. I knew I maybe should go...

There was only one place I wanted to go less than Florida: the Michigan technique camp.

I texted Gus: *I might have a plan.*

August 16th, 10:58 a.m.
O'HARE AIRPORT, PART XVI

My ass is killing me.

Just checked. No word on the flight. I am very stressed out.

Do you get stressed out, Aleah? The only time I'm not at least a little stressed is when I'm playing something (like football or Frisbee). Track is sort of stressful to me (not the practice part, but the actual events, because everything is riding on one shot—which I don't react well to sometimes—like when I false-started and barfed at Regionals when I was a sophomore). Even with football, recruiters stress me out, so I don't know if I'll enjoy playing this year.

Jesus, I really, really don't want to spend my whole life feeling like that. I don't want to stay awake half the nights of my freaking life sweating sweaty bullets, Aleah.

Do you ever wonder if you're not cut out for life? You probably don't. I know you don't. I wonder about my dad. Is this how he felt?

• • •

The morning Gus and I hatched our plan, I actually studied the one picture we have of Dad in the house. It's the only one Jerri saved, remember? As part of Jerri's new-style peacemaking with the past in February, she put the picture on the refrigerator. In it,

I'm like a toddler, blurry big head in the front left-hand corner. Jerri and Dad are behind me, him behemoth and square-jawed and happy, with the same Jewfro hair that I have. Jerri looks young and pretty and happy (which I know wasn't the case).

Dad looked happy.

He wasn't happy. He couldn't have been.

I want to be happy, not look happy.

Gus called while I sat at the table staring down at that thing.

"So, you have an idea?" Gus asked.

"Yeah, I think so," I said. I wasn't actually sure I wanted to say it. (I knew Gus would do something with it, start plan making.) I took a deep breath. "I'm supposed to go to a football camp at the University of Michigan this weekend. You want to drive me there, but not drive me there?"

"Oh," Gus said.

"Uh-huh," I said. I could feel myself flush. Fear.

"Oh hell, yeah." I could hear Gus thinking. Gus's gears turned. "I can work with that. Uh-huh. I think I need to make an academic visit to the University of Michigan," he said.

"Yeah. That makes sense," I said.

"Good school. Mama Teresa will like this…"

"Mama Jerri might not," I said.

"Call you back in a bunny breath, dude."

It took Gus ten minutes to get back to me. (The whole time, I stared at my dad's picture and got more and more hesitant to go to Florida and face my grandfather. *Why is Andrew so interested in the family*, I wondered. *Why isn't he scared?*)

"Okay," Gus said. "Michigan is the fourth-ranked public university in the country. I used that. The parents are in."

"Oh shit," I said.

"They're giving me a credit card for the gas and the Motel 6 I pretended to book, and a Triple A card, whatever the hell that is."

"Jesus," I said.

"Only one hitch—my dad wants me to meet up with an acquaintance of his from grad school. I'll figure a way around that."

"Why are they so easy?" I asked, really not believing it.

"You get near perfect on the SAT, you get what you want," Gus said.

It's true. He missed like one freaking question.

"How about Jerri?" he asked.

"She really wants to drive me. She wants to see Aleah's dad for some reason."

"Let me talk to her. You'll mumble and crap. You sound like a liar even when you're not lying."

He's right. I do sound like a liar. Also, isn't it weird that I didn't know about our parents' affair in June? Did you know, Aleah?

We decided Gus would come over before dinner to talk to Jerri. (He said flat out he wouldn't stay for dinner because he wasn't going to eat another shitbag, veggie-slop, Jerri-made meal ever again.)

• • •

Wait…

Someone is saying my name on the loudspeaker?

August 16th, 11:27 a.m.
O'HARE AIRPORT, PART XVII

I'm at a new gate. I'm flying to Charlotte, North Carolina. We're boarding in a few minutes. From there I'll go to Fort Myers. Fine. Who cares? I want to go someplace.

Cody just texted me to say Coach Johnson moved his son, Kirk—a stinking *sophomore*—from flanker to running back this morning. *Aaaahhh…I'm so, so, so pissed!*

Jesus. Makes me want to kick something. It's so freaking dumb. I'm the tailback, Aleah. I'm pretty good at it (duh). Why would Coach Johnson do that? Kirk is fast and super athletic (just like his brother Ken). If we have him opposite Karpinski in the passing game we'll be great this year.

When I wrote back *WHAT????* Cody texted: *Coach isnt sure you be back for game.*

Jesus.

You know, nobody forced me to miss practice. I made the decision to not be in Bluffton today. I'm fine with that. I'm fine that I'm not there. It was totally my decision.

Man, Aleah. I do worry. Am I destroying my football career?

• • •

Skipping Michigan hurt. After Gus asked his parents if he could take me to Michigan and they said yes, I emailed the offensive coordinator at Michigan to tell him I couldn't go due to family reasons. He called me up right away—I'm serious, like ten seconds after I hit *Send* on the email—but I didn't answer and I never got back to him. (I was lying on the floor on my stomach when he called.) A couple of weeks ago, Coach Johnson told me Michigan is no longer interested in me.

I worry. I worry. I worry.

Here's what I worry about most: I was so damn relieved not to have to go to that camp. How am I going to choose a college and go play football there? Why was it so easy for you to go to Berlin?

• • •

Okay. There it is. There's the call. I'm boarding a plane for freaking Charlotte, North Carolina. This is *now*. I'm on my way.

August 16th, 12:30 p.m.
ON THE WAY TO CHARLOTTE

Uh...Okay...

I'm sitting next to a very large man who is very unhappy to be stuck in the middle of two teens. (There's a girl in black reading a zombie book on the aisle). The man is wheezing and is very gross. He just ordered a tiny bottle of wine.

Go to Florida instead of practice football? This is where my good intentions get me: jammed against the airplane wall by a giant wine-sucking wheezer man. Huff, huff, huff. (Sound of him breathing while he stares at the side of my head.)

• • •

Okay, so Gus's parents were on board with the drive to Michigan. Right?

There was just the Jerri question left.

It was a big question too, Aleah. First, Jerri was stung that Andrew had requested a solo bus trip to his orchestra camp (although Jerri knew not the entirety of the situation). Second, Jerri had made plans with your dad to stop in Chicago on Saturday on our drive to Ann Arbor. I sure as crap didn't want to be at your apartment, but Jerri was very excited. ("I haven't *seen* Ronald in four months!") I didn't think there was anyway she'd let Gus drive me.

When Gus arrived, Jerri was in the kitchen making us some ugly looking hippie hummus and bean sprout sandwiches. (I like hummus, but I don't like sprouts—they get stuck in my teeth and then people make crap of me—at least Abby Sauter did one time in fifth grade—"booger tooth.") Jerri didn't act like a nice hippie, though. When Gus and I entered the kitchen, she smiled really fake and said, "If it isn't my favorite nicotine addict! Has your girl-friend gotten any tweens drunk lately?"

Gus stood there with his mouth open, his face turning red. "Um. Not that I'm aware of, Jerri."

"Great. Great to hear, Gus."

"That's not why we're here, Jerri," I said.

"Really?" Jerri asked. "Why are you here? Is it because you live here, Felton?"

"What's with the sarcasm?"

"I'm just a little angry with your little friend, I suppose," Jerri said, glaring at Gus.

"Jerri," Gus whispered. "I quit smoking. It's bad for me. I got a hacking cough. And Maddie? She's really crazy, you know? But she tries hard. And she's got a good heart. She's really a sweet person. I'm serious."

Gus was working Jerri. Jerri grew up a townie girl like Maddie. She couldn't not feel for her. Gus's lies actually made me feel kind of bad. He still smoked! Maddie did not try hard!

Maybe she does try hard?

Maybe she's like me who isn't Peyton Manning because her family (my family) is screwed up? Complicated.

Jerri nodded. She swallowed. She stared at Gus for a moment. Then she said, "Tell her not to get eighth graders drunk, okay? It really upsets me. It's also dangerous. Emily Cook can't weigh more than eighty pounds, you know?"

"I know, Jerri. Maddie feels bad about what happened," Gus nodded.

"That's not why we're here, though, Jerri," I said.

"Okay, then. Why are you here, Felton?"

Gus jumped in. "Something pretty cool happened today. My dad's friend at U Mich, Hector Johns—he's a professor there—invited me to take a campus tour while Felton's at football camp."

I nodded.

Jerri said, "Oh? That's nice…You're welcome to ride with us, if you'd like."

"That'd be great, but I actually need to have my own transportation because I'll be going back and forth from campus to the Motel 6 where I'm staying all week. So, I'll be driving."

"Yeah! Pretty great, huh, Jerri?" I piped in. Gus sort of kneed me in the thigh.

"I'll be driving, so really Felton should just catch a ride with me," Gus said. "No reason for us to pump double the carbon dioxide into the air. I guess more like quadruple, really, since you'll be driving back to Bluffton, then returning to Ann Arbor to pick Felton up."

This was very smooth operating by Gus. Best way to break a nice person like my mom is to make her think doing what she really wants to do is going to harm the environment and stop all future generations from existing.

Jerri shook her head, put her hands on her hips, and looked up at the ceiling. She said, "I was really looking forward to this drive for some reason."

Of course, I knew why. I didn't *know* know (didn't think they were going to be like...boyfriend and girlfriend), but I knew she wanted to see your dad. Before Gus could stop me from talking, I said, "Jerri, I think maybe you should just visit Ronald this weekend even if I'm not with you. You could stay a couple of days, then help him move stuff back here for the summer session."

Jerri looked at me. Squinted a little. "You think, Felton?"

"Oh, yeah. If I could visit Aleah, I sure as hell would," I said. (I really didn't know they were becoming a couple!)

"Nice language, son," Jerri said. "Maybe I will."

"Chicago's not far," Gus said.

"Shut up, Gus," Jerri said. "Enough rhetoric, okay?"

"Huh?" Gus said, as if he didn't know.

This was definitely the weekend when our parents became an official unit, Aleah. You have my lying to thank for it.

Anyway, it was a done deal. There. We did it. Gus was driving me to Ann Arbor, except not to Ann Arbor at all.

Out on our driveway Gus whispered, "What's up with Jerri? She's kind of mean these days."

True. Jerri was not acting the part of the Jerri I'd known my whole life. This was not a bad thing. "I think she's snapping out of the depression she's been in for like eleven years, maybe. I don't know, exactly."

"Oh," Gus said. "I like it."

So, we were all set up with lies and bull crap, all set to hit the road. Apparently I have enough courage to seriously, crazily lie to my mom, even if I'm scared to go to a camp by myself.

• • •

Oh Jesus, Aleah, the plane is bouncing up and down. I think we're possibly crashing. Seriously. The big dude just spilled a tiny bottle of wine all over himself. This is a disaster. Oh God. Jesus.

Turbulence. The big guy smiled at me. "F-bombing turbulence." Now he's reading what I'm writing: *Hello, man. My name is Felton.*

He just said, "Hiya, Felton!" I think he's had four tiny bottles of wine.

No, only three. "Three, Felton!" he said.

He is saying out loud anything I type.

I'm a big, drunk jerk!

He didn't say that.

Sorry.

He said it's okay.

The girl with the zombie book is laughing. Why can't she be my girlfriend, Aleah? She's right here. She's cute.

Sorry. I don't mean it.

The man just read that whole thing out loud to the girl. She laughed at me.

I'm going to close the computer.

August 16th, 2:35 p.m.

ON THE WAY TO CHARLOTTE, PART II

The big drunk guy is snoring like Grandma Berba when she has a cold.

Chainsaw McGraw.

I almost fell asleep, but then the little girl in front of me moved her chair back and smashed my knees at the same moment my favorite big drunk ripped on his chain saw. I woke thinking I was in a horror movie (with zombies chain-sawing through the door of the tiny, smashed closet I'm hiding in).

No. I'm just smashed on a plane, Aleah. (You should see how I'm typing—like a hobbit with arthritis, all bent up in a tiny hobbit-sized space.)

Also reminds me of being smashed in Gus's smoky car for like a thousand hours. Gus and I didn't get along very well on our trip. It started bad and got worse.

The start?

On Friday morning when we were supposed to leave, he was totally late to pick me up. He was supposed to get me right after he finished the freaking paper route. "Oh yeah, about six, man. I'll be there."

Jerri and I waited in the living room, my big bag filled with false football stuff and lying on the floor. And I felt horrible and guilty and sweaty and afraid. It got later and later. I called Gus at 6:40 to see what was the matter. He didn't answer. Why wouldn't he answer? Because he didn't want to.

Freaking anxiety! There were many, many lies afloat in the Bluffton air, Aleah.

As it got lighter and brighter and later, Jerri sat there in that same gross robe she'd worn all last summer when she was getting more and more depressed until she didn't get out of bed and didn't shower and just wore that ugly robe day in and day out, looking like a dead lady wearing a robe. I hate that robe.

I didn't say anything about her robe.

Jerri didn't say anything about anything for that whole hour we waited. Together, we stared out the window at the empty main road. Together we sat in silence waiting for the great, late douche Gus.

Then, after it became 7 a.m. and not the six o'clock hour at all, probably to break the tension she could tell was totally exploding inside of me, Jerri said, "Talked to Andrew late last night. He's having a great time. Really loves that Tovi girl."

"Oh-ho-ho," I said.

"Tovi is an interesting name," Jerri said. "I've never heard it except your dad's sister named her kid Tovi. Do you remember Evith, your aunt?"

"*No!*" I shouted.

"What?" Jerri asked.

"I don't remember her," I said.

"It's funny, you know? Evith and I got along really well back in the day. Why do people treat each other so poorly? I lost my husband too. They didn't just lose their son and brother."

"Wow," I said.

"It's been over eleven years now. I can't believe it."

"No!"

"Yeah, we've never talked much about your dad's family…"

"Never!" I said.

"It's high time. I don't know why I hid things. When Andrew gets back from camp, we should really sit down and try to collect all these bits and pieces and…Do you know Ronald and Aleah specifically sit down once a week to discuss her feelings about her mom?"

"Jesus!" I said.

"Felton?" Jerri asked,

"Wow!" I said. I could feel sweat beading up on my forehead. I jumped off the couch and started pacing around. Did Jerri know what was going on? What was this about you and your dad? Why was she bringing this family business up now? Did Jerri know something more? Had Andrew told her what was going on? Did Andrew talk to you and you talk to Ronald and Ronald talk to Jerri? "Whoa," I said.

"Uh," Jerri looked up at me, one eyebrow raised. "Are you okay, Felton?"

"No."

Just then, just in time—as I was just about to blow this whole wicked sham out into the open, drop the bomb, drop everything—an hour and fourteen minutes later than Gus was supposed to be, his Toyota rolled down the main road toward our house. The windows were down and smoke billowed out. Have you ever seen a Cheech and Chong movie? They're on cable sometimes. Billowing smoke.

"Ah, crap," I said. There were two people in the car. "Freaking Maddie."

"That Gus is such a two-bit sack of B.S.," Jerri shouted, standing up. "I don't want you to go with him."

"I have to go with him, Jerri."

"Does Gus take drugs?"

"No."

"You swear on…You swear on your Grandma Berba's grave?"

"Grandma Berba isn't dead."

"She will be one day. And she'll be buried. And you'll have to live with this lie for the rest of your life, kid."

This call to honesty was not exactly the kind of thing I needed to hear at that moment, but I kept my composure. As far as I know, dipshit Gus—who smokes and acts all irresponsible while maintaining excessively high grades—is not remotely on drugs.

"Jerri," I mumbled, my brow and hands sweaty and gross, "I swear on Grandma Berba's future grave. Gus is not on drugs. I haven't known him ever to take even a single drug. He is totally clean in that way. I say this to the best of my knowledge, okay? So you can't blame me if Gus does take drugs and I don't know about it, okay?"

"Okay." Jerri narrowed her eyes at me. "Grandma Berba can safely die now."

"Jesus. Shut up, Jerri."

Jerri blinked at me. "I'm just joking, Felton. No big deal."

"When do you joke?" I said.

"Whenever I want," Jerri said.

I was wound tight, I tell you.

Then Gus honked and Jerri flew out the door and started giving him and Maddie the wholesale business regarding smoking cigarettes and being late and getting little kids drunk on lemonade. By the time I dragged my bag out there, Maddie and Gus looked truly terrified, mouths opened, nostrils flared, like a great, terrible wind blew in their faces. Then Jerri gave me a big hug, helped me throw my gear in the trunk, gave me a hug again, pointed at Gus and Maddie and shook her head, then waved and smiled. Gus put the car in reverse and turned around.

"Your mom is a savage, savage woman," Maddie said.

"Who knew?" Gus said.

"I sure as hell didn't," I said. Then I looked back at Maddie. "Please tell me you're not coming."

"No," she said, her fake French face getting all pouty. "I have to stay in Bluffton to do Gus's stupid paper route."

"Come on, not just that…You have to baby-sit your cousin," Gus said.

"And baby-sit my diaper-assed, worm-filled, little skank of a cousin."

"She's a two-year-old," Gus said to me. "Kids are pretty damn gross, man. I saw her eat a cricket."

When we dropped Maddie off at her house, she and Gus made out for about ten minutes, all wound in a tight ball, falling over on the hood in broad morning light. While they made out, I sat in the passenger seat with squirrel-nut anxiety firing down my legs and arms. We needed to get the crap out of town before somebody stopped us or somebody figured out who Tovi was or somebody gave me enough of a brain to stop the madness and just go to Michigan. Gus and Maddie kissed and kissed. Ridiculous.

(Also made me miss you, Aleah. A lot.)

When Gus finally got back in the car he said, "Why are you so sweaty?"

My mouth took off! "Are you kidding? We lied to your parents and told Jerri that you were meeting up with some U Mich professor Hector dude, and Jerri wanted to talk about Dad's family this morning, and if you don't meet up with this Hector and Jerri sees your mom or dad and asks about how your visit with Hector is going and they call him to ask…we're totally busted. Totally screwed."

"Felton," Gus said. "Calm, buddy. We're going to be busted, okay? There's no doubt. Our parents aren't idiots. We said all that crap so we could get the hell out of town. Once we're gone, we're gone. Then when the crap hits, we'll tell the truth. It's not like they're going to call the cops on us, you know? So, just relax and enjoy the ride, okay?"

"Oh," I said. I took a deep breath. "Okay." I looked straight forward, not at Maddie, who was being bitched out by her mom on her front step.

And then Gus took off like a bat out of Bluffton (a very slow bat, because his Toyota is not a fast car at all).

• • •

Oh man. Turbulence. Chainsaw snoring man's head just bounced off my shoulder.

Oh shit. I hate this flight. I could be home. I'm so stupid.

Oh, now Drunky is awake. He's even drunkier than he was before he fell asleep. He's reading this again. He just told me I'm not stupid. The girl on the aisle just said, "Why do you think you're stupid?"

"Because I'm so dumb," I said.

"That's redundant," she said.

"Smarty pants," the drunk dude said to the girl. Then he laughed really hard. *Ha-ha-ha-ha-ha!*

I have to put the computer away. These people are in my business. (Trying to hide the screen.)

August 16th, 3:07 p.m.

ON THE WAY TO CHARLOTTE, PART III

Okay. Not so bumpy at the moment. The Big Drunkowski has fallen to his left on top of the zombie-reading girl. She's giving me the eyeball. I try to shrug at her, but I am cramped up and the air smells like cow manure. What am I going to do? I can't help her.

At least Drunky McFarts-so-much is asleep, so he can't read my screen.

Okay.

• • •

Even though Gus gave me the Google map he printed out, with our route computer-traced all the way down the middle of the dang country, I had a hard time believing he knew what he was doing.

We left Bluffton in what I was sure was the absolute wrong direction. Florida is south and east. We went south and west.

Instead of just cutting into Illinois, which is less than twenty miles straight below Bluffton, Gus put us on U.S. 151 and shot us toward Dubuque, which is in freaking Iowa, which is to our freaking west. And it's a place we go all the damn time so it didn't feel like we were going any place special at all, which I found very frustrating.

"What are you doing? Let's just go to Hazel Green and cross over into Illinois down there, man. That's more direct," I said.

"Have you ever heard of a map? It shows roads? It shows the big roads? Look! There are no big roads that cross straight south into Illinois. Do you see that? Look at the piece of paper I put in your big, dumb hands."

"Shut up, man."

"Dumb hands."

"Shut up," I said.

"Stop acting like such an ape all the time," Gus said.

Nice start to the trip.

We rolled off toward the Dickeyville bottoms. Gus's lateness and meanness immediately made me sleepy (daytime stress makes me sleepy—opposite of night), which immediately made me fall (half) asleep, which I assume made Gus happy because who wants to sit next to a stupid talking ape for like thirty hours straight in a tiny car? Maybe an ape biologist, but nobody else.

This was super too: while I was sleeping and waking and bumping my head on the window and drooling and opening my eyes and squinting at the bright sunlight and falling back asleep, I dreamed about Cody throwing me all these passes in games, about how I'd come out of my cuts and the ball would be in the air, but then I'd forget what I was doing and the ball would hit me in the chest or the face or on the neck, which is kind of impossible. I dreamed this same scenario over and over, and the miles went by and I woke and slept and drooled, and everybody was dream-screaming mad at me and then Gus hit me on the shoulder and I woke up.

"*Ma-koe-ku-tah*," he said.

"Cody thinks I'm on my way to Michigan," I said.

"What, dude?" Gus asked.

"What?" I rubbed my eyes.

"Maquoketa, Iowa. Gus need breakfast sandwich, Mr. Gorilla," Gus said.

"Why is everybody so damn mean?"

"What are you talking about, you freak?"

He pulled into the McDonald's in this small Iowa town.

While we were eating a couple of bacon, egg, and cheese biscuits, Gus talked about this movie he saw that showed where fast food comes from (giant death farms made out of razor blades where animals get really sick to their stomachs and then all fall over and sleep in their own feces until they die of cancer), and I sort of lost my appetite.

"Oh, it's gross, brother. It's wicked." He kept eating, though. His mouth was way open too, while he chewed, so I could see all the dead and mushed-up poop animals getting chomped up in there.

"Why don't you shut your mouth when you eat?"

"Because I can't get food in my mouth when it's shut, you dumbass," he said. Then he took another bite and made a big show of sticking his tongue through it all. He made this ahalahalahala sound in the back of his food-packed throat at the same time.

Totally disgusting.

At that point, he hadn't even begun the cigarette-smoking marathon. That particular start line happened to be at the exit of the McDonald's. He pulled out his white and blue pack of Parliaments, lit up, then offered me one. "Care for an after-dinner mint?" he asked.

"Yeah, not too much."

"I love me this abscessed filter." He spun the cigarette around to show me this sort of hole in the butt. "Love to stick my tongue in the groove, baby."

"I seriously have no idea who you are."

"You've missed it," he said. "I've gotten sexy."

Literally like three years ago, me and Gus were playing with Muppet dolls. I'm serious. We played Kermit and Miss Piggy in his living room and filmed ourselves putting on a Muppet puppet show.

Sing it, Gus! "*Why are there so many songs about rainbows, and what's on the other side?*"

We were immature eighth graders. We were funny, though.

"You want to drive?" he asked after he finished sticking his tongue in the groove.

"Yes. Please."

"You don't have to be short with me, Felton. I'm trying to show you a good time, okay?"

"I don't smoke."

"You don't have to smoke."

"Why do you smoke?"

"Because I want to." He handed me the keys. "Just stick to the map, Felton," he said.

"I go where the wind blows," I said.

"You used to be funny," Gus said.

"You used to think Miss Piggy was hot."

"That hasn't changed, Felton. Drive the car."

About twenty minutes later, on Highway 61 heading south, Gus put an old Green Day album on his iPod so it blared (I like Green

Day fine), then rolled down the passenger window and began smoking again.

Smoke means fire.

I could barely concentrate on the road because I was so nervous that his lit cherry would fly back into the backseat and turn the piles of newspaper and food wrappers and crap he had stuffed back there into a raging death inferno. I swerved around a little, keeping my eye on Gus's cigarette.

"You're a pretty crappy driver," he said. "I always thought good athletes were good drivers because they have a good sense of physics. Guess I was wrong on that count."

"I'm a great driver. Ask the lady who gave me my driving test. She said I'm fantastic."

"I believes what I sees."

"I believe you're going to start your car on fire."

"More with the smoking? Jesus. Fine." Gus whipped his cigarette out the window.

"Litterer."

"Felton, you're going to drive me freaking nuts."

"Who do you think is going to pick up after you?"

"I don't know, Jerri. The cigarette fairy?"

"You called me Jerri?"

"Yeah. Because you sound just like Jerri when we were kids. All preachy. And that's no good, Felton, because she went crazy, didn't she?"

"Why are you being such an ass?"

Gus paused for a second. He turned toward me and tilted his

head down so his eyes were covered up by his hair wad. "I honestly don't know, Felton. Maybe I'm pissed at you?"

"Please leave my poor mother out of it, okay?"

"Will do," Gus said. "Mind if I smoke?"

"Whatever."

He lit up again, Aleah.

Then, thankfully, he went to sleep.

There was a time—I guess through the first sixteen years of our lives—when Gus and me never fought. Not once. We were like synchronized swimmers on display in the dipshit tank at the freak show.

Still, he was never the social freak that I was. Kids sort of liked him even though he liked me. He was rebellious and an underhanded troublemaker and funny and dangerous (even though he was good in school).

While I drove, I eyeballed him sleeping there, his hair wad covering his eyes. This is what I thought: *He hasn't changed a bit. Of course he smokes and listens to punk music and acts all obnoxious and belligerent and shitty, even when he's really not such a freak. If he could've gotten his hands on cigarettes when he was ten, he would've smoked then. He was always on the way to being this rebel dude. He hasn't changed. At ten he was naturally cool. Really. You? At ten you were on the fast track to a mental institution for jelly-brained children. But he still liked you. Why?*

And how did you pay him back?

You changed.

Of course he's pissed at you for becoming Mr. Monster Jock out of no place. Of course...

We were just getting to the Quad Cities, where, according to Gus's map, we were to hit this major interstate (I-80) that would take us to this other major interstate (I-74) that would start us totally rocketing toward the Dangling Sack of America (Florida), when I reached over and nudged Gus awake.

"Are we lost?" he mumbled.

"No. We're cool. Hey, do you sort of hate me because I'm popular now?" I asked.

"What?"

"I'm popular, because…because of…" I realized maybe popular wasn't the right word.

"Jesus, Felton." He shook his head. "So arrogant. Popular? Jesus."

"That's not what I meant."

"Do we need gas?"

"Oh. Yeah. We're almost on empty."

"Well, pull over, man."

"Now?"

"When we get to an exit with a gas station. Duh."

"I didn't mean popular, exactly."

Gus didn't say anything. In about ten seconds we came to an exit and we pulled off and got gas, which I think smells great. I love that gas smell. Then we pissed, bought some chicken, and got back on the road. I stayed driving, because it hadn't really been that long since Maquoketa and McDonald's.

Already felt like a long day, though. (Not as long as today!)

"You know one reason I do like you?" Gus said, as I pulled onto I-80.

"No."

He gestured at me with a piece of fried chicken. "Because we go into a freaking Flying J truck stop like back there, filled with these redneckers who look like they'd like to stab me in the neck and cut me up, and crap, they see you and they just back the hell away."

"They do?" I hadn't really noticed.

"Yeah, man. You look like you could tear a rednecker to pieces and eat him for breakfast. Should come in handy in the Southland."

"Please don't cause anything in the Southland, man," I said.

Gus took a big bite of chicken. "Nop!" he said.

I wasn't sure what "Nop!" meant, but I felt immediately very concerned for our safety once we hit the Southland, wherever the hell that was. I didn't particularly like him calling people redneckers either. (Not honkies, not dirtbags, not redneckers…right, Aleah?)

Do you know what I mean by underhanded troublemaker? This: Gus causes trouble but the trouble he causes never causes him trouble. For instance, I was suspended in eighth grade for taking a bathroom stall apart with a screwdriver. It was Gus's screwdriver and Gus's plan—I was his worker.

Was he suspended? No.

Would I end up being beaten stupid by someone he called a rednecker in a truck stop? Probably.

• • •

Speaking of the Southland, the plane is going down. (Landing.)

Charlotte, North Carolina.

August 16th, 5:03 p.m. Eastern Time!
CHARLOTTE

Holy balls. This is it. This is really it. I can't believe this. I can't. I can't freaking take it, Aleah. The flight for Fort Myers left at 3:55. I'm done. There's another flight out tomorrow at 3:55 p.m.! What the hell? What the freaking hell? I can't take it anymore.

"Oh, honey, you'll be fine. Just fly into Atlanta and catch the early bird to Fort Myers in the morning," the desk lady said.

I'm going to fly to Atlanta, which I could've done yesterday, to catch a flight into Fort Myers tomorrow, two days after I was supposed to get there?

Aleah. I'm going crazy. Oh my shitting nards.

Bus Travel

August 16th, 6:12 p.m.
LEAVING CHARLOTTE

I am with the Zombie Girl.

We have just boarded a fugly Andrew-style Greyhound bus, which was suggested to us by the airline after I threw a fairly giant hissy fit, which I'm not entirely proud of, but sort of proud of, because at least I spoke up for my rights.

I'm a crazy man going all crazy on your airplane butt! Ahhhhh!

The Zombie Girl missed her flight too.

But she's going to Tampa, Florida, which is a bigger airport.

She could've gotten an 11 p.m. flight to Tampa but decided she'd rather take a bus that will get her into Tampa at 11:30 a.m. tomorrow?

Okay. Seriously. She is doing this for fun, Aleah. Why? To be with me?

I'll get to Fort Myers at 4:15, seventeen hours before Andrew and I are supposed to be on a flight back to Wisconsin. If I waited and flew, I might get there at 10 a.m. tomorrow, but I no longer believe that airplanes will fly when I need them to fly, so…

(Is Coach Johnson right about Kirk needing to learn my position? Will I get back to Wisconsin for our game against Lakeside Lutheran and my archenemy Roy Ngelale? Crap. I've never felt so far away from home, Aleah. My Jewfro is crazy in the wet Southland air…Sort of looks cool, I guess.)

Me and Zombie Girl shared a cab from the airport to the bus station. Zombie Girl made the arrangements. I followed. We saw the Carolina Panthers football stadium. That, I must say, was quite awesome.

We are sitting together on the bus.

Zombie Girl has a name. Renee.

Now she wants to talk.

I told her I'm working on a school project.

Astutely, she asked, "In the middle of August?"

"Uh-huh," I nodded. "Summer school."

Thank God Grandma Berba got me this computer for my birthday. I have about 80 percent charge, which, if I keep the Wi-Fi off and the screen dim, should give me about nine hours to not talk to Renee, because I think she wants to have sex or something. I'm serious. Or at least make out. She told me I'm sweet. She has a nose ring. Not that I don't like that. I don't trust myself to be true to you, because of my bad sex genes. (Dad cheated on Mom.) Who are you with right now, Aleah?

Don't panic…Don't panic…

Jesus. Okay. Renee is reading her book, not watching what I type.

Rolling out of Charlotte on a stinky bus.

• • •

Oh…I have covered so many, many miles this summer. I'm a rambling man, Aleah. Charlotte is hilly.

You know what's flat? Illinois. I know that from my trip with Gus.

The rest of Illinois is not Chicago. Did you know that? Illinois is huge and totally empty and windy like a hot blowtorch (when the windows were down because of smoking Gus). And it goes on and on and on. Illinois starts just a few miles from Bluffton. Then, because it seeps all the way into the south, Illinois goes on until the end of the great big flat world.

Around Peoria, which is not even halfway through the giant dead-zone Illinois, I started swerving a little because I couldn't keep my eyes focused anymore. Gus took over and smoked his bunghole Parliaments and drove, all slid way down in his seat.

We were on this stretch of I-55 that clearly made us both super crazy with anger, because after not talking for like an hour, Gus suddenly said, "Do you find it pretty weird that you weren't elected prom king?"

I shook my head to wake myself up. "Uh, no. I wasn't even on the prom court, so no, I don't find it remotely weird that I wasn't elected prom king."

"Did it totally hurt your feelings, though?"

"I had other things to worry about, obviously, since I didn't even go to prom." (I watched TV that night with Jerri.)

"Like bagging Abby Sauter?"

"Shut up, man." (Abby is just a friend, Aleah.)

"Have you tried to bag her? She's so pop-u-lar," Gus sort of sang the pop-u-lar part.

"No."

"Well…Just seems like the greatest athlete in the class, you know, especially because you got to be so popular last year and everything, would have his feelings hurt by not getting elected prom king."

"Jason Reese totally deserved it. He's a good guy."

"He's a fat-assed idiot."

"You don't even know him."

"He doesn't know me."

"He'd like you if he knew you."

"Everybody would. I'm great," Gus said.

"You're great?"

"Yes," he said.

"So you should be prom king? How come no one likes you?"

"Your honky friends are idiots. I don't want them to like me."

"You don't know crap about my honky friends. Anyway, Cody thinks you're cool." (Sorry about saying "honky," Aleah. I know you hate that term, but I'm just reporting the facts, okay?)

"I haven't ever said more than a sentence to him."

"That's because you're mean to everyone," I said.

"I don't even talk to people, man!"

"That doesn't make you nice."

Gus started driving really fast. "You're my prom king, Felton. Oh, I totally voted for you. You're the best looking jockstrap in the bunch too. And you only smell half as bad."

"What the hell, Gus?"

"I'm your chauffeur. I'm so lucky to be the king's chauffeur!"

"Jesus, shut up!"

"I should really turn this stupid car around, Felton. I should drive you home, you arrogant prick. What did you do to Andrew

anyway? Probably told him about how the whole freaking honky
world hates his guts and so he should just run the hell away, right?
Because he has no social future, right?"

"No."

"You tell him he's the jerk for being picked on? Did you tell him
it's all his fault? Because he's the idiot for being smart and great
at music?"

"No one picks on him."

"Yes they do, you idiot."

"No. Anyway, I didn't tell him he's an idiot. I told him he should
quit music and be a pharmacist."

"Oh. Whoa," Gus laughed.

"I know. Terrible," I said.

"Punched him in his tender acorns, hey?"

"Pretty much."

"His musicality not up to your professional standards?"

"I guess not."

"Did you say, 'Andrew, you and your gang of fourteen-year-old
musicians should throw in the towel, because there's little hope for
you ever being as great as me.' Something like that?"

"No."

Gus laughed, shook his head. "I'm laughing at you, you understand. Not with you."

"I get it."

"Wow, Felton, who died and made you king of the jerks?"

"I don't know, Gus. Maybe my dad?" I said.

"Oh," Gus nodded.

At least that shut him up. For a while, anyway.

Silence…Silence…during which I wondered if people picked on Andrew. I'd never seen it, but apparently I only see what I want to see, you know? This spring, Andrew did get in that weird fight. While in the car, Gus stewing and silent next to me, I wondered why Andrew had fought, what it was about. (It hadn't even occurred to me to ask him what happened—jackassed narcissist.)

About two hours after Gus and I fought about Andrew, the land finally began to give way around us. There were signs for St. Louis.

The first words Gus said? "St. Louis, home of the blues."

"No it's not," I replied. "Chicago."

"St. Louis Blues?" Gus asked.

We didn't turn and go into St. Louis, though Gus suggested he'd like to take pictures of that big arch.

No. I was angry. So, no.

We got some gas on what I assume were the outskirts of the city (using Gus's dad's credit card—I wasn't paying for this trip…Gus really wasn't either, though). Then more truck-stop greasy food that boiled in my gut (peeing, sweating, noticing Gus's redneckers back away from me). Then I took the next driving shift and nearly missed the exit for I-57 because Gus wasn't paying close attention to the map. If we would've stayed on I-64, we would have ended up shooting due east to Louisville, Kentucky, a place I'd like to visit for some reason (maybe because of the baseball bats?), so that would've been fine, but Gus grabbed the wheel at the last second and steered us into the correct lane so that we kept up our mighty plunge toward the Dangling Sack.

As soon as we got on I-57, there were actual sporadic clumps of trees here and there, some clumps pretty big and bordering almost on forest, which made me shout, "Hey, trees!"

"Ooh, you know your stuff, Felton. Those are trees."

I smiled. I like trees. I'm used to trees. Much of central Illinois is without trees, or at least the big-ass clumps of trees I'm used to. We shot past a giant lake like I've never seen too (not an ocean lake like Lake Michigan, but a giant lake that's still a lake).

"Check that out, man!" I said.

"Lake. Big lake," Gus agreed.

We kept seeing the lake for miles and miles. "It's really cool, huh?"

By this time, though, Gus wasn't paying any attention. He punched crap into his iPhone like a jackrabbit. "I didn't even have to print out maps, man. I got us on GPS right here! We're this little blue ball pulsing south! See?" He shoved the phone in my face. "Pull on back on the map…Hey, we're going to be in Nashville by dark. Nashville!"

"I like this lake," I said. Nashville made me nervous.

I was right to be nervous about Nashville, by the way.

We drove. More trees and hills. He smoked. He played with his iPhone.

Then he shouted, "Holy shit! Hazard Mountain is playing in Nashville tonight! At this place called the Basement!" He looked up from his iPhone, his eyeballs open, his cheeks on fire.

I looked at him, then back in front of us. "What?" I asked.

"Maddie is going to freak her damn mind, man! We're going!"

"Where? No," I said.

Then we drove through a storm that turned the sky green and fired lightning bolts into the big trees around us and cracked Gus's Toyota with giant hail. I thought we were dead. Gus kept saying, "Amazing. Amazing."

As soon as we were through it, Gus took the wheel and I passed out (fried nerves).

I awoke to him babbling at me about the big plan.

What a brilliant guy Gus is!

Not really. Not in this case.

His plan: "I will use my fake (fake ID, which he had, which I didn't know he had, which made me suspicious of him), and I will charm the crap out of the bouncer and he will look at you and you'll say…what?"

"I lost my wallet in the storm, officer."

"Hell no! You just lost your wallet. There is no officer."

Gus drove with his knee on the steering wheel all the way into the Nashville suburbs. With one hand he smoked (I was no longer nervous his cigarette would burn the car down, at least); with his other he kept flicking iPhone screens with his thumb (I was nervous he would kill us with his phone). His eyes were on the freaking phone more than they were on the road, and he was driving extremely fast because he was sure Hazard Mountain would sell out if we didn't get there by ten. (He'd read some review of the bar.) He was swerving in between lanes, and cars were honking.

"Gus. Gus, it's illegal to text and drive," I mumbled, terrified.

"Dude. I am not texting. I am using maps! Chill!"

"If we get pulled over by the cops, this jig is done, man. Cops will call our parents. We'll get sent home or to jail or to juvie," I said.

"You have no idea about how things work, do you, Felton?"

"No."

Gus threw the phone onto my lap. "Okay. You guide me in. When we get close to downtown, we have to slide over to 65. The Basement's off 65."

"I seriously don't want to go to a bar, man." I said.

"Guide me in…"

Nashville is pretty big, Aleah. Have you ever been there? It's kind of hilly and lush green, and it has lots of lights that were just beginning to go on as 9 p.m. sunset faded into 10 p.m. night, but I guided us in just fine, perfectly, because I'm not stupid.

Actually, at that point 65 and 24 were the same interstate and then 65 split to the right, so, boom, we just did that, followed 65. Then we crossed a river where you could see the lights of the city reflected and it was really, really beautiful. Clouds gone, sky dark purple, neon reflections…

"Eyes on the map, man! I need guidance!" Gus shouted.

Nashville is so good-looking, though, that I had to keep looking around. "Is there a university here? Is there a football team?"

"Vanderbilt. Ever heard of it?" Gus asked.

Just then we passed by signs for Vanderbilt University. "I think I might come here. I think this might be my destiny. Freaking Nashville. We're in Nashville, man!"

"You're star-crossed, brother. It's just a big city in the dark."

"You mind? Will you take this exit and head over to the campus?"

"Yes, you fool. Please. I love Hazard Mountain."

So, we didn't go to Vanderbilt, but I was pretty sure for the next ten minutes that Nashville was the place for me, Aleah. Maybe it still is? You could play your piano in a country band.

Gus rolled down his window, so hot, wet air streamed in over the top of the air-conditioning. It felt amazing. "I love Nashville, man." I rolled my window down too, and that Southland air just swept in. (Funny how I don't love that air right now.)

Even though I was staring around at everything, I did manage to guide us off the loop that circles the downtown and guide us farther south a little bit until we came to the right exit. And, in like a minute, we pulled up to a crowded parking lot in front of this brick house-like thing housing a music shop. A giant wad of Maddie-and-Gus-looking people (tight pants and weird hair with the sides all buzzed up or hair wads and plaid shirts and big glasses and crap) stood around in the front, all of them smoking and staring at each other.

"The Basement is in the basement of this place," Gus said.

We found parking around the corner, and I started to sweat like the total gorilla I am. "What are we doing? This is a bar. Did you see how old everybody looks?"

"Yeah, they look twenty. Totally ancient."

"Are you related to them? They all look like you."

"Ha. Good taste transcends borders, my man."

"Wait. Are we sleeping here? What do we…"

"We can sleep in that park." Gus pointed. Across the street there were some lit basketball courts with some dudes shooting hoops and a stretch of dark green behind it.

"Dude. I am not sleeping in a park."

"Just kidding. Let's go. Holy shit, I hope we can get in."

Yeah, holy shit, did I hope we wouldn't, Aleah.

Whereas my size and general bigness and jockiness seemed to make the "redneckers" of our nation's gas stations look away from me, something about my presence here among the young Gus-likes of our nation had the opposite effect. As Gus and I waded through the crowd of smokers in their tight pants, whispers arose, eyeballs fixated upon me, inaudible aspersions were cast (people called me names, probably gorilla, jockstrap, monkey, honky, etc., although I couldn't hear), and the Maddie-like girls all covered their mouths and giggled.

"Looks like a crew of angry librarians, huh?" Gus leaned to me and whispered.

That made me laugh. It did. Yes, all these mean girls looked vaguely like librarians.

"Makes me very hot," Gus whispered.

There was a short line actually waiting to get in. When we got to the front, Gus shouted, "Hazard's not sold out?" at the very fat, totally bald dude with the very menacing long goatee and pierced tattooed crap everywhere on his face and arms.

"No," the bald man said. "ID."

Gus whipped out his fake, gave the dude money, then walked in.

"Hey!" I called after him.

He backed up. "Oh. Right. Sir, my friend here is from the Czech Republic and he doesn't speak any English, so he had no idea he needed to bring his passport down from the hotel. We'd certainly be pleased if you would go ahead and show some mercy to him. He's a great fan of Hazard Mountain, and this is his only opportunity to see them before he has to…"

The bald man turned to me and said, "Go home."

"*Qué?*" I asked. (This is Spanish, by the way, and not Czech as far as I know.)

"No ID, you're shit out of luck, Vaclav," the bald man said.

"Look how big he is! He's on the Czech national tennis team!"

"I don't give a damn how big he is. There are ten-year-olds that big. You want me to let in a ten-year-old?" he spat at Gus. He turned back to me and said, "Go home, Vaclav."

"Aw, crap," I said.

"That Czech?" The bald man asked.

Gus paused, shrugged, mouthed *Sorry*, and then dove into the basement, leaving me there.

I stood for another second, sort of waiting for Gus to bounce back out, tell me he was joking or whatever, until Fat Baldicus said, "Move, kid. You're holding up the line."

Let me pause here to say something, Aleah: This situation is proof that Gus can be a huge, gigantic asswipe. Am I right?

What was I supposed to do?

I turned and walked slowly back toward the car, except I didn't have a key because my "best friend" took it with him into a bar.

I waded through the Gus-like people who stared and tittered, and I thought, *I wouldn't come to this crap town for college if you paid me a million dollars.*

According to my phone, which was totally low on battery, it was

10:12 p.m. Hazard Mountain was supposed to play at 11 p.m. That meant I had like fourteen years to kill on the mean streets. I tried calling Gus to set up a plan, but he didn't answer his phone, which is also not nice. So, I went over to the park to watch the dudes shoot hoops.

Think of me out there, Aleah. Czech dude named Vaclav. Watching dudes play basketball for no apparent reason.

Cursed. Czech. Dude.

I am simply cursed. I'm on the road to nowhere.

• • •

I don't want to type anymore. I am so tired.

August 16th, 9:20 p.m.
ORANGEBURG, SOUTH CAROLINA

We just stopped for like ever in a place called Orangeburg, South Carolina. I ate a chicken sandwich. Zombie Girl, Renee, thinks I'm too negative. I'm not the one wearing all the black, I pointed out to her.

While she stood outside the bus smoking cigarettes (it's like everyone I meet has forgotten how bad cigarettes are for you), I told her about Nashville, and she asked, "What do you have to complain about? I have friends who sleep in boxes. You played Frisbee."

Do you think she really has friends who sleep in boxes?

The truth: Nashville, after I got away from Gus, was actually fun, Aleah. Actually sort of great. Ultimate Frisbee is sort of who I am. Motion.

If you're standing around a basketball court staring at people playing basketball, which was what I was doing after I left the bar, either they're going to invite you to play or they're going to start staring back at you, and generally not in a friendly way.

The latter was the case in Nashville. The longer I stood there, the longer the six guys playing took to get the ball in play. They shuffled their feet. They looked over, one by one. Eventually, they were mumbling at each other and turning around en masse to look at me. So, I walked off. One of them shouted, "See yaaaaa," as I headed up the street.

If I could've gotten in the car, maybe I would've changed out of my jeans and done some running. No keys. I looked at that great stretch of grass to my left and thought, *Take off your pants. Nobody will notice you're in your boxers. Do something*...I couldn't get myself to pull my pants off. I've done that in the country (spring air in boxer peephole).

Not in Nashville. Someone would actually see me stripping down.

Oh yes, I cursed Gus's jerk-off name and wished him the worst time of his life in that terrible bar.

To kill time, I walked up around this giant sewer-treatment-looking place, then took a left onto another street that was lined on one side with pretty thick woods.

Big woods right there in the middle of the city, pretty cool.

All I've ever heard about Nashville is that it has a bunch of country music stuck in it someplace. I'm not a big a fan of that. (Grandma Berba is, by the way.) Anyway, who knew there were Nashville city forests and Nashville people with Gus-like hair wads and basement rock music venues that discriminate against big, young Czechs named Vaclav?

At the end of the city forest, houses started on one side, and the other side opened up into a gigantic park, even bigger than the one by the Basement. This park had all kinds of lit spaces. I was sort of drawn to it—like a mayfly to a purple bug zapper, I suppose. Rose Park.

People were playing tennis on weird-surfaced courts that didn't look like Bluffton's cement courts. Sort of rubbery or clayey or something. And, there was a huge pile of people watching teams in uniforms play baseball on a pretty big field with a fence that had to be close to 400 feet out. These dudes could seriously play too. I saw a couple of guys absolutely jack the ball.

And then there was an odd spectacle that really drew me to it. Something magical. Something I've never seen exactly (although sort of in a flimsy Bluffton way). On the outfield of a smaller base-ball diamond that wasn't in use, these hippie-looking people had set out traffic cones and they were sort of playing football or soccer except with a Frisbee.

Deep in my mind's terrible recesses, I vaguely remembered having seen Bluffton college kids playing this game too, but it was from when I was younger and couldn't have given two shakes of the shit pot about any sport.

It was seriously freaking incredible, though. The red disc hung in the air and then some hippie dude would explode from the ground and sail into the sky and grab it down and immediately whip it sidearm up the field so that some sports-bra hippie girl with pigtails could catch up to it and find herself in the end zone where she'd scream, "*Yeeeaaahh, boyeee!* That's it! That's it!" They were Southern sounding and muscly and excellent, so much better than the Gus-ly smoker people in those tight pants.

I was so psyched about this game that I barely knew what I was doing. I almost wandered right onto the field but figured out kind of where the sidelines were, even though there was no chalk. I watched with my mouth open, I'm sure, for like twenty minutes.

Then the magic really happened. A big guy with no shirt on and a red bandanna tied around his hippie head said, "I gotta run. My kids'll be up at the ass cracker, and I'm on duty tomorrow." Ass cracker! That's what I call dawn too! "Sorry to break it up."

Then someone pointed at me and the hippie-bandanna-dad man said, "You wanna jump in here, bud?"

I didn't even think. I was all like, "Uh-huh."

The hippie sports-bra girl who kept outrunning everybody said, "You know how to play?"

"Not exactly."

"Main thing: you can't run when you have the disc. You gotta stay put and throw it. And, if the disc hits the ground, it's the other team's, okay?"

"I can intercept, though?" I asked.

"'Course you can, boy!" a chubbier guy in a cutoff sweatshirt shouted at me. He had a blond Jewfro, which made me really like him.

And so I played. At first not that well, especially because I didn't really know how to wing a Frisbee sidearm. (I know now, I'll tell you that, because I got a big fat disc when I got home and started winging it around my yard.) When I'd catch it, I'd often blow it for my team because I couldn't get it fast up to the next player.

Then I started seeing crap develop in front of me, just like in football, and I started streaking out and taking the Frisbee out of the air and dumping it off to teammates and shooting down the field and jumping high off the ground to haul in big-time scores.

Someone said, "Intensity just got turned up a notch, hey?"

Another said, "Nice, man. Nice. You're a natural!"

Another said, "You play in the NBA or something, kid?"

I just said, "No. This game is awesome."

Best of all, there wasn't rest like there is in between plays in foot-ball, so I could just run and run and run—and I did run and run and run until an older guy wearing longer shorts said, "Too much youth talent on this field for me. I gotta call it or I'm gonna puke biscuits."

The guy with the blond Jewfro said, "Beers, anyone?"

Several raised their hands.

"You're a bit fresh for the bar scene, I imagine, aren't you, boy?" he asked me.

"I'm sixteen."

Then that fast hippie girl just bolted over to me. "You're sixteen? How is that possible? You're dang near the fastest mother I've ever seen in real life. Jesus, kid."

I nodded and totally blushed.

"You big-time?" she asked.

"Football and track," I said.

"Beautiful," she said. "I did field hockey at Vandy."

"Cool," I said. I blushed a hell of a lot more.

What a great night. I seriously might move to Nashville and just play Ultimate Frisbee for the rest of time. It's like distilled Felton poured into a game. I could be totally happy just flinging a disc and living among those country-sounding hippies. Listen to me, Aleah. I, Felton Reinstein, don't enjoy racing track anymore...I'm not sure I can enjoy football with everyone staring at me, but I seriously wanted roll all over the ground and make out with the hippie field-hockey girl to celebrate, because I was so happy playing Frisbee. It's weird.

I don't really mean make out. Just celebrate.

I said good-byes and walked off back toward the bar.

If I'd had a scissors, I would've cut my pants off right there because I was so damn sweaty and gross.

My phone had gone dead while we played, so I had no idea what the time was. But when I got back to the car, Gus was in there and he started honking the horn and he rolled down the window, and he flipped me off and screamed, "Where the hell have you been?"

"Playing some Frisbee." I walked up and pulled off my shirt and threw it in the backseat.

"What the hell?" he shouted.

"Yeah, I found this crew of running hippies. Unbelievable, huh?"

"Unreal, man." Gus glowered.

"Good show?" I asked, getting in.

"I only watched the first set—which was awesome by the way—because I felt sorry for you having to sit out here on the car waiting. Of course you weren't here. Why didn't you answer your phone, Felton?"

"I called you before it went dead, but you didn't answer."

"Whatever. We have to find some place to sleep."

"You ever play Ultimate Frisbee?" I asked as he pulled out of the parking space and up to Eighth Avenue.

"Jesus, Felton. Shut up."

"It's pretty awesome."

"You stink," Gus said. "Literally smell terrible."

"Not as bad as your cigarettes."

"Shut up."

"Is there such a thing as professional Frisbee?" I asked.

Gus didn't answer and then he drove way too fast all over the place.

I felt bad, but I wasn't sure why. (I guess I figured it out soon enough.)

• • •

Zombie Renee just told me, "You had a really fine time in Nashville. Your friend sounds like the problem."

I don't know about that.

No, that's not really true.

Oh man. I have to do it. I'm going back to the fugly, smelly, poo-crusted bus bathroom, Aleah. *So freaking gross.*

August 16th, 11:10 p.m.
BEAUFORT, SOUTH CAROLINA

It's dark as Bluffton out here, Aleah. The bus went way off the interstate and then we crossed a bunch of water. I have no idea where the hell we are, but Zombie Renee said Beaufort, South Carolina, is close to the ocean. She told me I'm a complicated person too. She wanted to know why Gus wasn't the jerk for going into that bar.

"Our history," is what I told her.

Gus and I stayed pretty close to Nashville that night, at a place called Murfreesboro. (I like that name—Murrrrrfrrrrreeeeesborrrrroooo.) We stayed in a Howard Johnson Express, "Because you're a total Johnson," Gus said.

"Wisconsin's biggest Johnson," I said.

"Not funny," he said.

I thought it was funny.

But then he booked us a room with only one bed and made me sleep on the floor wrapped in the bedspread, which I could only assume had been sat on by a million dirty and naked asses without ever being washed. (Sheets get washed, not bedspreads, right?) And I was pretty grossed out by the carpet, especially because it smelled like an ashtray, since Gus made us take a Tennessee smoking room.

And after all that—a day when Gus made fun of me for not being prom king and told me what a jerk I was to Andrew, then abandoned me at a rock club in Nashville—I decided I completely hated his guts and I'd be better off not being his friend anymore. Then I totally fell asleep in all that ass muck and ashtray dirt.

I woke up to Gus blasting hillbilly music from little speakers he attached to his iPhone. "That's Hazard Mountain, man! Country-fried punk!"

"Turn it off," I said.

"No. Let's get moving, okay? I've been sitting here staring at your curly gorilla head for like two hours and I'm ready to roll the hell out."

Apparently it was morning already.

I didn't shower because the bathroom was really gross (more gross even than me after Frisbee). But I pissed and pissed around. Read the Howard Johnson Express magazine a little. Pissed around with the coffeepot in the room (made a little coffee I tried to drink but couldn't, because I don't drink coffee, even though I keep trying). Then I got dressed real slow.

I eyeballed Gus, who eyeballed me. We didn't say a word. He pumped his chicken-fried steak music louder and louder. Then I reached into my bag to pull out my phone charger—because I needed to charge my phone at least for a little bit before we left, or I wouldn't have any way of calling 911 when I murdered Gus—but it wasn't in my bag. I dug deeper. Nothing. Nowhere. I sat down on the floor and emptied the entire contents (lots of useless football crap).

"Trouble?" Gus asked.

"I think I forgot my charger."

"Aces," Gus said. "Can't call home. Bet that will drive Jerri…"

"What? Crazy?"

"Just upset her."

"I swear I remember putting it in here. I think I pulled it out last night? Didn't I? I swear to God. Jesus, I'm an idiot."

"You can get a new one when we get to Fort Myers. Come on, let's go."

I stuffed my crap back in the bag and we left. It felt sort of like I was leaving my dog someplace, though. (Not that I own a dog.) Poor, dead phone.

It was only 9 a.m. when we left Murfreesboro, so we'd only slept like maybe five hours apiece. I was foul. Gus was foul.

The first thing he said when we pulled onto the interstate was: "Can't believe I missed the second set last night, man."

"Sorry," I said. (I wasn't sorry.)

"Best show I've ever been to, and I skipped out on half. Hard to believe." Gus shook his head and pursed his lips.

"Oh, have you been to a lot of shows, Gus?" I nodded, my eyes wide (sarcasm).

"Some."

"Really? Where?"

"Wherever. You don't know what I do when you're dicking around with all those honkies."

"No, I do know."

"No, you don't."

"Yes. You drive around in circles, then park next to dumpsters so you can make out with your prepubescent girlfriend. That's awesome, huh?"

"Shut up, Felton."

"Maybe not that awesome. You probably should seek some counseling because you love prepubescent girls so much."

"She's only two years younger than me, Felton."

"Yeah, but you only just hit puberty last week..."

"She is totally post-pubescent, Felton. I know! I know what I've seen!"

"Really? What have you seen, Gus?"

"I have seen everything."

"Everything?"

"Everything! Do you understand me, Felton? All of it!"

"Not surprised. Maddie's got some trouble in the family, like maybe with alcohol? Drunk girls are easy." As soon as this came out of my mouth, I wanted to stuff it back in. My stomach tightened.

"What did you say?"

"Um. Troubled family. So...not exactly..."

"You're going to judge her for having a troubled family?"

"We might have problems, yeah, but we're not trailer-park trash." (I paused here for a long second when I told this to Zombie Renee, so she could understand just what a jerk I'm really capable of being. She nodded, understanding).

And then, Aleah, while driving down the road at 80 miles per hour, Gus Alfonso, my best friend for my whole life, punched the left side of my face so hard I saw bolts of lightning and heard a screaming witch whistle in my ears.

For a second, I didn't know what had happened.

Then Gus was crying. I mean, like seriously sobbing and swerving all over the road.

Then I knew what had happened and thought to punch Gus back.

Then I didn't want to punch Gus; I wanted to cry—and not because it hurt either. Then I asked if we could stop because I wanted a Coke, which seemed like the only thing that could make this all better. Mainly I wanted to press a cold can to my head.

Gus did what I asked. We pulled back off the highway like ten miles after we pulled on.

• • •

Zombie Renee said, "Even if you were mean, he still shouldn't have punched you."

Yeah. He did, though.

It is so freaking dark out here. It's kind of funny because our next stop is in Georgia, and Gus and I went through Georgia.

Maybe it's not so funny. Gus and I were driving to Florida too.

But Georgia made me think that Gus is a good person because he actually thinks about stuff, like what kind of person he wants to be. I don't think about anything until like a month after it happens. Then I obsess about it but can't do anything about it, so I'm totally useless.

August 17th, 12:17 a.m.

SOMEWHERE IN GEORGIA

Renee is asleep. I don't think she likes me as much as she used to. Maybe it's not a good idea to spend several hours convincing someone you just met that you're the biggest jerk on the planet, huh? I've only talked about Gus with her too. Haven't really brought up you or Jerri or Andrew. I did tell her my life is an ongoing horror movie. She rolled her eyes, shook her head, said I didn't know crap about anything, and then she sort of passed out.

Now we're in Georgia.

Maybe I'll buy Renee something at the next stop. A candy bar? She's a vegetarian. Some broccoli? She seems pretty sad.

You know what I don't like? Being punched.

Back in the bad old days of Felton yore, I was shoved and elbowed and knocked on the ground at recess—and kicked in the gut while lying on the ground. Good times. I used to be angrier about it. Now I'm a different person (except when Gus punched me). Maybe I should do something for kids who get punched a lot. Like what? Buy them candy bars? Broccoli?

Here's weird: while that crap was all happening back in those bad old days, when the guidance counselor asked if I got picked on, I'd tell him no. "Not me! I'm grrreat!" I wasn't great. I was very, very mad. And also terrified, but not of other kids, exactly. Scared of not being able to do anything (like ask for help) about the crap without just catching more hell, maybe. Could a guidance counselor stop kids from hating me?

No. I don't know.

No.

Scared that there was no control, no stop button. I had no control over anything at all.

Do I have control now, or did I just get lucky? Clearly me turning into an athlete like my dad has nothing to do with control. I have athlete genes, that's all. Nobody caused it. I didn't try to become an athlete.

Now my oldest friend punches me?

Upside-down world. I got lucky for a while, but I'm still cursed. I still don't have any control. Shouldn't I be terrified?

I'm not. I'm riding a bus in the middle of the night in Georgia next to a girl named Renee. She's a good person. I can tell. I'm not afraid.

After Gus punched me, I asked to drive, because I wanted to be in control, I guess (so I could drive us off a cliff if he hit me again? I don't know), and then we drove in silence. He didn't say he wanted to go home. He didn't apologize. The side of my damn nut throbbed and the edge of my eye was kind of blurry because my face was swelling a little. (I pressed the Coke can on it.) Gus just sat there in a stupor.

The sun shone in the sky (total blue). We burned through some awesome, amazing, totally un-Midwestern hills and crossed over this big, fat chunk of forest-stuffed water called Nickajack Lake—which I've totally never seen anything like, except sort of by the Mississippi in Dubuque (and Nickajack was much bigger and grander)—until we got to Chattanooga, which actually has what I think are mountains. I think. Not like Colorado TV mountains, but there were pretty dang tall spots on these ridges.

Chattanooga. There's something funny about Chattanooga. Gus used to sing this line over and over and over to the tune of "Chattanooga Choo Choo": "Pardon me, Roy, is that the cat that chewed your new shoes?" He sang this dumb line instead of the "Chattanooga Choo Choo" lyrics (*Pardon me, boy, is that the Chattanooga choo choo?*). I looked over at Gus when we got to the "Welcome to Chattanooga" sign, and I sang it to him, "Pardon me, Roy, is that the cat that chewed your new shoes?"

"Yeah," Gus nodded. "I was just thinking about that too."

Then Gus's iPhone beeped. "Maddie?" I asked.

"Dad. He wants to know how the trip to Ann Arbor went."

"You tell him just super, okay? Really super."

"Ha." Gus swallowed and looked out to his right, stared off into nothingness.

Then I got a little worried about Jerri calling my phone. I'd really have liked to use Gus's to call her, but I felt nervous about asking him because he was a little psycho, apparently. Then I felt a bit anxious. Then I kept driving, feeling nerves about Jerri building up in my body until I was seriously anxious.

While the nerves built and boiled, we didn't say crap, just drove, for like two hours—all the way, Aleah, to Atlanta, Georgia, which is a freaking giant-ass city that doesn't look like Chicago at all (spread out forever and ever without the totally intense downtown or waterfront and rivers).

Right around the time we hit the first mighty Atlanta suburbs Gus said, looking down at his phone, "Oh. I think the time changed. Yeah, definitely. iPhone changed. It's an hour later than I thought it was. We're in the East for real."

I nodded and responded, "You know I could have you arrested for aggravated assault, you ass."

"Probably should add criminal damage to property while you're at it," Gus said.

"What?"

"Criminal damage."

"Really?" I was a little confused. "Did you take a dump in my shoe or something?"

"You left your phone charger out on the floor last night, so I cut it into little pieces and then flushed it down the motel toilet."

"Oh my God," I said. My hands and feet got icy, which I believe is an indication of complete terror.

"I've been kind of crazy today, I think," Gus said. "I've done some bad stuff." He started sniffling again. "It's…It's unpardon-able…It's…You're really my only friend, man. Not just today. Remember that poster of you and Roy Ngelale? That sort of gross sex picture that was all over the school?"

"Yes."

"Shit, man." Gus shook his head. "I did it."

"Well…" I didn't say that I pretty much knew it was him. For some reason, the poster didn't bother me that much. "Now you cut up my phone charger and punched my face."

"Yes," he said.

"What's next? Are you going to stab me or shoot me?" I asked. It was a serious question. I really wanted to know, so I could pull over, jump out, and run the hell away. (Not that I'd run away for real, just flag down the cops to get the necessary doctors to put Gus in a psych ward, I guess.)

"No. No, Felton," Gus said. "I don't know why you couldn't have just waited at the car last night."

"Because you were gone…"

"You're always going off somewhere. I just wanted to see a few songs and then come back out to tell you about how cool it all was, so you'd think I'm cool or whatever, and then take off in the damn car on our awesome trip, but you had to go and find a whole new set of friends in like two minutes, which…sucks. And then I waited for you for two hours in the car, which is what I always do—wait for you, man."

"Seriously?"

"Seriously," Gus said. "I seriously cut up your phone charger with my pocket knife."

"Ha-ha." I wasn't really laughing.

"I don't know…" Gus trailed off.

"Seriously," I said. "Are you going to try to kill me?"

"No. I want to visit Martin Luther King's grave. It's here in Atlanta."

"Seriously?"

"Yes."

"But you just punched me."

"Yes."

"Martin Luther King is about nonviolence."

"I'm aware of that, Felton."

Gus rolled down his window, and the hottest freaking air ever poured into the car. He lit a cigarette, then said, "I don't want to smoke. I want to be a good person." He threw the cigarette out the window and rolled it back up.

"Smoking doesn't make you a bad person."

"Not what I want. Do you mind if we stop at the grave?"

"I guess not," I said. This is not something I was expecting, Aleah.

Using his magical iPhone, Gus figured out where the Martin Luther King Jr. National Historic Site was and his birth house and grave site, and after some fairly craptastic traffic, we pulled off the interstate and got there in just about no time. All the MLK stuff is pretty much right off I-75 (the interstate that would take us all the way into Fort Myers in the south part of the Dangling Baggie).

Martin Luther King's grave is on this brick circle sitting in the middle of this cool blue pool. You can't walk right up and touch it or anything. It's weird to think Martin Luther King is in there. The real one, you know? Shot dead, Martin Luther King. A totally selfless person who gave up his life.

It's pretty sobering, you know? I sit around telling my brother he should be a pharmacist, while people are out there doing good until they get killed?

• • •

Shouldn't I be doing something for kids who get beat up? I have no idea what I'd do, Aleah, but here I am in the damn night with Zombie Renee. We're traveling through darkest Georgia. This is me. I can do things, you see? I can do different things with my time. I don't have to watch beach volleyball on TV. I don't have to sit on my ass with Jerri making snide comments about people on HGTV. Maybe.

• • •

It was too damn hot in that sun out at the grave, but Gus stood there letting all the rays beat down on him. He sweated so hard that drips started hanging off the end of his hair wad, which looked pretty funny. I might've mentioned this fact to him, but he was very serious and quiet. After awhile I said, "I've got to get some water, man."

He nodded and handed me the keys. "I'll meet you in the parking lot in a few minutes."

I didn't have to wait very long. Gus came stumbling out before I had even aired out the car from the ridiculous heat (doors all open). I handed him a bottle of water that I got at the gift shop.

"Thanks," he said.

"You feeling better?"

"A little. You know I wrote like a twenty page paper on Martin Luther King in seventh grade?"

"Yeah. Vaguely remember."

"I was totally set to try to be like him, to bring good shit into the world."

"That's good. You still will, man."

"Yeah, but I spend half my time chasing around a punk girl who thinks the height of awesome is drinking her mom's vodka, because all I really want to do…really, man, all I want to do is like put her in my mouth."

"Maddie? In your mouth?"

"Yeah. And I spent like thirty hours making a nasty poster of you, and I punched your face and cut up your cord."

"Yeah."

"I don't really know what I'm doing, man."

"Don't look at me. I have no idea what's going on ever."

"Yeah, Felton. I know that." Gus said. "I can't really blame you for anything, can I?"

"I don't know," I said.

"You have a curse," Gus said.

"I do?"

"Yeah. You have the curse of the monkey king."

"What?"

"You stopped riding your bike to school with me. You don't come over for movie night anymore. You missed my birthday. You don't answer my texts."

"Why did I stop doing all that?" I said pretty much to myself.

"I don't know," Gus replied.

• • •

But, Aleah, I do know. Here I am thinking about it a month or so later, and I do. I really can be blamed for stuff. I don't have a curse. I'm just me, the damn center of my own head-stuck-in-my-bunghole universe. Narcissus, the mythical dude who all narcissists are named after, loved himself so damn much he couldn't stop staring at his own reflection in the water.

Sorry. I'm so sorry for everything to everybody.

It's good I'm on my way back down to pick up Andrew.

August 17th, 2:55 a.m.
JACKSONVILLE, FLORIDA

Eighty-one degrees. I'm serious. Renee and I just woke up because the bus was pulling into a bigger town and there are lights. We're in Jacksonville, Florida. Back in the Dangling Sack of America. It's like three in the morning, but it's eighty-one degrees according to the TV in the bus station.

I just ate some of the Hickory Farms Sausage and Cheese Gift Platter, damn it. I'm weak! I'm also hungry.

Thank God I showered at the hotel in Chicago yesterday, or Renee would be dead from my sweat, probably. She had her head on my shoulder and my face was asleep on top of her brown-hair head and we are both seriously spritzed, which was sort of embarrassing. (I might have drooled on her head a little.)

We're in the bus station because our bus doesn't go any farther. Our new bus to Tampa leaves in two hours. I was just thinking: since Jerri and me left Bluffton like forty-four hours ago, I've slept probably a total of six hours. That's crazy. That's all. I keep flinching because I'm seeing things in my peripheral vision. (Little people, mostly.)

Renee is in the bathroom. She told me to come find her if she hasn't come back in ten minutes because there are some pretty weird, random people hanging out here, Aleah.

Before she left, she also said, "You haven't asked a single question about me. Aren't you curious?"

I answered honestly: "I am so hung up in my own crap, I don't even think."

"I'm starting my senior year at Gainesville in a few weeks."

"I'm a senior too," I said.

"Gainesville is the University of Florida, Felton. I'm twenty-two. I thought you were a lot older on the plane."

"I'm a lot older since the plane," I said.

"I do enjoy your peculiarity."

Now I want to know why she was in Chicago, Aleah. Now I want to know her story. Now she's in the bathroom.

I'll probably forget to ask her anything when she gets back.

I've been hung up in my own crap my whole life, you know?

It's some pretty serious crap, though. I just don't know if that's a reasonable excuse anymore. Dad died a long, long time ago. Jerri's in good shape. I guess I don't know if Andrew's okay, but I think so.

• • •

Gus and I went through Gainesville. (I actually called Jerri from there to tell her we'd made it to Michigan all right. She was relieved, as she'd been calling my dead cell. She told me she was having a great time in Chicago—your dad makes Jerri happy, Aleah). The University of Florida has contacted me about football too. They've sent me a bunch of emails. This is who I am. A top recruit. I'm not that little, shivering kid anymore. I have to get over the horror movie.

Speaking of the horror movie: Gus and I arrived in Fort Myers in the middle of the night.

Before we got there, as Gus's Celica barreled silent through the Dangling dark, I began to realize that I'd never been so close to my dad's people, at least not since he died.

My dad grew up in Chicago, you know, but his parents already had a place down here when I was tiny. I didn't really know where it was in Florida, but I remembered it a little. As we rolled, I figured it had to be Fort Myers. (It was, indeed, I found out.) Gus and I were barreling straight into the heart of my dad's family, and this was not a place where me and Andrew were ever welcome.

Why were we listed in Rose Reinstein's obituary, I wondered.

Talk about wanting to throw up, Aleah.

I thought, *How is this better than a damn football camp? You know how to play football. You can't talk to people who hate you, who go out of their way to show you they don't care, even though they should because they're your grandfather...*

Around 2 a.m. Gus said, "Here's the exit."

"Oh crap," I said.

"Where do we need to go?" he asked.

"How should I know? I don't know."

"Call Andrew. Get directions."

Gus tossed his iPhone onto my lap and I tapped Andrew's number and I couldn't breathe at all. "Are you serious? He'll know we're here."

"That's the point, Felton. We're here to keep him safe, to take him home if he's not safe. He has to know we're here."

"Right," I said. "Right. I know."

I pressed *Call.* Why would he be awake? Two a.m. Andrew's voice mail picked up, his high-pitched canary voice singing, "Leave a Message! Leave a Message!" (My God, I used to hate his little canary voice…so annoying—of course, things have changed.)

I left a message: "Okay. Andrew. You're going to be pissed. But me and Gus are here—I don't mean at your orchestra camp, okay? We're seriously here in Fort Myers, and I need you to call me right back and tell me where to find you. Thank you."

I hung up and shook my head. Half baked, you know, Aleah? What if Andrew never returned the call? He didn't have to if he didn't want to. Would I have to hunt down my grandfather myself? Would I call the Reinstein in the phone book? There probably wasn't even a listing. Not good.

"We didn't really think about this part, huh?" Gus mumbled.

Gus pulled off I-75 and aimed at downtown Fort Myers and "Beaches." There were a lot of cars out on the road for two in the morning. Gus smoked, and heat poured in (like in the 80s in the middle of the night, like tonight).

"We need to find a spot to park. I can't drive anymore," Gus said.

We drove through a wide and curving sprawl highway that went past shopping mall after shopping mall and restaurants and gas stations, and CVS pharmacies that were right across the street from Walgreens pharmacies, and gun shops and castle-themed minia-ture golf courses, and dark, empty retail spots that were sort of overgrown with Dangling foliage, but nothing that looked like any place specifically.

"There's no way we're going to find Andrew here," I mumbled.

"Yeah, man. Yeah. We have a problem," Gus nodded.

Finally, finally, after like a half hour of just sprawling crap (that looked exactly like the sprawling crap around Dubuque, Iowa, except with palm trees and thick shrubs), we pulled into a part of town that was older and sort of on a grid.

The giant palms bent over the car. Ranch-style houses sat back from the road in darkness. The houses got a little closer and older, but not like a hundred years old, more like from the seventies or something, and there were more and more old strip malls, and then a cemetery, and then we came to a sign that had an arrow pointing to downtown Fort Myers and one to the Midpoint Bridge and Cape Coral. Gus took a right to head toward downtown, because we couldn't leave Fort Myers.

But we never got to a downtown. About ten minutes later, Gus pulled into the empty parking lot of a closed restaurant that had thick bushes and trees all around it. He parked and shut off the car. We both stared into the dark.

"What are we going to do?" I asked.

"I can't drive anymore, man. I feel like I'm going to crash. We can hide in this overgrowth, man. We don't have any place to go, anyway. Try your freaking brother again."

Andrew didn't answer, of course. "We don't know where we are, Andrew…"

"McGregor Boulevard," Gus said.

"McGregor Boulevard…"

"In Fort Myers," Gus said.

"In Fort Myers, Andrew."

"Edison Restaurant, right next to the country club."

"Edison Restaurant. The country club. My phone's dead. Call Gus, okay?"

Andrew didn't call. We sat in silence for another ten minutes.

"I'm going to sleep now," Gus said.

Gus stuck his hand next to the seat and pulled a lever, and the shitty Celica chair fell backward and then he was out cold, I thought.

I breathed hard. My nerves sort of leapt. I didn't want to meet my grandfather, Aleah. I also didn't want to be stuck in a parking lot in the middle of the night in the middle of Florida where criminals might be hiding. (I've seen a lot of episodes of *COPS*.) I heard tree-creaking noises and cars driving past the entrance slowly. My muscles filled with juice. Had to do it. I got out of the car and pissed in a bush, and then I ran back and forth and back and forth across the parking lot like the total freak-show clown that I am.

After awhile, Gus rolled down his window and shouted, "Would you stop? You're like a freaking hamster on one of those wheels."

"This is what I do," I shouted.

"Freak, Felton. Wow," Gus said.

I ran back and forth until I could barely stand. *What the hell? Where's Andrew? Why am I here? I don't want to see my grandpa. I don't care about Tovi. This is stupid. Why aren't I in Michigan? Jesus Christ. Jerri? I'm sorry. Why am I here?* It took probably two hours, seriously. When I climbed back in the car, Gus was really asleep.

It was so freaking dark, and those thick palm tree bushes were bent over the car blocking out everything…

• • •

Wait.

Renee's not back, yet. It's been like twenty minutes. Should I really go find her? In the bathroom? Some more people just showed up. Like ten middle-aged African Americans. They're all wearing Hawaiian shirts like Andrew wears. They all look like they're going to fall asleep. I'm so tired too. There's one dude working the ticket window, and he's so tired he might not make it through the next couple of minutes.

Where the hell is Renee? I'm passing out. I have to unplug my computer and pack up if I'm going to find her.

August 17th, 3:41 a.m.
JACKSONVILLE, FLORIDA, PART II

Renee was smoking with a homeless guy outside. This station is just surrounded by empty parking garages and it's dark out there. I had to walk to this back alley to find her (because she wasn't in the bathroom when I called in for her). I crept around the corner, ready to punch and kick (my backpack on, which might have slowed me down). And there she was, smoking. I sort of freaked. I shouted, "What the hell are you doing?" at her.

She said, "Cool down, man child."

The homeless man laughed. "That your beau?"

"No, he is not," she replied.

I always expect the worst, Aleah. By the time I left the station looking for Renee, I expected I'd find her murdered body. Expect the worst. If things go wrong, I expect they will go very wrong. Yes, it will get dangerous. Yes, you will be terrified.

I expect the horror movie, which is seriously messing me up.

• • •

You can imagine how I felt, then, out there in that restaurant parking lot with Gus when someone started pounding on Gus's car window.

Murderer!

Okay. The passenger chair in Gus's Celica is broken, so it doesn't tilt back so I was asleep sitting straight up, my head lolled forward, drool flowing out of my mouth, I'm sure. And then, the pounding. Or, maybe, more like tapping. I flinched awake. "What?"

"Shit," Gus said, trying to sit up from his rolled-way-back chair.

"Does he have a gun?" I shouted.

"Cops?" Gus cried.

"Open the window," a voice came from outside.

"Don't. They might shoot you," I said.

Gus managed to get his seat up after kicking the steering wheel a couple of times trying. "They might shoot me through the window too. What's stopping them?"

"Let's go. Let's go. Drive out of here."

Instead, Gus rolled down the window. It was so dark in the lot that I couldn't see who was out there. "You're not a cop," Gus said.

"You're not Felton," a girl's voice said.

Gus reached up and turned on the dome light. I could see the girl had a hoodie on, but I couldn't really see her face. She could see me, though.

"That's Felton," Gus said.

"Oh. Shit. Yeah," she said. "That's a big bruise."

"I punched him," Gus whispered.

"Okay. Are you Gus?" she asked.

"Yeah." Gus nodded.

"You're not even close out here. We have to go to Fort Myers Beach. It's like a half hour. Follow me, okay?"

"Okay," Gus said.

She left the window and climbed into a car parked a couple slots away from us. Gus turned to me and said, "Did you see that?" His eyes were wide.

"Who was she?" I asked.

"Has to be your cousin. I mean, cuter, but looks like your sister. I can't believe she found us."

"How old is she?"

"She's driving. Maybe our age or something?" Gus said.

The car, which I could only assume contained my cousin, Tovi, backed up and then slowly drove out of the parking lot. Gus followed. The Celica clock said 5:05, so it was 6:05 Eastern time. 6:05 in the morning.

"She's driving a Beemer, dude. You think she has a Beemer?"

"Probably, since she's driving it."

"Nice car if you like that kind of thing."

Down McGregor my cousin drove, ten miles under the speed limit. Gus was on her tail like a dog nose to a dog buttock.

"Maybe she's underage, man. She drives like a grandma."

The word "grandma" freaked me out. "Oh shit," I said.

"Wish she'd speed up. I have to take a piss," Gus said.

For about ten minutes, we followed her back through the neighborhoods we'd been through a few hours earlier and then, for another ten minutes, into ones we'd never been in. My heart totally pounded.

Then at an open stretch of road, out of no place, the girl (Tovi) gunned it. She blew out to like 85 miles per hour.

"Whoa!" Gus shouted. He hit the gas but was behind her a long way immediately. "Definitely a Reinstein," Gus said. "Weird as hell."

I just nodded.

"At least she's moving. Bladder. Bad."

Tovi slowed down and we caught up. (Gus said, "Nooooo....") The sun started lighting the sky all blue, orange, and purple. Tovi slid around a right curve in the road, gunned it like crazy on a straightaway, and then slowed way down so we could catch her as she slid around a left curve.

"Another straight run of road now. Wonder if she'll hit a hundred?" Gus asked. "Go, girl!" he begged.

But she didn't go fast. She went very, very slowly so we were right on her tail. There was enough light that I could see she was alone in the car, no Andrew. I could also tell that she was staring up in the rearview, on occasion. Looking at me?

It was light enough that I could see we were on the water. Between little ramshackle buildings, great stretches of water appeared.

The sight of it made my heart pound. (Even though I was plain freaked about this girl, I still felt excited.) "Is that the ocean, man? Is that what that water is?"

"It's attached to the ocean," Gus said. "Or at least to the Gulf of Mexico. This isn't really the ocean, you know."

We rolled past sort of dumpy resorts and then past a tennis court that was filled with eight old ladies whacking balls at the ass cracker of morning. "Lot better than the old ladies in the nursing home on your paper route, huh?" I said.

"They'll be there one day. We'll all be there."

And then there was more water, everywhere, water on both sides of the land. "We're on the ocean, man. Holy shit."

We were following my cousin, who I'd never met, out into the ocean, maybe to meet my grandfather who hates me or not... Crazy, Aleah. I was totally shaking.

We came to a giant bridge that shot up like ten stories into the air. The actual sun, not just its light, came up over the side of the earth. Giant bodies of water rippled on both sides of us and under us. "This is awesome, Gus."

"Yeah. Pretty," Gus said. "I don't like water that much right now. Pee."

The sign at the end of the bridge said "Welcome to Fort Myers Beach." It was resort-y like the Wisconsin Dells, but with lots of palm trees and white sidewalks and lots and lots of swimsuit stores. A couple of old guys ran past on a morning jog when we stopped at a stop sign. They were shirtless and were tanned this dark orange color I'd never seen before.

"Someone left the steaks on the barbie too long," Gus said.

Then Tovi veered to the right and there was a pier—which I recognized from a certain photograph of a pelican that had been on display on feltonreinstein.com—but I couldn't see the water because there were some stores and some dunes and thick vegetation in the way. I really thought I might throw up.

"I totally have to piss very, very bad," Gus groaned.

Just as he said it, Tovi pulled left into the parking lot next to a hotel called the White Shells.

"*Ah!*" Gus shouted.

He pulled into an open space a couple of cars down from Tovi. Then he shut off the car, burst out, and ran toward the hotel.

Then I got out of the car.

I could hear Tovi get out of her car.

I didn't want to look over at her. Instead, I looked at my feet, which were in my stinky running shoes (Ultimate Frisbee, running in that parking lot), which were on pavement that was covered in a thin film of sand and crackly stuff I later figured out is broken seashell.

Dizzy. My throat felt like it might close down and kill me. Tovi didn't say anything either. We both stood next to the cars for way too long.

Then she said, "Hey, did you like my driving?"

"Yeah," I said, looking at the ground. "Pretty funny."

"I can't help it. Papa's car is so fast. It's so fun. Sometimes I just got to go."

I lifted my head and turned to the right in time to see Tovi pull back her hood. "Papa?" I asked.

"Our old granddad," Tovi said. "You know it's me, right?"

We stared at each other. Seriously weird.

"Yeah. I know," I said. "You ever look in a mirror?" I asked.

"Do I look like a boy?" she asked.

"No," I said. "I didn't know you existed."

"Felton," she said, shaking her head and talking really quiet. "I almost don't believe it. You're real, man."

We stood there facing each other, and I guess we were both sort of crying, which was weird, and then she came up to me and hugged me and then she whispered, "But seriously. Why are you here?"

I felt heat rise in my face. "Because…I don't know."

"What are you doing?"

"I'm worried about Andrew."

"This sort of sucks. I mean, don't get me wrong…I'm glad to see you. Totally. We're like a…a…"

"Freak show."

"Right, because we look so much alike, but why you're here…"

"Andrew didn't tell me not to come."

"It never occurred to him you would, dude. He freaked when you called. Threw a fat fit. Then he fell on the bed. When I left he was in a state of shock. Like, comatose staring up at the ceiling."

"Why?"

"Let's go in."

"Okay."

"Papa's going to know who you are, man."

"Is he in there?" I said, nodding at the White Shells.

"No. You're safe for now."

"Safe. Shit."

"It's gonna be okay. I made a promise to my grandma to take care of this. I'm gonna take care of…"

"Okay," I said.

Tovi exhaled and nodded at me.

. . .

Ow. My head, Aleah.

I must be getting to the end of my rope. What am I even writing? I am so sick to my stomach. Why did I eat all that Hickory Farms sausage? So freaking salty. The drinking fountain is filled with mushy Kleenex. I'm totally dizzy. But there's no way I'm going to fall asleep in this bus station. Renee's asleep. I don't want to go to sleep.

August 17th, 7:18 a.m.
ORLANDO, FLORIDA

I'm in Orlando. Not at Disney World, though. At another ugly bus station.

I might sleep here. I did it before; I can do it again.

I slept in the Jacksonville bus station for like an hour. No one murdered me! I did not die of summer sausage intake! There is still half the sausage left too. That's good. I think. Or is it rude to give somebody a gift of half-eaten cheese and sausage?

We'll find out.

I am alone now, but the sun's up.

Renee woke me up when it was time to get on the Tampa bus, thank God, or I might still be sleeping on that bench (totally stretched out with my head on my backpack and my Stan Smith tennis shoes dangling out into the aisle).

Renee and I boarded the bus and sat down together toward the back. She said, "You're really, really young, do you know that?"

I said, "No."

She said, "I could tell when you were sleeping. You really look like a little kid."

I said, "Oh."

She said, "Tell me exactly what you're writing."

I said, "I don't know."

She said, "Use your words."

I said, "I guess it started out to be an apology to my girlfriend, but now I'm trying to explain to her how I don't know anything but am really trying to be a better person."

She said, "Have you been a bad person?"

"Not intentionally. But I might be bad genetically."

She said, "No. No." She shook her head. She whispered, "No." She pulled my head onto her shoulder.

Then we fell asleep. When I woke up, Renee was on the phone to her sister. Instead of riding all the way to Tampa, she got picked up a few minutes ago here in Orlando. (There's like a forty-minute layover here—this is sort of the nicest, cleanest station I've been in so far—will use bathroom several times.)

So, Renee's gone. I miss her. She was my partner, I guess. She didn't leave me without telling me something.

"I broke up with my boyfriend in Chicago."

Me: "Oh. Sorry."

Her: "I'm not pregnant."

Me: "Uh...That's good?"

Her: "I had a miscarriage."

Me: "What do you mean?"

Her: "I lost my baby because it died inside of me."

Me: "Oh shit."

Her: "I don't want to be with my boyfriend if he's not the father. I don't want to be with my boyfriend at all. I took the bus the whole way with you because I told my parents I was pregnant two weeks ago. My mom's been reading wedding magazines and calling me every night. Now I have to tell them…her. I just wanted to delay getting home…"

Me: "Oh crap."

Her: "I'm going to graduate from college this year. My mom thinks I'm bad, though. She thinks I'm…I'm just wrong. I don't know why, really. Me telling her I'm pregnant and telling her I was getting married…that made her happy. And now this…my sister, Janey, is coming to get me. I told her about the miscarriage on the phone."

"Oh shit," I whispered. "I'm sorry. I'm really, really sorry."

"I was right about you. You're a sweet kid, Felton. You're not a jerk, okay? I think it's really cool you're writing an epic letter to your girlfriend."

"She might not be my girlfriend," I said.

"Sucks," she said. Then she reached up and touched my cheek, which was weird, because it's something Jerri would do.

A few minutes later, Renee was gone. I think her sister, Janey, weighed over four hundred pounds. She is really big.

I do know something, Aleah: most people are in a horror movie, at least sometimes.

It doesn't matter that Renee's sister is big. (Why would it matter?) It was nice of her to drive over to get Renee.

(I thought Renee wanted to have sex with me, Aleah.)

(I guess I think about sex a lot.)

(Not as much as Gus.)

August 17th, 7:39 a.m.

ORLANDO, FLORIDA, PART II

You probably want to know about Andrew—how he greeted me and crap, huh? Here it is in sum: Andrew was *pissed*.

On the way into the White Shells, Tovi again tried to warn me, but I couldn't really get my head around how bad it was that I'd shown up.

As she opened the door for me, she said, "Remember. Be ready. Your little brother threw a hissy when you called."

"I don't get it. I'm here to look after him."

"No you're not," Tovi said.

"Uh," I paused. "Why would you say that?" I thought maybe she knew that I'd used his disappearance as a convenient excuse to skip Michigan. Freaked me out.

"You didn't ask him if you could come. You didn't leave a message saying you were thinking about it. I don't see the big deal…or didn't until I saw you in person and realized you totally, one-hundred percent, look just like your dad. Plus, Andrew…Andrew's trying to escape you, you know?"

"Me? Why escape me?"

"You'll have to ask him," she said.

I walked in. Tovi followed.

The White Shells does not have what I would call the nicest lobby in the world. Sort of looks like it was built in the '80s for, like, gold-chain-in-their-chest-hair, cocaine-smuggling dudes. It's white and faded light green and pink and a little stinky, at least in the morning. It smells like moist, mushy dog carpet, probably because there is mushy green carpet.

And this was weird: even though it was pretty early, four dudes wearing Hawaiian shirts (like Andrew does constantly, now—I have pictures to prove it) sang around a piano in the corner of the restaurant. (This was the first time I saw the Golden Rods in action—more about them in a moment.) They sang a Beach Boys song, which is pretty much all they sing, except for other beach music, like from that guy who sings about margaritas and cheeseburgers. I can't remember his name.

"Those guys saw Andrew playing the piano last week and asked him to help them out," Tovi said, pointing at the old farts.

"Andrew plays with them?"

Then she said, "Yeah." Then she stopped. She said, "Do you have any idea what's going on, what we're doing?"

I shrugged at her. "Maybe."

"You've been left out of a lot."

"I have?"

"Duh."

"About, like, Randy Stone?" I asked.

"No. That's done. That stupid Randy Stone crap. Andrew threw his cigarettes in the ocean."

"Andrew really smoked? Are you kidding?"

"He couldn't smoke. He looked ridiculous and coughed, and I yelled at him for being an idiot. Plus, his cigarettes were Steve's…you know, your dad's? I guess Andrew found them in a crawl space in your house last summer."

"My dad smoked?" I said. *What?* "He was an athlete."

"Right. I don't know, man. That's what Andrew says. Anyway, the cigarettes were like twelve years old or something, really dry. When he'd light one, it would catch fire instead of smoke, and he'd have to throw it on the sand so it wouldn't burn him. He and Big Rod—the lead singer of his band—threw the rest of the pack in the gulf yesterday."

"Littering."

"I know, but it's good, you know? He says Rod taught him he doesn't need to hide behind a fake detective. He has to take responsibility for his emotions."

I paused and stared at Tovi. She sort of mock-stared back at me (bulged out her eyes and opened her mouth). "Okay," I said.

"What?"

"I guess I don't really know Andrew."

"Me either. But whatever."

Then I started nodding really fast, because Andrew's a nut. "It's possible he'll drive us totally crazy. Do you understand?" All the crap he'd pulled last summer flew through my brain, Aleah. The fire where he burned his clothes? The pirate shirt? The shaved head? The constant digging through boxes in the attic and garage? The screaming matches with Jerri? The vegetables? The shoving? The locked bathrooms? Holy cats, you know? Remembering this, I wonder why I think of Andrew as the sane one in our family.

"If this was going to be easy, it wouldn't be worth doing," Tovi said.

"What does that mean?"

"I don't know, Felton. Ask Andrew. That's the kind of crap he says. At least before you called saying you were here. Now, maybe he's come to the end of his ability to deal with hard stuff."

"Why should me being here be hard?" I said.

"Because everything's so easy for you."

"It is not."

"Andrew thinks so."

"He doesn't know crap then," I said.

"I don't know crap, man. Other than we look like twins."

I nodded at her.

Tovi guided me over to a big, cracked, white leathery padded bench across from the bathrooms. She told me to sit and wait. I sat. Then she walked a couple of steps to this counter, pressed some coffee from this urn thing into a Styrofoam cup, and handed it to me.

"You want me to drink this brown stuff?" I asked.

"Trying to be a good host," she said. Then she smiled really big. "Enjoy your coffee, Felton. I'm going to go get your little brother."

I nodded. I sipped bitter freaking coffee. I waited. Andrew? Crazy Andrew?

You know what tastes bad, Aleah? Coffee. It made me gag. But nerves made me keep sipping. Then my legs started twitching.

I thought: *How the hell did Andrew find this girl? Our cousin? This girl has a whole life in our family that isn't our family but is our family? What am I doing here? What is Andrew doing? How am I such a big problem? I have it easy? Ha! What if this girl is my twin and there are more terrible lies? What if she and Andrew were switched at birth? Wait, that would make her his twin…*

These crazy thoughts kept flying.

Freaking out, Aleah.

Wait. Where the hell's Gus?

While I sat there accidentally drinking terrible coffee, I looked around for Gus. He hadn't left while Tovi and I were in the parking lot. He wasn't in the lobby. *Did he leave? Why is he here in the first place? What the hell?*

Fifteen, twenty minutes had passed and he hadn't returned from the bathroom.

Did he just say, Done? *Did he leave me behind? Jesus!*

Then I wondered why the hell those dudes were singing at like seven in the damn morning. Then I wondered if Tovi would even come back. I could feel the big bruise on the side of my face throbbing. Then I got a little dizzy and wondered if any of this was really happening.

Have you ever actually paused and thought, while your eyes are wide open, "Is this now? Am I here right now? Is this a dream?"

• • •

I'm sort of doing that at this moment, here in the bus station, Aleah.

• • •

About twenty minutes later, I suppose, although it felt more like several days (me bouncing up and down on my ass cheeks), the elevator doors opened, and Andrew and Tovi stepped out.

I stood up fast.

Andrew wore a Hawaiian shirt like the singing dudes, which might have made me laugh if I weren't going crazy with coffee, etc.

He stopped and stared, his glasses slid down his nose so he looked like an owl.

My heart pumped harder.

Heat rose on my neck.

Without smiling he said, "Good morning, Felton. What's wrong with your face?"

"Gus punched me."

"I'm not surprised," he said.

Then I became a rambling man. "Andrew, you're totally crazy… you're in Florida…what the hell are you doing…this could be dangerous and I'm not a fan of flying off the handle on some kind of wild adventure without even notifying the authorities, i.e., Jerri about the fact that you've made contact with our family that always hated us…and now what? Are you trying to kill our grandfather or something, or are you trying to rob…"

Tovi shouted, "Stop, man!"

I did.

Andrew stared for a second, then said, "Why are you here?"

"Why are you here?" I shouted.

"Because I ran away," he said. "I took Greyhound buses here, all the way from Green Bay. It was disgusting," he said. "An old man put his feet on the window next to my face," Andrew said. "I earned being here. I earned being away from you."

"Why don't you dudes go to the beach and hash this out," Tovi said.

"There's nothing to hash out," Andrew said. "Go home, Felton. I'll talk to Jerri about this when I'm ready, so leave her out of it."

"I wasn't going to tell…"

"I'm going to practice my crappy music now," Andrew said.

"What?"

"Stick it in your butt," Andrew said. "You're a giant pecker." Then he turned and walked to the dudes in Hawaiian shirts who were not singing but staring at us.

"Jesus Christ, Andrew. Come on," I called after him.

He flipped me the bird, Aleah. It felt like a kick in the nuts. Not Andrew-like.

The big singer (the one I found out is named Big Rod and is Andrew's new best friend), gave me a weak wave.

I sort of waved back. The room spun.

"Come on," Tovi told me. "We should hit the beach or something."

I followed her. None of this felt real.

• • •

Nothing feels real right now. I'm going to grab some water.

August 17th, 8:11 a.m.
ORLANDO, FLORIDA, PART III

Whoa. The bus leaves again in a few minutes. I'm very, very sick to my stomach. It's totally rumbling from downing the gift platter (and probably from not sleeping very much forever, you know?). My calf muscles are bubbly. It's like there are little mice underneath my skin running up and down from my knees to my ankles. Trembly.

The last bus I was on had rainbow stripes running down the center of the seats and it smelled like somebody had been cooking bacon. So, so sick.

This is the second to last bus, though. This should just about do it. I just texted Tovi and told her I'd be in Fort Myers in a short six hours.

Man, I think I could fly from Madison to Fort Myers twice in that time. How did this happen?

Karpinski, Cody, and Reese keep texting me too. Kirk Johnson couldn't stay behind his blockers in practice yesterday. The offense is all off. What if I can't get back in time for the game Friday? What if there are more power outages and crap? Roy Ngelale will beat us for sure.

I hate this.

There are about twenty people going on this bus. I hope I can get a seat by myself.

Oh, Renee. You are gone.

I really miss her. I hope she's okay.

Oh, look: Disney posters.

Normal kids go to Disney World.

Andrew and I take days-long Greyhound bus rides.

August 17th, 10:04 a.m.
TAMPA BUS STATION

Holy crap, Aleah. I can't believe what just happened!

On the trip just now between Orlando and Tampa, I was a few rows behind this guy with a mullet. I noticed his shirt when he got on. It was a tank top with a Budweiser can emblem, except instead of Budweiser, the can had "Go Gators" written on it. And I could smell him from my seat. Cigarettes and armpits and dirty shorts, and he was all jumpy, so I couldn't stop staring at him.

He kept asking people around him their names. "What's yer name?" and they'd all have to answer, because if they didn't, he'd keep asking them (in a meaner and meaner voice) until they did. "What's yer name, I said." (*Scary.*)

Then he tried to light up a cigarette! On the bus! But the bus driver, who was obviously staring at him in this mirror because the dude was so weird and scary, shouted, "No smoking in here, son." And the mullet guy shouted the f-bomb back at the driver and then, as we pulled into Tampa, a couple of cop cars started driving next to us, which made the mullet dude just freaky.

"They following us, man? You see them cars?"

"Don't know," the lady next to him said.

"Fuzzy Wuzzy was a bear," mullet man said. "Fuzzy Wuzzy was a bear." He said it like twenty-five times.

When we pulled into the station, the dude jumped into the aisle (said, "Excuse me," to people he bumped) and went barreling to the door and out, and then two cops tackled him on the sidewalk!

The woman in front of me said, "Thank God."

By the time I got out there to go into the station to use the bathroom, the dude was in handcuffs and he was crying. I mean totally sobbing. And there was a German shepherd dog sticking its nose in his bag and barking.

He was trafficking meth! I heard one of the cops say that! *What the hell?*

Now I can't stop hearing his sobbing, Aleah. It was terrible. It was like Jerri in her bedroom last summer, when she was totally out of control.

COPS isn't that funny.

Is the whole wide world filled with all this craziness and broken crap and crying?

Yikes. Jesus.

That guy was way worse off than Renee.

I'm going to swim in the gulf when I get there, even though there are stingrays and other terrifying fish in the water. I like the water. It's cleaner there than out here.

Beach.

Okay, okay, okay…

Everything is weird, Aleah.

August 17th, 10:12 a.m.

TAMPA BUS STATION, PART II

Bus station.

Smells like a manure spreader. Cow crap. Weird. At least there's a place to plug in my computer.

• • •

Speaking of weird. You know who else is weird?

After Andrew told me that I'm a giant pecker, Tovi took me out to the beach.

We left the White Shells from the back door and walked out onto a patio, then past an unstaffed tiki bar and a pool area (with pool) where a couple of grandpa-aged old people were floating (swimming).

Tovi walked fast (faster than me!).

From the White Shells we took a boardwalk path between dunes and then, there it was, the ocean. (Okay, okay, the Gulf of Mexico, but dudes like me can't make too fine a distinction or else we might have to say we've never seen anything at all.)

"There it is," I said.

"Uh-huh," Tovi said.

The sand was really white and soft, and the water was really, really blue because the air was still and there weren't really waves, and the morning sky was totally blue, no clouds anywhere. Little birds ran on the sand. Pelicans dove into the water. Really cool.

Both Tovi and I sat down and pulled off our shoes, and we paused for a moment and stared at our feet. They looked like the same feet except hers are a little smaller and she has no hair (but long toes like me).

"Pretty weird," Tovi said.

Then I said, "Will you please tell me exactly what's going on with Andrew?"

She stood up, so I stood too. "Let's walk. I can't sit still." (Sound familiar?)

As soon as we were walking, she started to spill, speed talking.

"Okay. So here's the deal, okay? Andrew's here because I asked him to come down. But Papa has no idea Andrew is his grandson. I've been bringing Andrew over there every couple of days or so…"

"Over where?" I asked.

"Fiddlesticks. It's the golf community where Papa lives."

"Oh yeah. That was a clue. That was in a Randy Stone email. Fiddlesticks."

"Screw Randy Stone. Andrew's a freak. Anyway, Papa always asks questions of Andrew, like, 'Where you from again?' 'How do you know Tovi?' 'You like Bach, huh?' but just sort of looks through him for the most part. Papa's not doing so great. Gram (Grandma Rose) was pretty much his whole life after he retired, and he's always been a sad guy, anyway. So he's not behaving that weird."

"He's sad, huh?" I asked.

"As long as I can remember, anyway. Since…" Tovi paused and looked at me.

"Since my dad killed himself in my garage," I said.

"Yeah, man," Tovi nodded.

"Jesus," I said.

"I know," Tovi said.

"So, you asked Andrew to come down?"

"Well…he wasn't my first choice, Felton. I didn't really know about him. I knew about you. And I remembered you."

"We met?"

"Here. Right here, man. When we were like four."

"I sort of remember." I nodded. I did remember too, Aleah. I could picture a little curly-head girl and this beach. Hazy. But there in my head. "Why did you ask Andrew, then?"

"He emailed me like a day after Gram died. Out of no place. I was supposed to contact you…I mean that's what Gram wanted. But then, Andrew's all…*you don't want Felton around this.*"

"I think the day he found out about Grandma Rose, I told him he should stop worrying about crap and should just shake it off."

"Oh." Tovi nodded. "Okay."

"I have to apologize to him. Seriously apologize."

"I don't think it's going to be so easy, man. Andrew's pretty much straight-up anti-Felton Reinstein right now."

"Jesus. I don't know why he's so mad."

Tovi shrugged. Then she said, "You're pretty fast, right? You want to race to that umbrella?" Tovi pointed down the beach about sixty yards to where an old lady in a black bathing suit had just jammed her umbrella in the ground.

"You want to race me?" I asked.

"Yeah. Your hamstring healed?"

"How do you know about…"

"I read the Internet, man. 'Reinstein Runs over Cuba City!'" she shouted (a headline from last fall's football season). She took a couple of fast steps down the beach. "Andrew isn't the only detective in the family. Go!" Then she was off. Fast. Very fast. Very fluid like a gazelle, even though we were in sand. I actually had to turn it up to catch her.

I passed her about fifteen yards from the umbrella and the black swimsuit, biscuit-butt lady and then Tovi did something so weird, Aleah. She totally dove into my legs and sent me twisting through the air onto the back of my head, about five yards from the poor old lady who screamed ("*Ahh!*") when we both hit the ground rolling.

"Ow. Shit!" Tovi shouted. She grabbed the back of her head. "Damn! Why would anyone play football?"

"Helmets," I said.

"Damn!" she shouted, squeezing her eyes shut.

My mouth had sand in it. My face and hair were covered in white sand. I chewed and spit. Then I looked over at Tovi and said, "Who are you?"

Tovi rolled onto all fours and spit sand, then swallowed and spit again, then said, "You think you're the only jock in the family?"

"I don't know."

"You're not."

"Oh."

"You have to be careful with your hamstrings. That's genetic."

"You have a lot of sand in your hair," I said.

"That's genetic too. Your 'fro is totally crusted, dude."

"You look like an old lady," I said.

Then the old lady yelled at us. We picked up our shoes and walked again.

"Actually, Andrew's more of a Reinstein than we are," Tovi said. "We're more like Gram, Rothenbergs. The fighting Rothenbergs of Prague! Andrew's all Papa Stanley. You'll see," Tovi said. "Except Papa has some curly hair, not totally straight like Andrew's."

"Rothenberg."

"Yeah. That's her maiden name. Gram was the real athlete. Papa just whacks tennis balls around and shouts at people for not playing as well as he'd like to, even though he can't."

"Oh," I said.

"He's teaching Andrew to play tennis."

"No way."

"Yeah. He's teaching him to play like John McEnroe. I'm a tennis player, you know? I won't let Papa tell me anything because he'd drive me crazy like he drove your dad crazy."

I stopped. "What do you mean he drove Dad crazy?"

"I guess Papa just rode Steve hard all the time, just took all the fun out of the game for him."

I stared at her for a second. "Is that why Dad killed himself?"

"Jesus. I don't think so. No. There had to be a hell of a lot more to it than that."

As we walked on, Tovi told me that she'd become aware of me again during track season last year, when out of no place I was running some of the fastest times among sophomores in the country. (She had a Google Alert, like Andrew). She showed her mom the articles, and her mom was like, "Oh my God. That's Steve's Felton," and her mom totally broke down and cried. They decided they'd print articles and bring them to Grandma Rose when they visited her during the summer. But then Grandma Rose got the cancer diagnosis and Papa Stan fell into a worse mood than ever, so they didn't do it.

Apparently Grandma Rose had been saying for several years that it was time for Stan to get over my dad's death and reconnect with us boys. Grandma was waiting for him to feel better, but he never did.

"Papa sort of hates your dad, I think," Tovi said.

"I don't understand," I said.

"I don't know. I think Papa's really just heartbroken, but it comes out as anger," Tovi said.

In the fall of last year, while I was getting more and more sort of famous from football, Grandma Rose's health went downhill fast. Tovi decided Rose should know about me, no matter what. Her mom, Evith, wasn't so sure. She thought it might be too late.

"Gram was having all kinds of chemo and she lost all her weight and she was so weak she could barely get up from her lawn chair… but I brought it up to her anyway."

"You mean, you brought me up to her?" I asked.

"Yeah. I printed out a bunch of articles for her, and it was all kind of sweet and great to start out with. Gram was lying down on the couch in the living room, then Mom told her that I had something to show her and Gram stared at the articles and read them really close and smiled and got teary-eyed and said, 'He's an athlete! He's my boy!'

Then her hands started shaking and then she started coughing and sobbing really hard, and then she went completely crazy screaming at Papa, who was in the other room listening to classical music like he does all the time, that she was going to die without her grandkids ever knowing she loved them and it was all his fault for not forgiving…it was bad, Felton. We had to call the ambulance because she couldn't breathe or sit up or swallow. Oh man. It was scary. And Mom was super pissed at me for coming up with this lame-brained plan."

"Oh God. Oh shit. I killed my grandma."

"No, she didn't die then. But I decided to forget about it. Papa told me if I ever brought you up again, he'd disown me too."

I felt so weak. "Why did Andrew come here?" I asked.

"Because," Tovi said. "Gram wanted him to come."

In March, about three weeks before Grandma Rose died, Tovi got a card in the mail. Inside there was a check for ten thousand dollars (yes, $10,000). Grandma Rose wrote about how it was so terrible and heartbreaking for her because it was too late. She couldn't ever fix the family. She always thought she had time and that she'd let Stan heal, but then this? *It's not too late for your grandfather, Tovi. You can make this happen for him and for me. He needs to make amends with his grandsons.*

"She asked me to bring you guys down. She told me to use the money. I would've made a plan, man. I would've contacted you. But Andrew beat me to the planning stage. He knew right when Gram died. He told me you were a jerk and weren't interested in us, Felton. Then me and Andrew spent a couple of months planning out how we'd slowly introduce him to Papa. We're using tennis and classical music. That's why he's here."

"That little asshole," I said. "He tried to cut me out of the family." I could feel the heat rising in my face.

"Don't be too hard on him, man. He's had a rough run, you know?"

"No."

"Being your younger brother."

"That's ridiculous."

"I don't know," Tovi said. "He is a little nuts."

"Well, I'm here," I said.

"I'm glad," Tovi said. "But now I don't know what to do about our plan. Papa is going to know you're Steve's kid, man. He's going to recognize you right away. There's not going to be any more easing in."

Well…

• • •

We tried, Aleah. We tried to ease in. I wore a costume.

I shit you not.

I'm like a freaking Scooby-Doo cartoon.

August 17th, 10:49 a.m.
SOUTH OF TAMPA

Here's a question: is it weird to like your cousin too much? I don't mean in a gross way, but I mean, I really, really like Tovi. Is it weird?

I don't even freaking know because I've never had a cousin before, Aleah. Jerri was an only child and Dad whacked himself. Where were all my cousins supposed to come from? Cody seriously has like eight hundred and forty-two cousins. If his mom wants to have a barbecue, she puts a post up on the family Facebook, and she can't blink before they're all rolling down from the hills in their big-ass pickup trucks bearing bratwurst and potato salad.

I texted Tovi from the airport in Madison and told her I was bringing her a huge box of cheese and sausage from Wisconsin. (I bought the Hickory Farms at the airport. I needed to give her a gift. She texted back, "You are such a freak, dude.")

I know she's really going to love it, though. (I guess what's left of it…sort of gross—like a half-chewed stump of sausage.)

Also, Tovi told me about my hamstring. The little man that blew me up? That's a tweak. Tovi gets hamstring tweaks and she rests for a week and she's fine. My dad had tweaks too. Ruined one of his tennis seasons in college. What if I knew that this spring? Took a week off? Victory.

Right. If Dad hadn't killed himself and I had Tovi in my life forever, I don't think I'd have ever felt so out of place on the planet. I might be more like Peyton Manning.

What if I always had Grandma Rose? She was an accomplished track athlete and tennis player in her youth. Remember that from the obituary?

If I want to make myself really sad, I think about how I never got to hang out with my Grandma who was like me. Grandma Berba is great, but she doesn't know a touchdown from a home run from a three-pointer from a…total shuttlecock master spike in badminton. Grandma Rose played sports and watched sports, I guess. Back when she was Rose Rothenberg instead of Reinstein, back when she first got to the U.S. from Eastern Europe, she totally killed everyone in all these New Jersey Jewish sports leagues.

Who would I be if she had been in my life, Aleah?

They just called my last bus. Thank God. It's going to be great to see Tovi (for about an hour before I have to fly back to Wisconsin for the game).

August 17th, 11:40 a.m.
JUST LEFT ST. PETERSBURG

Hey! Believe it or not! It's hot as shit!

We pulled off to pick up passengers in St. Petersburg, which is pretty much just another part of Tampa as far as I can tell, and the hot air poured, poured, poured into the bus.

I need to change my freaking clothes, Aleah.

I bought a Snickers bar in the bus station. It was so melted I threw it out, but not before chocolate got spread all over my shorts. I look like I pooped the front of myself. Nice, huh?

Onward. We're rolling again.

• • •

Andrew was not acting like Andrew. When Tovi and I got back from the beach, the Golden Rods were done practicing. We went up to Andrew's room, but Tovi's key card didn't open the door.

"What the hell?" she said.

We went down to the lobby, and the front-desk person said, "Mr. Andrew has changed rooms."

"Well, Mr. Andrew is an idiot, because I'm paying for the room, so you have to tell me what room he changed to," Tovi barked.

"Fair enough," the front-desk dude said.

Andrew had moved two rooms down the hall. We went back up the elevator with the new room key in hand.

"Andrew's giving me a big headache," Tovi said.

When we got up there, Gus was hanging out in the room watching TV and Andrew sat in the corner on the floor reading that same fat Spinoza book he'd had in Bluffton. (Library book! Fines!). He didn't look up at all.

Gus lifted his hair wad out of his face, gestured with his eyes at Andrew, and shook his head really fast (I believe saying, *Crazy*).

Tovi didn't care if Andrew was crazy. She started screaming immediately. "You think you can just do whatever you want? You think you're entitled to just run and hide from me?"

Andrew looked up. "I'm not running from you."

"Did you tell me you were moving?"

"I knew you'd tell Felton if I did."

"Did you think I wouldn't figure it out?"

"It was a flawed plan, I admit," Andrew said. "I need to register with my brother the seriousness of my anger."

"So registered," I said.

"Don't talk to me," Andrew said.

Then Gus said, "Hey Felton, can we talk?" His eyes were wide, his skin sort of gray.

"You two stay in here. I'm going to take Andrew into the hall and beat the shit out of him," Tovi said.

"I'm not moving," Andrew said.

"Now, you little ass, or I'll call your mother!" Tovi screamed.

Andrew put down his book, stood, pushed past me, and followed Tovi into the hall.

When the door slammed behind the two of them, Gus jumped off the bed, fast. He said, "Okay. Okay. Felton, man. We have trouble on many, many fronts. First of all, my dad called Hector Johns, that professor, who said he hadn't heard from me. Then dad looked at his credit card statement on line and saw gas stops all the way from Iowa to Florida. Mom is out of her mind. They're trying to get ahold of Jerri."

"Oh shit!"

"Secondly, Andrew is a total lunatic. I don't even recognize him, man. He almost took a swing at me in the lobby. I swear to God. That big, old dude singer with his band had to lift him up and carry him away from me. After he calmed down, he told me he'd take me out if I blew his plan. I don't even know what his plan is, man, but I think I'm going to blow it."

"Okay, okay," I said, trying to get anchored. "What's going on with your parents, first? Do they know where Jerri is?"

"I don't know where Jerri is," Gus said.

"She's in Chicago until Tuesday. She's with Aleah's dad."

"Oh yeah. Why?"

"I don't know why."

"Does anyone else know?" Gus asked.

"Maybe Grandma Berba. Would your parents know how to get ahold of her?"

"I don't think so." Gus shook his head. "They want us back in the car immediately, Felton. Mom said she'd call the cops if we're not home tomorrow."

I thought about Andrew's reaction to me being there. I thought about the possibility of Jerri finding out about my treachery. I thought about having to meet my grandfather who hated my dad (and me). I said, "Okay. Okay. Let's go."

Gus squinted at me. His eyes watered. "Are you sure?" he asked.

"Yes."

"I don't know, man."

"Seriously. Yes."

"You don't have to go, Felton."

"I'm ready."

"But, you have some stuff going on."

"Yes. Some."

"Really, man," Gus said. "I totally underestimated the shit you have going on. I sort of forgot about your dad this spring…"

"It's okay," I said.

"No," Gus shook his head.

"We can leave."

"You're family is totally screwed," Gus said.

"Yes," I agreed. I wanted to leave very badly.

"Oh man." Gus shook his head more. "I'm so sorry I punched you. I'm sorry I checked out on you this spring. I got pissed because you weren't paying enough attention to me? That's so weak…Why wouldn't I be happy for you for finding your…destiny or whatever?"

"We can leave, Gus. Let's do it."

Gus shook his head a little. "You need to deal with this."

"No. No. This isn't real. This isn't mine, man. This is Andrew's war. I don't need to be here. I have a life of my…of my…"

"Listen," Gus spat. "This is the shit you'll be running from forever if you don't deal with it."

"Really?" I said. Was it true? Horror movie!

"I'm going to get my ass grounded. I drove you all the way here. This is huge, man. The time is now. You need to stay."

"Okay."

"Okay," Gus breathed deep. "Okay. I'm going to help you." Gus nodded.

"Holy shit," I said.

Gus and I stared at each other for a moment.

Then Gus said, "Are we supposed to hug or something?"

At that moment, Tovi came crashing through the door. Andrew crept in behind her, his head hung low. "Here's the deal. Listen. Right now, Felton, you and Andrew are going to get a hot dog. You're going to talk. Tomorrow morning, we're going to Papa's house. Felton, you'll wear a disguise. We're going to do this. Do you understand?"

I looked at Tovi. I looked at Gus. Gus nodded at me.

I said, "Okay."

Andrew grimaced.

Tovi said, "And you. Whoever the hell you are."

Gus said, "Me?"

"We're going swimming. Right now. I've totally had it."

"I don't know," Gus said.

"Come on," Tovi shouted.

Gus shrugged and looked at me. I shrugged.

He went swimming, Aleah.

August 17th, 12:23 p.m.
NEAR BRADENTON

Here's something I started thinking about that day, something I've been thinking about all summer, Aleah: my actions have an effect on crap. For my whole life, they really haven't, but now they do.

When I was a little kid, I couldn't really do anything. I had no power to change anything. Gus and I were always there for each other because there weren't any other choices. I had no other friends. He didn't either. He didn't have a girlfriend. We just were together. I didn't know much and I couldn't do much and whatever I did didn't matter much. (Nobody got hurt; nobody got better.)

Now I know about my dad and I have a weird brother who depends on me and I have teammates and I know that Jerri isn't remotely perfect, and all the stuff I choose to do—like miss a camp at Michigan or go to Florida with Gus or miss my brother's concert—makes all this other stuff happen or not happen.

I have all this responsibility. Seriously. It makes me want to throw up sometimes. And it isn't going away, I don't think. I'm not ever going to brainlessly ride my Schwinn Varsity over to Gus's house to watch a Muppet movie again, you know? That's all gone.

I want my family to be okay. I need them to be okay.

Action, reaction. Whatever I do makes it better or worse. It took me many weeks to figure this out. I wasn't ready last time I was in Florida.

Just like Tovi told us to, Andrew and I walked to the DQ near the pier to talk. We walked in silence.

We ordered our hot dogs (what Tovi ordered us to order) in silence.

We sat and ate our hot dogs in silence.

Finally, as Andrew was finishing his, while staring at the table in front of me, I said, "How can I help you?"

"Fail to be born," he mumbled.

"What?"

"Disappear," Andrew said.

"I can't," I said.

"Go home," he said.

"I might. I really might. But I want to know why you're so pissed. Then maybe I'll make a decision."

"It doesn't matter, Felton. I can't get my old life back."

"What old life?"

"The one where I don't feel like a failure just for existing," Andrew said.

I didn't know how to respond. Nothing like that had ever come from Andrew's mouth. "Why would you say that?" I asked, after staring at him for like ten years.

"Because," Andrew said.

"That's a lame answer."

"You're a lame answer."

"That's not nice."

"You're not…"

"Don't do that," I spat.

"Go home."

"I can't."

"You should. You're not wanted here," Andrew said.

"You're not wanted here either. Tovi told me that our grandpa doesn't even know you're you."

"I have a better chance with him than I do in Bluffton."

"Everybody loves you in Bluffton," I said.

"No they don't," Andrew said. "They hate me to my core."

"Jesus. What's wrong with you, Andrew? Not true."

"Yes. That's what I feel. I'm claiming my emotions," he said. "I have a right to my emotions. Big Rod said I don't have to hide behind you or Jerri or…or…"

"A child detective?"

"Right. I can just be as mad as I am. And I'm very mad about how you've treated me, and I'm not just going to roll over and be happy to see you, okay? Because you're terrible to me and just being related to me isn't good enough anymore."

"How am I terrible to you?" I shouted. (What a dumb thing to ask, Aleah.)

"Concert. Pharmacist. Tell me to get lost when I need you. Say 'shake it off' when I'm very worried. Don't listen when I talk. Don't thank me for working all night on your website. Run fast…"

"Run fast?"

"Run! Fast!" Andrew shouted so loud everybody in the DQ stopped eating and started staring.

"I can understand how it might make you feel pretty freaking crappy when I don't show at your concert or when I call you a pharmacist or am ungrateful and mean, but I can't really help it that I run fast."

"Are you going to apologize?"

"For running fast?"

"For everything else!" Andrew shouted.

"Everything?"

"You're a big, fat, stupid jerk all the time!" Andrew screamed.

Then came another voice. "You two. Get out. Now. Door. Go." It was a man in a DQ hat and apron. He also had a mustache. He walked toward us fast, shaking his finger at us. "Door! Door! Now!"

I jumped out of my chair and was out the door in a blink.

I waited for like a minute. Andrew didn't come out. I pressed my face to the glass. Andrew sat inside and shook his head at me. I opened the door and poked my head in. The mustache man was back behind the counter. He yelled, "Get out!"

"What the hell?" I yelled at Andrew.

"You just abandoned me again, Felton. Ran away without me. Left me to the dogs. But this isn't Bluffton. This gentleman is making me a Heath Blizzard."

"Jesus Christ," I shouted. All the people stared at me and shook their heads. "Did you tell him our business?"

"Get out," Andrew said.

So I left. In retrospect, I failed my test by not getting Andrew out of the DQ with me.

I have no idea what he told the mustache man to get a Heath

Blizzard. But I was pissed. I vowed never to go to a DQ again (a vow I have since broken sixteen times).

Then I sort of realized what I'd done by bolting so fast.

Oh yes, it was a long, sad walk back down the beach to the White Shells. Here's what I thought: *I'm not only too fast, I'm a really terrible person and Andrew has finally figured it out. Now he's gone completely apeshit in Florida, and it's my fault.*

See how my actions create reactions? (A boy calls his brother a pharmacist; the brother turns Super Crazy-Ass.)

I have responsibilities, Aleah. I do.

Andrew didn't come back to the room that night.

"He's started staying at Big Rod's when I'm at Papa's," Tovi said. "He's there, I'm sure. Don't worry."

Gus looked worried.

August 17th, 1:00 p.m.
JUST LEFT BRADENTON

Just a little more than two hours to go. I'm dreaming, Aleah. That's what it feels like. The Florida ditches are dark green pools (water is everywhere) and the palm trees are bent and the clouds are blowing up and turning and look like crazy cartoons, and the stringy-haired woman in front of me is eating a whole bag of Utz potato chips—crunch, crackle bag, smack lips—which would normally make me hungry, but now makes me want to totally barf. Whoa.

Andrew just texted that he's coming with Tovi to the bus station. Nice.

• • •

More reaction: Boy misses brother's spring concert; brother throws boy's shoes in the ocean.

Sound crazy? Yes. Crazy.

Even though Andrew didn't spend that night in the White Shells, he was there briefly, very early in the morning. I have a vague memory of him coming into the room at the cracker of dawn. I was on the floor, half asleep. Gus slept on a foldout cot Tovi ordered. Tovi slept in the bed. The door opened. Andrew tiptoed past me. He dug around for a moment, then was gone. I shut my eyes.

About an hour later, Tovi woke Gus and me up, and we went for a swim in the gulf. It was amazing in there—warm like a bath and rolling and perfect, except Tovi told us we had to shuffle our feet going in so we wouldn't step on any hidden stingrays. I asked her if she was kidding. She said, "Why would I kid about stingrays?"

Scary.

Out in the water, I told Gus that he was right. I had to deal with this crazy shit. I had to stay in Florida. "But you should go," I told him.

He didn't really respond. He kept his eyeballs on Tovi the whole time, which sort of grossed me out because Tovi's my cousin. (Of course she looks like a tennis player in a bikini, and I look like a freaking lumberjack or something.)

The three of us didn't talk much, just floated around in the warm water.

I tried to relax but knew what was coming…a trip to Papa Stan's. *Gus is right. You have to deal with this shit…*

Not relaxing.

When we got back to the room from swimming, Andrew was in there. He was dressed in tennis whites like for Wimbledon, except in the 1970s. He had on a collared shirt and short shorts and a red headband and red wristbands.

"I was worried about you. Why didn't you come back?" I asked him, my throat tense.

Andrew didn't respond.

"Nice outfit," I whispered. He looked up briefly, then went back to tying his white tennis shoes.

"I wear this because Papa Stan would like me to play a classical game, like John McEnroe," Andrew said.

"Okay," I said.

"Those are Papa's old clothes," Tovi said.

"He's as small as Andrew?" I asked, not believing a grown man could be so small.

"I threw your running shoes in the ocean," Andrew said, still not looking up.

We all paused for a moment and stared at Andrew.

"Mine?" Tovi asked. "I don't have running shoes here."

"No," Andrew said. "Felton's."

"What?" I stood there staring at him, mouth dropped open. I'd worn flip-flops out to the beach, so I hadn't looked for my shoes. That's apparently why he'd come back to the room briefly. To get my shoes. "What?"

"Oh crap, Andrew," Tovi said. "Why?"

Andrew sat up. "They floated for a long time. I thought they might wash back onto the beach, but then they went out to sea. I don't really understand how the ocean works."

"It's the gulf," Tovi said. "You know that."

"Whatever."

"My shoes?" I shouted. "Why would you?" Adrenaline pulsed through my veins.

"You still have your flip-flops," Andrew said. "You don't have to go barefoot."

"I can't run in flip-flops, you jerk!"

"I know. You can't run and you can't play tennis either."

"Andrew," Tovi said, "you know Papa is going to want to hit."

"Yes," Andrew nodded. "This will keep Felton from looking like our dad on the tennis court."

"Goddamn it, I love those shoes," I said.

"They're on their way to Cuba," Andrew said.

"You didn't have to throw his shoes," Tovi said. "Felton wouldn't have to play."

"If there are balls around, Felton is going to chase them," Andrew told her.

"What are you talking about?" I shouted.

"Lots of things," Andrew said.

"Papa should see him play sometime," Tovi said. "Maybe not today, though, huh? Better ease in."

"My shoes." I walked to the door to leave, to what? Go swim around in the Gulf of Mexico to find them?

I stopped. I turned around and pointed at Andrew. "I should throw your big book in the ocean!" I shouted. Action, reaction. Bad reaction.

"Poop flinger," Andrew said.

"You guys are so nuts," Gus said.

"We should go soon," Andrew said. "I can't stay for very long today. I have to be at sound check at six."

Yes, Andrew and the Golden Rods had a gig that night on the White Shells' pool deck. (Wasn't looking forward to that, Aleah.) I exhaled and shook my head. Very confused. "I'm not going anywhere," I said. "I can't believe this." I sat down on the bed and put my head in my hands.

"Ridiculous, Andrew," Tovi said.

"No, not," Andrew replied.

I have to shower," Tovi said. "The gulf is gross." Then she dropped the towel she was wrapped in, and Gus almost fell on the floor. Tovi blushed because of Gus's reaction. "What's wrong with you?" she said.

"I'm sorry," Gus said.

Then she went into the bathroom.

I almost cried about my shoes. I said, "I feel shackled."

Andrew whispered, "Join the club."

August 17th, 1:16 p.m.

A LITTLE FARTHER
FROM BRADENTON

It just occurred to me that "shackled" is a good word for how I've been feeling ever since you stopped talking to me, Aleah. Recruiters watching me. Hamstring hampering me so I couldn't race for State or run to feel good. Worried about football camp. Worried about Andrew. Even when football practice started a couple of weeks ago, I didn't feel right.

Everything seems like it's moving faster than it's supposed to because so much crap is crammed into every moment. At practice, the ball flies out of Cody's hand, which is one thing, but at the same time I'm thinking about college and Andrew and you and Gus, and I can't just catch the ball Cody throws. I have to catch it and think about all this other stuff, and that makes everything hard.

Ultimate Frisbee in Nashville. That's the only time I've felt unshackled since you've been gone. Maybe I need to stop thinking about you, Aleah.

Jesus God, there's a little kid in the seat behind me. He's kicking the crap out of my seat. My head…my head…my head…

August 17th, 1:23 p.m.
EVEN A LITTLE FARTHER
FROM BRADENTON

The poor kid who was kicking my seat got screamed at and probably spanked (hitting of some kind). If you want to feel like your life isn't too bad, take a Greyhound bus, Aleah. We should all take Greyhound buses.

• • •

Need a good friend? Call Gus.

Andrew left the room while Tovi showered that morning.

As soon as Andrew left, I turned to Gus and said, "He threw out my shoes."

Gus said, "This is trouble."

"Can you believe it?" I asked.

"I've decided to stay."

"Dude, no. You have to go. This isn't your problem."

"This is our problem. We're brothers," Gus said.

"Your parents are going to call the cops, man. You have to drive home now." I didn't want to take Gus down with me.

"I have to believe Teresa will understand. She's a good mom. She worries about you too. I'll call them today, okay? I'm not going to abandon you again, Felton."

Just then, Tovi opened the bathroom door. She wore a tennis

skirt, which clearly made Gus shiver.

"*Jesus*. Child abuse," Gus whispered.

"Jesus. Thank you, Gus," I whispered.

"What?" he asked, staring at Tovi.

"Where the hell's Andrew?" Tovi barked.

We found Andrew in the lobby playing the piano. He had a big white straw hat and a giant pair of sunglasses on the bench next to him, which Tovi had directed him to buy at the gift shop.

"Good. Here's your disguise," Tovi said.

I put the junk on, but looked totally ridiculous. (There's a big mirror in the lobby.)

"This is crazy," I said.

"He still looks like our dad," Andrew said.

"It's better," Tovi said. "It's better."

A few minutes later, we were in the Beemer (the car Grandma Rose once drove) and were rolling over bridge, past water, into sprawl, into crap ranch homes and more sprawl and the CVS pharmacies across from the Walgreens pharmacies, and past Winn-Dixie grocery stores in giant strip malls.

And, Aleah, I was completely petrified. I couldn't not go but I totally didn't want to go, plus I had on flip-flops, which I hated because they harmed my escapability. I was dizzy. I wore sunglasses (over a black eye). I wore a big hat. (I'd never worn a big hat before.) Nobody talked. Nobody really breathed. The energy in the car was totally, wickedly foreboding, like when the teens in a horror movie know who the psycho mass murderer is and have made a plan and are on their determined way to kill him (even though they could turn the car around and just go to the beach and forget about it). Crap. Scary.

Eventually, like forty minutes later, we drove through what looks like a Florida Dangling Sack version of a California TV ghetto—lots of seriously run-down ranch homes with cars parked on the lawns, and then, out of no place, came the giant black-and-gold-painted gates of the Fiddlesticks Golf Community.

"Why is this place stuck in the middle of hell?" Gus asked.

"It's how Florida works," Tovi said.

Tovi pulled up to security. A giant dude in a uniform leaned out the window of the gatehouse. "Morning, Miss Tovi. You know all these boys?"

"Not intimately," Tovi smiled.

"Thank God for that," the gate man laughed. "You kill me, girl." Then the gate went up and we were in.

Inside, we followed a winding road past Spanish-looking mansions with those clay-pot-planter roofs (as seen on *COPS*). We rolled past fountains and swimming pools and past the tennis courts and the country club. I felt ill, like I'd throw up hard on my flip-flops, and my straw hat made my head itch and the glasses made the world dark. Gus said, "Reinsteins have some cash, I guess."

"Hey, yeah," Tovi said. Then she pulled up to a two-story behemoth with a Honda parked out front. "Why doesn't he park that shit in the garage?" Tovi asked. "The sun's going to melt all his gum."

"This is it?" I asked with no voice to speak of.

"Yes," Andrew said.

"One little old man lives in that thing?" Gus asked.

"Except when I'm here," Tovi said.

"It's like Southern Gothic with you guys," Gus said.

I sweated great bulbous drips of viscous liquid that got hung up in the mounds of man hair on my legs.

My dad's dad. Dad.

I don't know Dad. My dad's dad hates my dad. My dad's dad hates me. I'm in a costume. I'm going to die. I'm going to die. Om shanti. *It's okay. Jerri, Jesus. Okay...*

My very capable squirrel-nut brain began to take off on the angry hamster wheel, and I couldn't even move my body as the others climbed from the car.

Tovi leaned back in. "Come on, Felton. It'll be okay."

"Can't we just tell him the truth and get it over with?" I asked.

"We're in process here," Andrew shouted at me from outside the car. "Don't destroy our work, Felton. Please."

I almost had to lift my legs with my arms. *You're a football player. You're a damn star. Every school in the country wants you. This is nothing...* I swung my big legs out and stretched up to standing, so that I towered over Gus.

"You are a big man, Felton," he said.

"Yeah."

"You look like the white Ray Charles."

We walked up the sidewalk. (I stumbled along in the Dangling Sack heat.) Tovi opened the front door. (I stumbled behind her.) *Mass murderer. Why don't we turn and run?* Gus and Andrew entered before me. Cold, cold air-conditioning blasted us. We walked into a museum filled with that blobby painted art that is just colors, not actual pictures of anything. (I shuffled, my legs almost giving out.) *Phantom of the Reinsteins…*

Music came from a room deeper inside. It was Bach. Andrew's favorite.

"Good. Pretty music. He must be in an okay mood," Tovi said. Then she shouted, "Hey Papa, I'm home!"

"You're here?" A voice came from within. *The horror…*

"Yeah. I have some friends with me."

And then he came. A little old man in a pink polo shirt, a man with owl glasses slid down his nose, a man wearing shiny track pants and a very big watch, a man with wisps of white, thin, curly hair. He shuffled into the room, talking to the floor.

"Always with the friends, Tovi." He looked up and saw us. "And they're multiplying! All boys too. Your grandmother would be very proud."

"This is Gus," Tovi said.

"Nice hair, you sheepdog," the man smiled.

"You know Andy," Tovi pointed to Andrew.

"Johnny McEnroe!" the man said.

"And this is…this is Ricky Martin."

"Big guy. Is he Australian? What's with the hat?"

"Sun sensitive," Tovi said. "Ricky, this is my Papa Stan."

"Oh shit," I whispered. I tried so hard not to tremble.

"I'm Venezuelan," Gus blurted.

"Must be tribal hair, sheepdog. Come in, come in. Go ahead and use the pool. I'm paying my bills!" Papa Stan said, sticking his pointer finger into the air.

"We'll knock around for awhile, Papa. You want to hit some balls later?"

"Maybe, little girl. My back doesn't feel straight today. Slept funny. All right. Bills! Good to meet you all." He shuffled back into the house.

"That was totally anticlimactic," Gus said. "Tribal hair? That's funny, don't you think, Ricky Martin?" Gus grinned at me. "Nice one, Tovi."

"He's in a good mood, man. Don't let your guard down. Let's look at some pictures upstairs," said Tovi.

We followed Tovi up some brick stairs and into a large room at the front of the house. We sat down on a couple of couches. Andrew seemed relaxed. Gus was relaxed. I thought I'd vomit. Tovi pulled two photo albums off a shelf and handed them to me.

"These are pretty neat, Felton," Andrew said. It was the first kind-sounding statement he'd made to me in months.

The first one had pictures of my dad and Evith, Tovi's mom, when they were in high school. Lots of prom and beach (Fort Myers— they always vacationed here) and messing around with friends and tennis tournaments. Dad didn't look exactly like me.

"He had a bigger forehead, huh?" I said.

"Bigger than what?" Tovi said.

"I seriously wouldn't know that wasn't you," Gus said, looking over my shoulder. "He looks a little off, but seriously, man. That's like 1980s you."

There was a great shot of high-school Dad holding a trophy and smiling his head off. I could see me. I could see a picture from the fall Jerri took of me, Cody, and Karpinski standing in front of the scoreboard after the Richland Center game. I could be Dad in that shot.

"He looks so happy, you know?" I said.

"He really does," Andrew said.

"Maybe he was then," Tovi whispered. "But not a couple of years later. Mom told me that Papa just rode him constantly. He'd pull Steve out of bed at like 4:30 and make him run. If Steve didn't get all As, Papa would ground him. If he played bad in a tournament, Papa would make him hit balls half the night. Mom said it was pretty terrible. After he left for college, Steve wouldn't come home for anything."

"Shit," I whispered. "Then why are we here?" I glared at Tovi.

"You saw him, Felton. You saw Papa. He's nice, okay? He lost Steve. He lost Gram."

Andrew nodded next to her.

"You think this is good for us?" I asked Andrew.

"Don't you want to know what happened?" Andrew said.

"No." I shook my head.

"Look at this," Tovi said. She handed me the other album.

These were pictures of me—three-, maybe four-years-old, with Dad, Jerri, and Grandma Rose at Fort Myers Beach. There were a couple on the same pier where Andrew first photographed a pelican, me in Dad's arms, staring up at birds, me pointing at a boat on the gulf behind us. There was one close-up of Jerri and Dad cheek to cheek.

"Weird to think he was romantically with other women," Andrew whispered.

"Shut up," I whispered back.

There was a picture of me nuzzling my head into Grandma Rose's cheek, her laughing. "I sort of remember," I said.

Felton in diaper. Felton stares at shells. Felton chases seagulls. Felton in surf with dead father. Felton and Tovi running into the water. Felton hugging dead grandma's leg. Felton lifted into the air by Jerri, who is right now probably holding hands with your dad, Aleah. And then, just one shot from ten steps behind: *Felton holding hands with an older guy named Stan. Felton looks up laughing. Stan looks down making some kind of goofy face. That guy, the old one, is alive but will not talk to, look at, acknowledge Felton's existence any more. That guy thinks Jerri is trash and Andrew is unworthy of attention. That guy is downstairs in this house.*

"Hey," Tovi said. "Compare this picture to that one of your dad when he was smiling after his match in high school."

Tovi pulled an 8x10 out of the album. "Look. You can see that he stopped enjoying playing. It's from when Steve won the National Championship. He beat Guillermo Pender, see?"

"Yeah?" I said.

"Pender made it into semifinals of the Australian Open the next year," Tovi said.

"Yeah? Okay?"

"So, Steve was like beating dudes who were amazing, like tops in the world. But look at Steve's face."

Guillermo Pender smiled in the picture, even though he took second. My dad, though, wasn't smiling at all and was staring off into space. If anything, he looked a little mad, or maybe sad.

"He was awesome," Tovi said, "but he totally didn't care by the time he was champ. You have to pretty much kill yourself to play at that level, but your dad didn't care."

"Pretty much kill yourself," I said.

"I didn't mean it like that," Tovi said.

"I have to leave. Right now," I said.

"Now?" Tovi asked. "Don't be dumb."

"*Now*," I said louder.

"No," Andrew said.

"I want to go." I stood and handed the picture to Tovi.

Gus said, "It's okay, Felton. It's okay, man." He nodded at the others. "Felton found Steve hanging. Don't take this stuff too lightly. This is rough shit."

I stood there. Gus. Man. He's as good as it gets, Aleah.

Tovi said, "You're going to be all right, Felton."

Even Andrew nodded at me.

"Okay," I said. "Can we do something else at least?"

"Let's see if Papa wants to hit," Tovi said.

We all followed Tovi downstairs. Charming Grandpa Stan was eating green melon balls in the kitchen when we entered. "All these boys," he said.

"We feel like hitting Papa. You interested?"

"Oh, my poor back." He shook his head.

"Come on. At least you can coach Andy," Tovi said.

"All right. For the youth!" he said. He held a fork up in the air with a melon ball spiked on it. Then he glanced over at me and paused. "Why don't you take off your glasses, Ricky Martin? I can't see your eyes. Do you have eyes?"

"Light," is all I could get out.

"He has dilation issues," Tovi said.

"Hmm." Grandpa Stan shrugged. "Maybe if he stayed off the cocaine?"

"Bahahahahahaha!" Gus laughed.

"The Venezuelan has a sense of humor," Grandpa Stan said.

Then Stan looked at my feet. I got worried he'd recognize them, so I curled my toes. "Ricky Martin is going to play barefoot?"

"I can't play," I said. "I have leg problems."

"What leg problems?"

"Hamstring," I said.

"We know a little bit about that in this house," Stan nodded. He wasn't smiling this time. "We sure do. Right, Tovi?"

"Yeah," she said. "The Reinsteins have short hamstrings."

"That's what I hear," I pretty much shouted.

Everyone stared at me.

"Tovi has short hamstrings," Grandpa Stan said. "So did my son."

"Yes," I nodded.

And then we were following Grandpa Stan and Tovi on a path outside the house. And then we were next to the golf course, so green compared to the country club in Bluffton. And then we were pulling racquets out of lockers, and my grandfather grabbed my hand and stared at it, paused over it, which made me shake.

"Do you play when you're healthy?"

"No," I said.

"You have athlete's hands. Not like this one," he pointed at Andrew. "He has ballerina's hands. Ha!" he laughed.

Andrew nodded.

"Too bad, Ricky Martin. Wish you had some shoes. I could teach you the game. I'm a good coach. Just ask my daughter over there."

"Granddaughter, Papa."

"Right…right," Stan mumbled.

He passed out racquets to Andrew (Here you go, McEnroe!) and Gus. Tovi had her own racquet in the locker. Then he handed me a metal basket full of balls ("Relegated to ball boy, big fella"), and then we headed to the courts.

Tovi and I fell behind as we walked along. "This is terrible," I said, my voice weak.

"No," Tovi said. "This is the plan, okay? He's teaching Andrew to play, and when Andrew gets good enough, we're going to tell Papa who he is."

"That's it?"

"Andrew also listens to music with him."

"Jesus. Andrew can't play. He's the worst athlete in the world."

"He's smart. The game is half smarts, Felton."

"That's your plan," I mumbled.

Ten minutes later, Tovi was smacking balls at Gus and he was tripping all over himself. She moved so quickly and beautifully that I wanted to play. ("If there are balls around, Felton will chase them…" Remember that Andrew said that?) And Stan was hitting balls at Andrew, who stood a few feet from the net. Andrew actually managed to take the ball out of the air and drop it softly back over the net half the time.

Stan yelled at him, "That's right, kid! Use what you've got. Soft hands! Kill the point. Kill the point…"

My leg muscles twitched. I did want to play. I love to play stuff. The seriously hot sun beat down on these beautiful, rich-person courts. I sweated. I felt like I should be moving. I couldn't move.

Then Andrew went on a streak of missing the ball or hitting it way off the court. Stan got more and more wound up, the more Andrew blew it. He barked at Andrew to focus. I could see Andrew get frustrated. I could see him tighten up and miss because of Stan's yelling. Maybe it was because I've hated being the focus? Maybe it was because I've felt all this pressure to do well? Maybe it was because I'd just seen that picture of my dad looking sad after winning the NCAA Championship? I don't know. But…

After watching Stan yell for ten minutes, "Focus, kid. Come on. Look at the ball!" After Stan screamed, "Your concentration is for shit…"

I stood up and shouted, "Lay the hell off him!"

Gus and Tovi stopped playing. Andrew's mouth hung open, and his eyes bulged.

Stan cocked his head and stared at me. "I'm just coaching here, Ricky Martin. This is what coaching sounds like."

"It's okay. I like being coached," Andrew said.

"You play sports, right? What do you play?" Stan asked me.

"Football," I said.

"Of course, big guy. Do coaches yell at you?"

"Yes," I said.

"Okay," Stan said. He stared harder at me. "Okay, Ricky."

"Andy has to get home," Tovi said. "Good time to stop!"

"You're going to have to do better tomorrow, Johnny McEnroe, or I'll bring out my whip. Got it?"

"Yes, sir," Andrew said.

"Time for my nap," Stan said. "Tovi, bring back some chicken, will you? There's no food in the house."

"Okay, Papa," Tovi said.

We left.

On the way home, we almost didn't speak. At one point, Tovi said, "Hope Papa forgets about the chicken. No way I'm missing Andrew's gig."

"Doesn't he notice when you don't come home?" Gus asked.

"He's never mentioned it if he does," Tovi said.

After a few minutes, I noticed Andrew staring at me. He said, "You don't have to protect me."

"I'm sorry," I said.

"Thanks, though," he said.

We rolled silently through the sprawl until we hit the beach again.

• • •

We're pulling off the interstate in the bus.

August 17th, 2:17 p.m.
NEAR PORT CHARLOTTE

When we got back to the White Shells, Tovi turned right back around and drove to Stan's. "I want to get him his chicken. I've got enough time. I'm going to do it." She took off.

Gus said, "I have a phone call I need to make. You guys go up." He was talking to Andrew and me. I knew what the phone call was. Parents. I knew it wouldn't be easy on him.

There were still a couple of hours before Andrew had to meet with Big Rod and the other guys to sound check. On the way up in the elevator, an almost cordial Andrew asked, "What do you want to do?"

"Relax. Veg, okay? Maybe watch some *COPS* on TV."

"Tovi watches that terrible program all the time. It's one of the reasons I feel at home here. It's like I never left you in our basement."

"Me and Tovi are really alike," I said.

"She's a bit more thoughtful," Andrew said.

The elevator opened on the fifth floor, and we got out and walked to the room.

"She's more thoughtful?" I asked. (Of course she's more thoughtful.)

"The truth hurts, right, Felton?" Andrew stared at me. "Remember when you said that to me? The truth hurts?"

"No."

Andrew let us into the room. I didn't have a key.

"You said it the day you hurt your leg. You told me I wasn't that great a pianist. You said the truth hurts."

"I'm really sorry, Andrew." What's weird is that I didn't remember saying that to him. I know I've thought it. But jeez, am I really that mean?

"Felton, I don't want to just hang out here with you," Andrew said, looking around the room. "I don't want to forgive you at the moment. I'm going to go."

"Don't. Please."

"You can hang out with Gus," Andrew said.

We stared at each other a moment.

"Okay," I said. "He'll be back in a second."

Andrew squinted at me like he was staring into my freaking soul. Spooky.

"Who is Gus calling?" he asked.

"Well…" I can't lie very well, Aleah. Heat rose in my face. "He needs to talk to his parents, okay?"

Andrew leaned his forehead in. He whispered, "Why is Gus talking to his parents?"

"Shit. Well…because they figured out he came here. They figured out we lied," I said really quietly.

"Do they know I'm here?" Andrew asked, very slowly, very quietly.

"He's going to tell them what's going on. He wants to help us."

Andrew stood straight up. His face turned red. "He wants to help you! He doesn't want to help me at all. If he tells his parents, they'll tell Jerri and then I'm completely screwed, Felton. *God Damn Cock Snap!*" he shouted.

"No. I don't know. I can stop him."

"Everybody helps somebody!" Andrew shouted.

"That's good. That's good, Andrew."

"I helped you my whole life. Tovi is here all summer to help Papa Stan get better. Gus is helping you."

"They're good people. They're good," I said.

"Nobody…nobody…nobody ever helps me. They just screw me. They just screw me over and over."

"No." I shook my head. "I don't know."

Then Andrew was out the door. He flung it open and tripped running out so that he sort of smacked into the wall across the hall, and then the door gently shut itself.

My heart pounded. *Oh no.*

When Gus said at the beginning of our trip that we'd definitely get busted, I didn't think for a moment about what getting busted might mean to Andrew.

Action, reaction.

I jumped off the bed to follow Andrew out, to apologize, which wouldn't help—I just needed to do something. He wasn't in the hall and the elevator was gone. I ran down the stairs, but he wasn't there. The kid is quick when he wants to be. I checked through the lobby and restaurant. Nothing. I found Gus by the pool. He was smoking a long, thin cigarette, something he hadn't done since we got to the White Shells thirty-six hours earlier.

"I had to bum one from an old lady," he said.

"Have you seen Andrew?"

"No."

"I need to talk to Andrew."

"So do my parents. They want to know what he's up to."

"Shit. Are they hunting down Jerri?"

"Not at the moment, man. But they are seriously concerned about you guys. If you don't tell Jerri what you're doing, they're going to," he said.

"Oh man. Oh shit. I blew this. I didn't even think."

"I'm going to be violently grounded. Apparently telling the truth after the fact only counts for so much. Man, my mom is a freaking firebomb. She's going crazy on me."

"Gus, I'm so sorry."

"My bad, man."

"No," I shook my head. "You're the best."

"I have to leave in the morning. I want to stay, Felton. I guess Maddie is messing up my paper route and Mom had to deliver it this morning. I'm so sorry, man."

"Gus," I said. "I'm serious. I love you."

"Uh, I'm just going to smoke my cigarette."

"Okay."

"But thanks." Gus sort of smiled at me. "Thanks for noticing, man. Maybe you're not a narcissist after all. Ha-ha."

"What do you mean by narcissist?" Yes, Aleah. That's the first time I'd ever heard the term.

"It's pop psychology, man. Doesn't mean anything."

"No, seriously. What do you mean?"

"A narcissist is someone who's so damn full of himself, he doesn't notice what people around him are doing. Like, you know, how you forgot my birthday and stuff."

"Oh my God."

"Dude, relax."

"Oh shit. I have to find Andrew right now."

"I'll be here, man."

I walked out to the beach, but he wasn't there.

I walked over to the pier. Andrew wasn't there.

I looked in swimsuit shops and clothes shops and an art store featuring paintings of sharks and stingrays and sailboats and dolphins. I poked my head into a Greek restaurant and into a bar that was playing beach music, but found no Andrew. I looked in the DQ as I passed (saw the mustache man, but no Andrew). And finally I walked into a sports shop, not that he would be in there…

I hate to say it—then I spent twenty minutes staring at new running shoes. They were beautiful. I even tried a pair on.

Here's what's crazy, Aleah. When I went in the sports shop, I totally forgot I was looking for Andrew. He disappeared from my brain. Then a skinny kid with glasses walked passed me (Andrew-like!). Then I totally freaked. I stood and ran out of the store. (Thank God I'd removed the shoe I tried on.)

I took off running down the main street on Fort Myers Beach toward the White Shells. The flip-flops flapped, and sand got between my skin and the rubber, and it just burned. About a hundred meters down the road I stopped where I was running, next to two skater-looking twelve-year-old dudes who were sitting on a cement wall. They stared because I was probably mumbling to myself, which you know I do sometimes, Aleah. But I didn't care at that moment because I knew something very big and terrible: I don't try hard for anyone but myself, which is the root of my trouble. I act. Shit happens because I act. Everyone suffers. I don't notice.

I'm selfish. I'm self-absorbed. I'm a narcissist.

"Do you know what selfish means?" I asked one of the dudes.

"Uh, yeah," he replied, raising one eyebrow.

"It's when you don't do crap for anyone but yourself."

"Thanks, Einstein," the other said.

"You're welcome," I said.

They both laughed. I didn't.

"Narcissist." I nodded.

"Uh-huh," one said.

There was only one thing for me to do. I couldn't find Andrew—and if I couldn't find Andrew, he might totally leave my narcissist mind and I might start thinking about my own junk while he went off and drowned or something. I had to act. I had to act immediately on his behalf. I had to call Jerri to tell her what we were doing, tell her to leave Andrew alone, tell her that I'm the one to blame for all of this.

August 17th, 2:51 p.m.
PORT CHARLOTTE

We're stopping here in Port Charlotte for twenty minutes because apparently we're ahead of schedule. Ha-ha. That seems totally impossible. I'm two days late.

I had to eat. It's possible I made a terrible decision in the convenience store just now: beef jerky (chewing). Salty. More crap.

Narcissist! It makes me feel smart to say that. Narcissist.

After I said "narcissist" to those two skater dudes, I ran back to the White Shells (on burning flip-flop feet). I found Gus listening to music on his iPhone, curled up on the same deck chair. Workers from the hotel were setting up a small stage for the Golden Rods gig at the other end of the pool. Made me feel sick. I didn't want to see Andrew play music. But I would go and I would cheer and I would support him. I stood over Gus.

He pulled the buds out of his ears. "Don't you think 'the Golden Rods' is a pretty porny name for a band?" Gus asked.

"Yes," I said. "That has occurred to me. Hey, can I use your phone, man?"

"Why?"

"I'm going to call Jerri and admit everything and make sure she knows Andrew is a good kid and beg her not to get in the way of anything that…that is going to happen down here."

"Yeah, yeah…That's good." Gus handed me his phone.

"She's in Chicago. I have to call Chicago."

"You can do it, brother," Gus said.

I nodded and took ten fast steps away, toward the gulf side of the pool. Without pausing to think another second, I pressed in your home phone number, Aleah (yes, I have it memorized, even though I almost always called your cell) and hit *Send*. It rang five times and I said, "Please. Please…" and then your dad picked up.

"Hi, Ronald," I said. "It's Felton."

"Hey there, my boy! Football camp going well?"

"Ronald. I need to talk to Jerri right away. She still there?"

He clearly heard the seriousness in my voice. "Yes. Right here."

Jerri got on the line. "Are you okay? Is everything okay?" she asked, her voice sounding shaky.

"It is, Jerri, but things aren't what you think." My heart pounded. I took big breaths.

Jerri didn't say anything for a moment. I heard her breathe. Then she said, "What?"

"Not what you think. It's all a…a sham. I'm involved in a sham, but for good reason."

She breathed very deeply. "What in the world are you talking about?"

"Okay, Jerri. Okay. Remember the pelican? From my website? Andrew put it there?"

"Yes."

"Right. Exactly," I said. "It wasn't a migratory bird."

"Oh?"

235

"It was…Jesus. I'm in Florida with Andrew," I spat out.

"Oh my…" Jerri exhaled. "What now? What is this?" Her voice trailed off.

"Florida with Andrew, Jerri."

"Uh-huh. Andrew. And he's there because…? Are you with Stan and Rose?" she asked.

"Sort of," I said, "except Rose is dead."

"Oh no."

"And Stan doesn't know who we are."

"Oh God."

"But…Tovi, Andrew's new friend…Tovi is the Tovi you remember, Jerri."

"She's Evith's?"

"Yeah. Yeah, she's actually Tovi our cousin."

"Okay…Okay…Okay…Why is this happening?" Jerri began to ramp up. "Why are you lying to me? Why are you boys faking going to camps and traveling across the goddamn universe? Why are you lying to your grandfather? Why…"

"I don't know, Jerri. I'm a narcissist."

"You're what?"

"I'm self-involved."

"Felton, I'm just not interested in your philosophizing right now, okay?"

"Okay. But this is my fault. Andrew made the plan, but this is my doing."

"No it's not," Jerri said. "You're not capable of this, Felton. You're not…"

"That smart?"

"You're not curious and you're not wild and you're not…"

"That smart."

"No, Felton. Andrew is just a very, very special boy and I want to kill him. I really do, Felton. You put him on the phone right now, okay?"

"I can't. He's not here. He doesn't know I'm confessing, but we're going to be busted because Gus and I drove down here and… and…I think Andrew's doing the best he can to make things good for himself, you know? He's not really happy, I don't think. I've caused him some problems by being a narcissist. He's just…"

"He's just a maniac," Jerri said.

"Yes. He threw my shoes in the ocean."

"If you're in Fort Myers, it's the gulf, Felton."

"I know."

"You have to take it easy on yourself, okay? Not for the lying. Beat yourself up for that. Please do. But Andrew isn't your responsibility. He's mine."

"I don't know, Jerri. I don't agree."

"I'm coming down there."

"No!"

"No?"

"No, Jerri."

"Oh, I'm coming down, Felton. Don't you tell me no."

"No. Please, Jerri. Don't freak. Don't come. Andrew needs this. I really think so. I think we need to let Andrew follow his plan. He's not in any danger. You can kill him later, okay?"

"He's not in danger?" Jerri said. "Of course he is."

"No. None that I can see."

"Okay...Okay," Jerri breathed out. "So? Tell me his plan."

"Well, Grandma Rose gave the money for this when she died."

"Money."

"Yes. And Andrew's using tennis and classical music to introduce himself to Stan."

"Jesus. Good luck. Oh shit, Andrew." I could almost hear Jerri shaking her head. "Jesus. They never gave you two money before."

"I know. But, I think Stan caused that, not Rose."

"And that's Andrew's plan?"

"Yes."

"He's just hanging out with Stan, pretending not to be himself?"

"Yes."

"It's ludicrous."

"Yes."

"He could get his feelings hurt, Felton."

"His feelings are already hurt."

"Yeah...I know," Jerri whispered. "I know. That's fair, Felton. You two have earned your hurt feelings. You've been through a lot."

"Yes. Yeah, Jerri. Plenty."

"Oh shit." Jerri paused for a second. "*Shit,*" she shouted again. Then she said, "You make Andrew call me every day."

"He'll be lying to you about orchestra camp."

"Fine. Whatever. I just want to know he's okay. I will kill you both when you get back."

"Okay," I said. "That's good."

"Oh God. I'm so pissed, Felton. I am so freaked out."

"But you're going to be okay, right?"

"Yes. You boys don't have to protect me. I'm better now than I've been your whole lives. Okay?"

"Okay, Jerri."

"Jesus. What in the hell? Fine. Love you. Okay…"

When I got off the phone, I walked back over to Gus. He nodded at me. My hands trembled. He saw. He said, "Jerri all right?"

"Uh, I think so. I think she's all right," I said.

"Good work, brother. You did it."

• • •

Why is this bus not moving!?!?!?!?! I can't sit any longer!

August 17th, 3:16 p.m.

PORT CHARLOTTE, PART II

There is something wrong with our driver, Aleah. I'm not kidding. The bus station (like most of the stops we've made) is really a gas station and store that sells beef jerky and candy bars and pop and crap. The bus driver went into the store like fifteen minutes ago and he hasn't come out, and I can't even see him in there. The woman behind me keeps saying stuff like, "Aw, Lord, no. Come on, bus driver. Get your ass out here. Lord, no!"

At least the air-conditioning is on. Do I text Tovi to tell her I'm going to be later? Yeah. I better.

The whole big world is weird. Did you notice that in Germany? Weird stuff happens everywhere.

Want to hear weird? Want to hear about a concert?

• • •

A few minutes after I got off the phone with Jerri, Tovi got back from her chicken delivery to Stan's and found us by the pool. "He was a little weird," she whispered in my ear. "He asked some questions about you."

"Really?" I asked.

"I'm sure it's nothing," Tovi said. "He's asked questions about Andrew before too."

The dudes who were setting up for the show asked everyone to get out of the "venue" for the sound check, so the three of us spent an hour or so walking down the beach and going out on the pier, just to bide our time until Golden Rods go time.

All this crap going on, Aleah. And a concert? I seriously didn't want to sit through another concert highlighting Andrew's lack of talent. I'd been there and done that enough in my life.

The sun was going down and lots of people were gathered out there on the pier. It was pretty, I guess. Lots of orange and purple. Freaky pelicans and other pointy birds barreling into the water to kill fish. I stared down and couldn't see stingray shadows (Tovi said you can sometimes see them), but I figured they were down there. When the sun hit the horizon and popped out of sight with a flash, the old folks and Germans all cheered. (Lots of German tourists in Fort Myers—maybe you know some, Aleah.)

"What's the big deal?" I asked. "Sun goes down every day."

"Grumpy," Tovi said.

"I don't enjoy Andrew's concerts."

Tovi said, "You're in for a surprise, man. I'm going to run ahead and get us a table, okay? I had to stand through Andrew's first concert last week. What a pain."

Tovi took off jogging.

"She's beautiful," Gus whistled.

"Yeah. I suppose," I said. I tried to keep my mind on Andrew, send him good vibes, keep up my energy for cheering for crap. I was so exhausted, though.

We wandered back slowly along the beach.

Because it was the off-season, not many people were staying at the White Shells Hotel and Resort, which is apparently how the super wily Tovi had gotten Andrew booked into a room for cheap. (Don't get me wrong, Aleah. Andrew had done most of the work—setting up the camp to get confirmations and receipts, canceling the camp, catching and shredding the cancellation letter from the camp before Jerri could see it—but Tovi did the money stuff.)

During the day, the White Shells was pretty much empty. At the tiki bar that night, however, ten million people were crammed into every damn corner of the pool patio.

"Jaysoos Chreestmoos," Gus said, lifting up his wad so he could eyeball the place as we walked in. "Ees ay mad henhouse een heere, no?"

In the ninety minutes we'd been gone, the patio had been transformed. There were lots and lots of middle-aged women drinking drinks from ceramic coconuts and ceramic pirate heads. There were many mumbling middle-aged men wearing Hawaiian shirts and sipping cold, crisp cans of Coors Light beer. There were several soaked old biddies dipping their biscuits in the middle of the blue swimming pool. Out of the corner of my eye, I caught the waving hand of Tovi, who was on the opposite side of the pool. "There. Tovi," I said to Gus.

When we got to Tovi, she was excited. "Just got off the phone with Mom. She's coming down on Friday. She really wants to meet you and Andrew."

"Oh. Okay. Good." I nodded. Crazy. Evith knew the plan? And the notion I would be meeting my aunt, who knew who I really was, sent a shiver down my back. I shook my head to stay in the moment, to be there for Andrew. The drunk crowd made me nervous. They might boo him.

Then there was applause. Then cheers.

And then, out of nowhere, Andrew and the Golden Rods climbed up on the stage. They were all wearing those crazy Hawaiian shirts. The whole mumbling, middle-aged and biddy crowd cheered and clapped. I thought of Andrew last summer with his shaved his head and skull and crossbones T-shirt that he wore for like six weeks straight without showering. He sure looked healthier in that dumb Hawaiian shirt.

"Good evening, White Shells!" Big Rod shouted.

The crowd whooped and wooed.

"I know you already know that Andrew's great," Tovi said, "But you're really gonna enjoy this, man."

"Uh, yeah," I said.

"Did y'all have a good day at the beach?" Big Rod cried.

People called back, "Woooooo."

"Let's keep the good times rolling!"

Andrew sat behind an electric keyboard aimed out at the pool. He played like a five-note chord, and all the Golden Rods hummed, including him. And then, the lowest singer started singing *Bah bah bah, bah bahbrah ann,* and then all the other three guys jumped in with this crazy harmony, *Bah bah bah, bah bahbrah ann,* and then maybe the weirdest thing I've ever seen happened.

Tiny concave Andrew stood up to the mike while the other guys *bah bah bah bahhed,* and he sang this super-high part in the song

"Barbara Ann." He sang in his canary voice, which has driven me nuts in the past, you know? He took the dang melody, while the other dudes sang in harmony below him and it was perfect, Aleah. He was perfect. It was so good.

"*Holy shit!*" I shouted.

"I know!" Tovi cried.

"Andrew sounds like a disco singer!" Gus said.

"Oh man!" And then, Aleah, I felt this pain in my chest because I am such a bad brother and I, you know, just act so terribly, and the pain sort of flowed up and out, and tears exploded from my face. I seriously lost it and had to fold over and hold my head in my hands. The song went on and Big Rod took over the vocals and then handed them back to Andrew when the super-high parts took the melody, and I just burst snot and spit and tears everywhere because I'd told Andrew he should be a pharmacist and told him the truth hurt, and he wrote all that great stuff on a website about me and I think he's nothing? And he's not nothing. He's so good singing like a canary. Oh, man. I can't see what's right in front of my narcissist face...

"Jesus, Felton! Are you okay? Are you bleeding? What's going on?" Tovi shouted.

I put my finger to my lips and made a *shh* noise. Tovi nodded.

Gus, who was a little in front of me and to my right, so he didn't see me break, sat with his mouth open, his hair wad lifted up out of his eyes. When the song ended, and the cheers and the hoots and the whistles and the screams all began to subside, and after Big Rod pointed at Andrew and said, "Andrew R., the little keyboardist who always can!" and the crowd screamed so loudly that little Andrew had to bow like five times, Gus leaned back to me and said, "I am so glad I'm here. It's worth all the beatings and berating Teresa's going to dish out. That's the best thing I've ever seen in my damn life…are you crying?"

I shook my head no, but I sure as hell was.

The whole night went like that and my love for Andrew grew and grew, and the middle-aged ladies with their coconuts whistled and screamed stuff like, "Kiss me honey," and the middle-aged mumbling men shouted, "Hell yeah, man!" between beer swigs, and the old biddies bobbed on their biscuits in the blue pool. And I loved my little brother so much, I thought I might die.

"They're pretty good, man, huh?" Tovi punched my shoulder hard enough to hurt.

"Uh-huh." I nodded.

Middle-school orchestras aren't that great. They're not old enough to be that great. Sixty-year-old rockers can be the best thing you've ever seen, even if they're not nearly the most talented people on the planet, especially if they have a fourteen-year-old keyboard player with them, one who can still sing as high as a beautiful yellow canary.

After the Golden Rods gig, which ended in a bunch of encores— lots of drunk ladies shouting for more—Andrew slowly worked his way back to us. Gus jumped out of his chair and shouted, "Dude, I had no idea!"

Andrew smiled at him, "It's very fun."

I stood up to hug him. He backed away. I paused and said, "You're awesome, Andrew. Seriously. You're great. You're amazing. I wish Jerri could see…"

Andrew said, "No. I just want to be here. I just like it here. That's all."

"Okay. Okay. That's fine," I said.

"I don't care if it's fine," Andrew said.

"Andrew. I'm just…I'm proud of you. I want to make you a website or something, you know?"

Andrew paused for a moment and took a really deep breath. Then he shouted so we could hear him over the crowd noise, "All happiness or unhappiness solely depends upon the quality of the object to which we are attached by love, Felton. That's Baruch Spinoza. He's a philosopher."

"Oh?" I said, very confused.

"What the hell?" Gus said.

"I don't want to love or hate what people think about me. I want to stop worrying about that. I want to play Beach Boys music now," Andrew said.

"Okay," I nodded. "Okay, Andrew. I get it." And I did. I really did. I want to play Frisbee without recruiters judging me, Aleah. You know what I mean?

"Okay?" he said.

"Yes."

"You understand, Felton?" Andrew's face was all twisted up, like he couldn't believe someone as dumb as me could possibly get it.

"Yeah," I smiled. "I'm so glad you had fun playing. It was really fun to be here," I said.

"Okay, Felton." Andrew smiled. "I'm glad you're here. I really am. I'll buy you shoes, okay? I'm…"

"It's fine," I said. "It's okay. Thanks for singing so damn high."

Andrew stepped up to me and hugged me around my middle.

"Reinsteins are the weirdest people on the earth," Gus said. "Baruch Spinoza."

"Dude. I know." Tovi nodded.

Andrew let go of me and said, "You're not an idiot. You have very common problems, Felton."

"I am an idiot," I said. "But it's going to be okay."

Andrew nodded. "Thanks, Felton."

• • •

Wait. Here's a text. Tovi.

August 17th, 3:56 p.m.
PORT CHARLOTTE, PART III

Tovi says that if it's going to be more than an hour, to let her know, because she'll drive up and get me.

I don't know how long it's going to be. The bus driver has been taken to a clinic because he broke out in hives. Allergic reaction! Action, reaction. He probably ate a bad walnut. We're all sitting on the bus, which is running, which seems kind of crazy, because it seems like any freaking yahoo could just go up there and drive it away.

The lady behind me is all, "Lord, no! Bus drivers falling over ill on a day like today…"

I totally agree with her. I will be with Tovi for like ten minutes before we have to go home. Oh well…

• • •

So, the morning after the Golden Rods concert (three of the old dudes in the band are actually named Rod—thus the porny name), I woke up to Andrew quietly digging in my bag, which was at my feet. Gus sawed logs on the foldaway. I could hear Tovi breathing in the bed. I blinked, then mumbled, "What are you doing?"

Andrew whispered, "I'm glad you're awake. Will you come with me?"

"Uh-huh," I said.

A couple of minutes later, we were walking in the opposite direction from the pier down the main road on Fort Myers Beach. (I think it's Estrada Street or Estado or something.) The sun was just coming up, the sky all orange and purple, and the air was super still. We walked, totally quiet, down the side of the road (my flip-flops flapping on that broken shell-sand kind of gravel).

Andrew carried one of my black Under Armour T-shirts, which I'd packed so Jerri would believe I was headed to football camp. I figured he would soon throw it in the ocean.

After passing another couple of resorts, we came to a stretch of sort of shacks, except nicer. I guess one-story beach houses. The third one we came to, Andrew took a left onto the property, toward the beach. I followed him, although going onto private property made me very, very uncomfortable.

"Don't worry," he said. "This is Big Rod's place."

I nodded.

I followed him along the left side of the house. There was almost complete silence, except for the faint sound of the gulf lapping at the beach. Then a small dog with pointy ears came tearing down the sidewalk behind me. It circled Andrew, jumping up and down, wagging its tail.

"Hi, Brian," Andrew said. "This is Brian Wilson, the dog," he told me. Then the dog noticed me and realized I was a stranger and began barking like crazy and growling and hopping up and down. I sort of freaked and ran from him, saying, "Shit. Good dog. Crap!" because I'm sort of afraid of dogs, especially little ones, because they're pretty quick.

I ran around the corner of the house, Brian Wilson on my tail, and right up to Big Rod, the big-assed singer from the Golden Rods. He was drinking a glass of orange juice, standing next to a round, white table with a bowl of bananas on it.

"Well, if it isn't the famous Felton Reinstein," he said. "Brian. Calm, pup."

Brian Wilson sat down on his dog butt and sort of smiled at me.

"Hi," I said. "Great show last night."

"Thank you, sir. Fun times."

Then Andrew came around the corner. "Morning, Big Rod. You mind if Felton comes out with us today?"

"Best news I've heard in a while." Big Rod nodded. "Welcome to my cottage, son."

"Thanks," I said. I had no idea what 'come out' might mean. "What are we doing?" I asked.

"I'm trying to say good-bye," Andrew said.

"To what?" I had a bolt of fear, because in health class we'd learned that one of the signs to look for in kids you think are suicidal is a penchant for dramatic good-byes and for giving their stuff away. Andrew was actually giving *my* stuff away...to the ocean (gulf)...but the behavior seemed kind of similar, right?

"To old ways of being," he said.

"Oh. Okay." Yeah, I didn't know what he meant.

"Let's do this," Big Rod said. "I'll row. There's not much wind to work against today."

A couple minutes later we were shoving a rowboat from Big Rod's house across the beach toward the water. Brian Wilson tailed us, occasionally barking at me as I helped. We pushed the boat into the water, climbed in, and then Big Rod rowed us through these little waves out into the gulf.

The water was fairly still and the sun was low, so that the water reflected a dark, morning-sky blue. As far as I know, I'd never been on a boat (no memory of ships, boats, paddle boats, canoes, etc.). I grasped the side of the rocking thing as hard as I could.

To be honest, it didn't seem that stable and I'm not the best swimmer.

"Dolphins to the right," Big Rod nodded.

Holy crap, Aleah. Not more than fifty feet away, two giant dolphins bobbed up and down in the water, swimming on by. "That's real? Those things are in here?" I said.

"Man, of course. They're about the friendliest buggers around. Lot worse than dolphins out here," Big Rod said.

"Pretty neat, huh?" Andrew said, smiling at me.

Rod rowed on in silence.

After we got out a couple of football fields from the shore, Big Rod said, "Don't have a lot of time. Might as well do it, buddy."

Andrew pulled my Under Armour shirt out of the cargo pocket of his shorts. Looked at me. Shrugged. Then said, "I throw this athletic shirt, my big brother's stinky football shirt, into the great Gulf of Mexico to say once and for all and with complete peace: This shirt is not mine. I am not like Felton. I am not a great athlete. I am just me, Andrew Reinstein. Just some kid. And that's okay. I embrace my fate."

Then Andrew threw my shirt into the water.

"Man," I said.

"I'll get you another one," Andrew said.

"That's not it. I just don't understand, Andrew."

"Spill it, boy," Big Rod said.

"Felton." Andrew shook his head and paused like he didn't want to say what he was going to say. "Nobody really knew you were alive before last year. My classmates mostly didn't know I had a brother...and I liked it because I was just me, you know? I was just Andrew who played piano and was smart and kind of funny and that was very nice, in retrospect."

"You just described yourself, Andrew. That's who you are."

"Yes. But...not anymore, really. Kids in gym class this spring started making fun of me for not being like you."

"What? Who?"

"Some kids, just regular kids in my grade, make crap of me because I'm not fast like you. I trip over my own feet. I can't catch. I throw, and I quote, 'like a girl,'" Andrew said. "They mess with me at lunch...Do you understand?"

"Oh." I nodded. Andrew always seemed immune to other kids. "I'm sorry. I didn't know. You should've told me...I'd...I'd...scare them...scare those kids?"

"No. You wouldn't have done anything," Andrew said.

"I'm so sorry."

"Here's the thing, Felton. This is what Big Rod and I discuss all the time. That stuff shouldn't matter, okay? I don't want to be like you. I don't want to be a jock and I don't want college sports coaches calling me ever and I don't want to worry like you worry about everything, but I've started worrying and I just don't want to waste another second of my life wondering if I'll go through a growth spurt and suddenly be another human being, like you did, so people like me...because I've become some freaky genius that I don't even want to be."

"Uh-huh, uh-huh," I said. I totally understood.

"I'm not like you. I'm not going to suddenly gain more control over my fingers and play like Aleah either. It isn't going to happen, and it's not even what I want."

"Okay," I nodded. My Under Armour bobbed along in the ocean just like the dolphins.

"I want to like doing what I like doing, but everyone wants me to be like you or to talk about you, and meanwhile you won't even show up at my concert..."

"I know. I really know," I said.

"So, I'm trying to let it all go," Andrew said. "Which isn't easy because I also really like you, Felton, because you're my brother."

"I row out here anytime I need the gulf to carry my worries away," Rod said. "This was my idea."

"So I threw away your shirt," Andrew nodded.

"My shoes? Same deal?" I asked.

"Sort of," Andrew nodded. "I worry that you like your jock shoes more than you like me."

"No." I shook my head. "No way."

Andrew's face turned red.

"I don't want to worry about you not liking me or about what people think. I just want to be with my family and to...to be happy..."

"You boys got some trouble," Big Rod said.

"I'll help you, Andrew. I'll be a good brother. I'm just beginning to understand all this…"

"Thanks, Felton."

"It's so complicated, huh?" I said.

"It's not really, but it seems like it," Andrew nodded.

"Say it," Big Rod said. "Be a man and say it."

"I love you, Felton. My happiness is not your responsibility. My happiness is up to me. I love you."

"Uh, I love you too," I said.

"Breakthrough." Big Rod nodded.

When we got back to the beach, Andrew hugged me and I hugged him back. My poop-flinger self wanted to go beat up his classmates. I don't think that's what Big Rod meant by a breakthrough, though.

Andrew thanked me again on our walk back to the hotel.

August 17th, 4:19 p.m.
PORT CHARLOTTE, PART IV

Okay, I got off the bus and am now sitting on my backpack next to this Shell station. (Gift platter is one small wad of sausage—I threw out the box, so nothing's getting hurt from me sitting on it.) Tovi is driving up from Fort Myers to get me. She said it won't take long.

Of course as soon as I got off the bus a new driver showed up and drove off. The lady who was sitting behind me waved. So, now I'm alone at this gas station. I have been in these now chocolate-covered shorts for thirty-six dang hours. Hope Tovi makes it. She has a GPS in the Beemer. And I've got about twenty minutes worth of battery left, Aleah, so I guess I'll tell you the rest of the bad story, huh?

• • •

Bad.

When we got back to the room, Andrew changed into his McEnroe tennis outfit. I showered and put on my big glasses and hat, my disguise. Tovi sat on the bed in her tennis outfit, watching TV and waiting for the rest of us to get ready. And Gus slowly packed his junk in his bag.

"Long damn trip," he said, shaking his head.

When we were all set, we took the elevator down (in silence).

Even though we'd only been together for a few days, it felt like forever and this felt huge, losing Gus. There would be a hole.

Out at the Celica, Gus threw his bag in the passenger seat, then turned around.

"Wish I could stay," he said.

"Thanks for teaching me what a narcissist is, man," I said.

"Thanks for not punching my face when I punched your face," he said.

My black eye had improved, but it was still there. Felt like the punch was so, so long ago.

"I will never punch your face," I said.

Then Andrew said, "Gus, I know you think I'm just a little freaky kid, but will you please keep your parents from telling Jerri where I am?"

Gus lied: "They don't even know you're here, dude. You're safe. They just think me and Felton took a joyride."

"Jerri might ask you, though…" Andrew said.

"Don't worry. It's all under control, muchacho."

"Thanks."

"You got it, Randy Stone, you freaking dork." Before he climbed in, he asked Tovi if she wanted to go with him. She said she did but she wouldn't, and then he blushed really hard and drove off fast.

Tovi said, "That boy has a serious crush on me."

I nodded.

"He comes up to my neck. Is he too short for me?" she asked.

"I don't think height matters."

"Oh. Good," she nodded.

Before we got in the Beemer, I said, "Okay. I'm ready for this. I'm looking forward to this."

"Just be ready for a mood swing, okay?" Tovi said. "Papa was a little weird when I brought him the chicken, and Andrew can tell you, Papa's not always as smiley as he was yesterday."

"He actually told me to get the f-bomb out of his house once the first week," Andrew said.

"And you went back?"

"I feel sorry for him," Andrew said.

"You're braver than me."

"Duh." Andrew smiled.

Tovi was right. When we got to the house, something in Stan's demeanor had changed. When we walked in, he was sitting up front in the living room instead of back in his den (where he generally spends his time, apparently). There was no music playing. He was wearing athletic shoes and a white baseball cap.

"Look who's here," he said. "The Australian returns. Where's the Venezuelan? He decide he has better things to do than sit around in an old man's house?"

"Gus had to go home, Papa," Tovi said.

"Caracas?" Stan said.

"No. Wisconsin," she replied.

Andrew shot her a glance.

"Hmm. The Dairy State?" Stan said. "Looks like Andy is dressed to play. You want to hit some balls, Andy?"

"Yes, sir," Andrew replied.

Then he turned his attention to me. "How about you, Ricky Martin? Did you know you share your name with a homosexual pop singer? I looked you up on my computer. Good-looking boy."

"Uh…"

"You want to hit?"

"No shoes," I said.

"I have some shoes. Follow me." Stan got up and walked toward the stairs.

"He's not going to fit in your shoes, Papa," Tovi said.

"Who said they were my shoes? I said *some* shoes."

I looked at Tovi. She shrugged a little. Maybe more flinched. Stan gestured for me to follow, so I followed him up the stairs. There, at the end of the hall, he dipped into a room and popped back out immediately with a beat-up pair of green-and-white tennis shoes (the same ones I'm wearing right now).

"These are Stan Smiths," he said. "Classic shoes for a classic game. What do you wear, size thirteens?"

"Twelve"

"Perfect. These are twelve and a half. Funny I should have the right size just lying around my house, don't you think?"

"Yes."

"They were my son's, Ricky. He was a remarkable tennis player. So good."

"I don't want to wear them."

"Just wear them. Did Tovi tell you what he did to himself? Don't worry. There are no ghosts. Here. Take them. These shoes are yours."

Stan handed them to me and I took them.

"I'll get you some socks too. And, one of my son's racquets will fit you just right, I'm guessing."

"I can't play. I have a leg problem…"

"I'm not saying you have to play a championship match. Just hit some balls, Ricky. That's all."

I followed Stan down the stairs. Tovi and Andrew hadn't moved. They were standing straight as nails in the living room, both of them pale.

"Let's play!" Stan shouted.

"I'm not feeling it, Papa," Tovi said.

"You think just because your grandmother died I'm going to let you go soft?" he asked.

"I don't know," Tovi said.

"The hell I will," he said.

At the clubhouse, Stan pulled a racquet out of his locker. "It's from the '80s. Not high tech, but a good stick. Big grip for a guy with big hands like yours." He handed me the racquet.

"I'm going to hit with Andy over here. Tovi, you show Ricky how it's done. He might want to lose the hat and glasses, though."

"Okay, Papa," Tovi said.

I was very relieved he didn't want to play with me.

As Stan and Andrew warmed up, I sat at the edge of the court and pulled on the socks and the old Stan Smith shoes that were my father's. Yes, of course they fit me perfectly.

Tovi said, "That's Steve's racquet, man. You don't have to do this. Just fake a hamstring right away. Don't do this, okay?"

"I'm fine," I told her. I wasn't fine, but I didn't want to draw attention to myself for refusing or for being hurt, you know? I didn't want to engage Stan by not playing.

I kept my hat on. I pushed it down hard so it stayed glued to my head. I kept the glasses on. We took to the court.

When I was very small, my dad had given me a racquet and lobbed balls over the net at me. I remember him telling me to concentrate, but I was maybe four and there were clouds in the sky and birds, and I remember the fluff from cottonwood trees blowing around. That was the last time I'd hit a tennis ball. For most of my life, Jerri had told me he was a chubby, gentle guy. I still picture a chubby, gentle dad in that memory. My dad was neither.

And then there was my cousin, who I hadn't known until a few days before, standing across the net from me. She said, "You ready?"

The racquet felt good in my hand. I nodded.

She hit the ball spinning toward me. I stepped to my left and awkwardly doinked it back. Tovi bounced lightly to the ball and hit it back softly. I hit the ball a little harder, and it flew long over her head. "Feels weird," I said.

"Not for long," she told me.

On the other court, Stan hit balls at Andrew. Andrew bounced balls back over the net from where he stood up close, and Grandpa Stan called, "Look the ball into the racquet, McEnroe, feel it in your hands! That's it. Stay square. Backhand!" Andrew didn't look like he was having any fun, like he did early the day before. But I noticed that he was surprisingly quick to get his racquet on the ball. (His stupid classmates should've been there, should've seen him doing it.)

Tovi and I hit back and forth. The motion got less and less strange. The racquet felt like an extension of my arm.

Stan shouted at Andrew. Andrew moved back in the court. Stan ran him back and forth, and Andrew hit.

Tovi picked up speed, hitting balls that whirred as they approached me. I hit some back. Others I hit long or into the fence next to me or over into Stan and Andrew's court. But some, I just hit right, and that ball just spun perfectly off my father's racquet and shot low over the net.

"Yeah, Felton, you're all right," Tovi shouted.

I shook my head no. She'd called me Felton. She froze. I looked over at Stan. He was hitting a ball at Andrew, which Andrew missed. And then Andrew, sweating bullets, said, "Um. Stan, I need some water, okay?"

"Go get it, you wimp."

And then Stan looked at me. "Get over here, Ricky."

I gripped the racquet hard and looked at Tovi. She didn't move. Then I wandered over onto Stan's court. I didn't know what else to do.

"Lost duckling," Grandpa Stan said. "Go stand at that back line," he pointed. "That's called the baseline. Right there. Okay, good. I'll just hit a few at you, see what you got."

I nodded. He hit a ball right to me and I swung half-assed because I was so weak in my body, so gone, and missed it all together.

"No, no, no, Ricky. See the ball off my racquet. Prepare yourself for where it's going."

I nodded.

He hit a ball and I lumbered over to it and hit it back, but it was way long.

"You're faster than that, right? Get to the ball. Get prepared."

He hit again and I sped up. I turned quick and hit a ball just over the net that ended up about a foot wide of the court.

"Better. You get perpendicular to the net next time and that…" and then I remembered. And then I saw him and my dad, clear as everything, my own dad big like me, powerful, running, hitting spinning forehands over the net, right here, right in this place thirteen years ago when I was a wee shit, before everything went to hell, everything broke to pieces.

He hit a ball at me. I turned, crouched, hit it back.

"Better," Stan said.

He hit another at me and I took two big steps because this thing, this game, is in my body and I know it, and smacked the ball the hell back. And I liked it. I liked the ball coming square off the racquet and ripping the air over the net.

"Jesus Christ," Stan said.

He pulled another ball out of his shorts and hit it into the corner of the court. In a broken second I was there, and I rifled it back over the net, the ball buzzing as it spun away.

"Water break?" Tovi shouted. She shook her head, *no*, at me.

"I don't think so," Stan said.

He bent down and picked up another ball. This time he hit far from me, to the far backhand of the court. I turned and leapt and dragged the end of the racquet backhand across the surface, catching the ball before it bounced twice and sailing it with backspin over the net in front of Grandpa Stan who hit it again, hard into the center of the court. I exploded and caught the ball rising up and fired it screaming right past his kneecaps.

Grandpa Stan stopped. He shook his head. "Yes? Do you have something to say?"

"No," I said.

"Nothing?"

He hit another ball at me, and I cracked it back so hard the air around it screamed.

"Are you saying something?" Stan shouted.

"No!" I shouted back.

He hit another ball right at me and I stepped, turned, and fired it back a million miles an hour.

And then Stan stared at me.

I stared back.

He said, "You," quietly.

I couldn't move.

"You!" he said. "You!" he repeated. "Take off that hat. Take off that goddamn hat!"

I didn't.

"I know this. I know this goddamn game. Take off your hat!"

I pulled it off. Then I stood straight with the hat in my left hand, my father's racquet in my right.

"Oh, you. Oh, Tovi," Stan cried. "How could you do this, Tovi? How could you do this to me? You…you ambushed me! You!" He pointed his bony finger at me. "Get out. Get off this court." He turned to Tovi. "Take this dead boy and get out of here!

You little…You did this? Get off of my court. Tovi. Tovi…you did this?"

"Hit me a ball," I said.

"Get off my court, kid!" Stan shouted.

"*Hit me a goddamn ball!*" I screamed.

"Tovi. Take this person away. Take him away!"

My hands shook. My brain screamed. My heart exploded. "You did this. You did this. You killed him. You did this," I started shouting. "And now you want to kill us. You've tried forever to kill…"

"Felton, don't. It's not…It's not true," Andrew shouted.

"You murdered him and now you want to kill us. You want to kill Andrew."

"Tovi. Why?" Stan pleaded. "Why would you do this to your grandfather?"

"You're my grandfather!" I screamed. "You're mine…"

And then Stan crumpled to his knees. He cried, "Get off my court!"

Tovi and Andrew ran to him.

And I was gone. I dropped the racquet and ran through the gate and out toward the car, my Grandma Rose's damn Beemer. No place to go. I climbed into the back and fell to my left. I broke the big, stupid glasses with my hand, then gripped my head and cried for my dad.

Moments later Tovi got to the car.

"Get me out of here, Tovi. Get me out of here. Please. Please," I said.

"Okay. It's okay, Felton. It's okay."

"It's not." I didn't know what was happening, Aleah. I'm still not sure. I don't know what happened to me. But I was sort of convulsing, crying.

Tovi started the car and pulled away from the curb. Andrew got there and said, "Tovi. You have to come back. Stan's really losing his mind. Somebody might arrest him."

"Can you stay?" Tovi asked. "Can you do it?"

"Me?" Andrew asked.

"I have to drive Felton out of here."

"Get in the car, Andrew," I shouted at him. "Get in the fucking car right now. Please!"

"No," Andrew said. "I'm going to stay." He backed away from the car, and that was the last I saw of him.

"Andrew. Goddamn it…" I sobbed as Tovi pulled away.

I was totally inconsolable. Tovi asked me if I wanted to go back to the hotel. I told her no. I wanted to leave. I had to leave. I was so freaking crazy and burning, Aleah.

"What do you mean?" Tovi asked me. "You want to go the airport?"

I said yes. I probably wouldn't have thought of it on my own. But that's where I wanted to go.

Tovi (who was pretty shaken up too—this was bad Reinstein stuff) used Gram's money to buy me a ticket home, a flight that left two hours later, connected through Chicago, and landed me in Madison just after 9 p.m.

This ticket cost over $600. It makes me sick. Gram gave Tovi ten thousand to put us back together, and I used over five percent to run away. Jesus.

Before I left, I called Jerri on Tovi's cell and couldn't say much.

She didn't ask much, just told me Andrew had called her and she knew what was happening and that she'd be at the airport when I got there.

Even before I flew in, she'd talked to Stan too, Aleah. Somehow this whole thing wasn't between Andrew and Stan. He was somehow comforted that Andrew stayed behind with him. It was between Stan and me. Or, really, between Stan and my dad, a dude who was so much like me. My dad, who wore these shoes I'm wearing.

Jerri said she screamed at Stan. Jerri said he took it and didn't scream back.

I don't know.

In the airport, even after we had the ticket, Tovi kept grabbing my hand, saying, "Are you sure you have to go? Are you sure?"

I couldn't really respond. My brain shut down.

From the plane I could see the huge expanse of the gulf stretching across the underbelly of the country. I hadn't flown since I was a kid, since the last time I flew back to Wisconsin from Florida. Then I was with my dad, my poor dad. And only then, only when the plane was off the ground and there was no way I could return, did I feel this huge remorse.

Here's a big part of my curse, Aleah. At important moments I can't think. I can't think ahead. I just react, just fling the poop that's in front of me, fight or flight, which maybe makes me a good football player, but it kills me in real life. It breaks crap and there are consequences for my actions. I left Andrew behind. I left Tovi alone. Poor Gus drove for thirty hours below me.

I couldn't even talk to Jerri when she picked me up, I felt so terrible. I was still the bad brother. I hadn't learned anything. Half my football crap is still at the White Shells Hotel and Resort, which has caused me trouble all summer. My dead cell phone was in my pocket because Gus had hated what I did to him so much that he cut up my charger. We barreled west through the Wisconsin night, fireflies lighting the ditches on Highway 151, the silence only cut by the sound of Jerri sniffling, Jerri crying.

• • •

I don't want to be that guy, Aleah. I don't want to be a narcissist or a dude who just chases balls or flings poop because that's what's in front of him.

I still run, because I have to run, but I don't want to live my whole dang life running. That's what I've decided.

And that decision led me here to this corner of a Shell gas station parking lot—because there is absolutely no way I'd have stayed on the phone with Stan when he called a few weeks ago if I was still that guy.

I don't want to be afraid of my own grandfather (or my dad). I don't want to be afraid of Andrew or you, Aleah. I don't want to be afraid of going to a football camp or on a recruiting trip or to college next year.

And I've had the rest of the summer to think.

When Stan called on my birthday, I said yes. Yes to coming back here, even though there were about a billion reasons not to, including me missing practices right before a game.

• • •

Oh. Hey. I think that's Tovi. Yes. Beemer at the stoplight a block away. Yeah, Andrew's in there. They're rolling…Jesus, Stan's in the backseat. Okay. That's good. Okay. Gotta run, Aleah.

Whoops they missed the station. They'll turn around…

Tovi and Andrew. I have to pull out the last little stump of Hickory Farms summer sausage. That'll make them laugh.

Oh my God, I have never been so happy to see human beings in my whole damn life.

Gotta go.

I miss you.

Bedroom

August 20th, 12:48 a.m.
BLUFFTON, WI

So...I've been back in Wisconsin for a couple of days.
Yup. Here I am again. Basement bedroom. I have welts on both my forearms. My right hand aches because it got stepped on.

Good! That's football!

Hi, Aleah. It was so awesome to see you. It was such a shock, and it put me in such a good mood. I was already in a pretty good mood this afternoon, but you really sent me into...I guess, elation? Elation is a word, right? I was very jacked.

I wasn't the only one who was excited. I knew you were there but hadn't told anybody. When Cody (who thinks you're so awesome—which is true, in fact) saw you in the stands during warm-ups, he said, "Hey! Hey! Dude! Aleah's here! Jesus!"

Cody doesn't get emotional about anything. "I know," I smiled.

"Why didn't you tell me? Man!" he shouted.

He's been worried all summer that we'd break up. He figures we'll be coming over to his house for barbecues in twenty years, so it's very, very important we stay together as far as he's concerned.

"Thought I'd let you have the joy of discovery," I said.

"Cool," he said, getting his shit back under control.

You waved and we both waved back and really we shouldn't be

waving at people during warm-ups (Coach talked to me about that last year), but I waved and you smiled so big and then I just started jumping up and down like I did all the time last year, back when I was an innocent boy.

It was really cool to see you sitting next to Gus and Maddie.

Did you see the Wisconsin coach a couple rows in front of you? He can't talk to me right now because of NCAA recruiting rules. But he was there. Makes me happy. Coaches don't get to Bluffton very often. We're in the middle of nowhere if you haven't noticed.

Hey, do you remember? Exactly fifty-one weeks ago today I played my first football game. You were there. Tonight I started my second season. And you were there, again.

Man, Aleah, thank you. You were so whacked from travel, so jet lagged, we barely had time to talk after the game before you passed out. Weird that you're up there in Andrew's room. If Ronald and Jerri weren't upstairs too, I'd lie down next to you. Of course I wouldn't be able to sleep and I'd annoy the crap out of you.

So, I've read some of this notebook you gave me. Berlin sounds dang cool. I do understand why you wanted a break. I really appreciate all the thinking you've done too. You're very, very smart. Have I told you that?

I want to finish mine by tomorrow so I can surprise you with a bunch of pages. (Let's be honest, an absolute crap ton of pages—I probably should just email this to you…not enough paper in the house.) Funny to think you were writing to me while I was writing to you. Of course, you wrote during your whole summer in Germany.

I wrote all of this in just a few days, and honestly, I didn't think I'd ever actually give it to you. I want you to know, though, that even when I was lifting weights, running routes, flinging around my Frisbee in the yard, hanging with Gus and Cody and those guys, I was thinking about you, constantly.

Thank you for writing to me.

The house does feel pretty empty without Andrew. Yeah, you're right. It *is* pretty weird.

Pretty funny that you asked me, "What in the world happened while I was gone?" I've got it for you. I wrote it all out.

How did this happen with Andrew being gone? Keep reading.

• • •

You know, Tovi and I talked just about every day after I left Florida that first time, after what we've come to call "The Great Reinstein Tennis Court Disaster." (Stan freaking at me on the court.)

At first, she just wanted to make sure I was okay. I was, I guess.

More than anything, I felt really embarrassed for having run away like I did. Think I could stand up, right? After all that I'd been through, after going out on the boat with Andrew?

Be strong. Don't freak out. Stay there like Andrew stayed.

Wrong. Squirrel Nut Felton took control. The bad squirrel nut, the one who runs when he should stay and be strong.

I freaked and ran at the first sign of danger. (I mean, my fight with Stan was pretty intense—Jerri, Tovi, and Andrew have all told me to stop beating myself up about it—and I have stopped.)

For the last few weeks, I guess Tovi's been trying to break some different news to me. "Papa and Andrew are so good with each other. Andrew didn't leave his side for a week after you took off, man," she told me.

"Great," I said. "That's really good." I didn't understand what she was getting at. Nothing occurred to me.

Maybe I should've gotten the clue when I finally took that call from Stan.

It was my birthday, a few weeks ago. Tovi said she wouldn't speak to me ever again if I didn't talk to Stan. She's still doing Grandma Rose's work. Trying to make the family all right. Tovi actually didn't have to threaten me. I wanted to talk to him (even though it was scary).

Jerri and your dad had already taken me for lunch and a movie in Dubuque. I'd already told Cody, Karpinski, and those guys that I'd be hanging with Gus that night. Gus and I planned to watch movies at his house and eat a whole store-bought cake, just like we used to do on movie nights back when we were in eighth grade. Stan hadn't called yet, and I was beginning to think he'd chickened out (which bummed me out).

But as I was biking over to Gus's, my phone rang. I pulled over and pulled the vibrating phone out of my pocket.

It was a 239 area code. That's Fort Myers. I almost fell off my bike with nerves.

I answered, "Hello?"

"Felton?" the old man's voice said.

"Yes?" I waited. He didn't speak right away. I held on—this was a big deal because my squirrel-nut, bolt-up-a-tree sensors were firing pretty hard. "Yes, this is Felton."

"Felton?"

"Yes. I'm here."

"This is your grandfather. This is Stanley."

"Okay," I said. I'm sure my voice was shaking.

"Are you having a good birthday?" he asked, as if we'd always talked and this wasn't the actual first conversation (other than him screaming at me to get the hell off his court) we'd ever had.

"Yes," I said.

"Good…Good. That's good to hear."

"Thanks," I said.

"Your brother has really made great strides on the tennis court. Quite impressive. You should really see him play, Felton."

"Okay. Um. I'll…I'll watch for that…"

"Felton?"

"Yes?"

"I bought you a ticket to come back here. I want you to see Andrew play tennis. And I'd like to take you out to dinner for your birthday."

Football was about to start, Aleah. A ticket? What was he thinking? Just like that? I was totally unprepared for the invitation. "I don't think I can," I said. "Not right now."

"I'm sorry?" he said.

"I'm not available at the moment. Thanks for asking."

"It would mean a lot to Tovi. Andrew would like to see you. It would be very nice."

"No," I said. "I really can't."

"Felton?"

"Yes?"

"Damn it," he mumbled. "Felton?"

"What?"

"Do you know what I did?"

"No?"

"When I yelled at you? On the court?"

"No."

"I wasn't yelling at you, Felton. I knew it was you and not your father, but I wasn't yelling at you. Do you understand?"

"No."

Stan's voice began to warble, which made me lose my balance, so I had to step off my bike and sit down on the curb. "Your father, Felton. Your father killed himself."

"I know."

"Your father hurt me and your grandmother very much. I would suggest, Felton, that I won't ever recover from…I won't ever be okay again, do you see?"

"Yes," I said.

"And he was, Felton, a good, big, wonderful guy just like you. I don't know…" Stan was gulping for air. "I don't know, but he was so far away in that little town where you live?"

"Yeah."

"With your mom who was just a kid. She was a little girl. What was he doing?"

"I don't know."

"I couldn't help him. He wouldn't let me. And I am so angry at him, Felton. I am so angry, but I've got to stop because the costs of this anger are enormous. Do you know what I did to your grandmother?"

"No."

"I made it so she'd never meet Andrew, so she'd never spend time with you, because I was so angry. Tovi should have her cousins, you know?"

"Yes."

"I wasn't yelling at you on the court, Felton. I was yelling at your father because what he did...it's been too much for a small man like me to bear and I've broken everything. Do you understand?"

"Yes."

"Will you please come down here and see Andrew play and have some dinner for your birthday?"

"Oh shit. Oh shit. Oh shit," I cried.

"It's not just for...I would like to see you, Felton. I would like us to be good friends."

"I don't know..."

"Andrew is such a good, good boy. We're friends, Felton. He's my grandson. I have a grandson. But I don't know when I might see you again. We don't know. We need...I would like so much to be your grandfather. Please come."

I lay back in the grass, Aleah. All these birds were flying overhead like stingrays below Tovi and me in the gulf. I shut my eyes. I thought of Gus and what he did for me. I thought of Tovi taking off a whole summer of tennis to do Gram's work. I thought of Andrew and how I want to be the brother he deserves. And so I said, "Okay. Okay. I will."

Happy birthday. He got the damn ticket for the week of my first game. Jerri had to change the return date so I at least had a day back in Bluffton before playing. Then it took two and a half days to get there? Happy birthday, Felton.

It's okay. I'm glad I made the stupid trip, you know? It wasn't stupid at all, really.

The big casualty of me being so late to get to Fort Myers was that there wasn't time to play tennis. When they picked me up at the Shell gas station, Andrew was in his Golden Rods Hawaiian shirt.

"We've got to get to your birthday dinner, so I can't show you my tennis game," Andrew said.

"We can play back in Bluffton," I said.

Stan jumped in: "The boy is good! He's gotten good at the net. Such a technician!"

"Uh, yeah. Pretty good," Tovi said.

"I'm nothing special," Andrew said.

"Baloney, kid. You set up points like a chess player now," Stan said.

"No. I just like to play. I'm nothing special," Andrew said more pointedly.

"Say what you will," Stan said.

Instead of driving to Fiddlesticks or back to the White Shells, Tovi drove the Beemer out to Sanibel Island and then to Captiva. For my birthday dinner, they took me to a restaurant right on the beach called the Mucky Duck. The bad part of this was that I hadn't showered in days and I had chocolate melted all over my shorts, so I didn't exactly feel comfortable walking into a restaurant.

Nobody seemed to give a crap, and even though the food seemed ridiculously expensive (I guess I got used to restaurants being super cheap from my truck-stop stops on the way down to Florida with Gus), almost everybody in the place was in shorts and T-shirts and sandals.

I ordered a filet mignon. It was quite tasty. I have never eaten such a fancy-pants steak. Andrew, Stan, and Tovi all got seafood, which smells like boiled nut cup. I guess I'm not exactly an ocean dude, yet. It sort of grossed me out, especially Stan's lobster tail—very graphic crushing of shell…gross.

During the meal, Stan, Tovi, and Andrew laughed and talked and told me about all the crap they'd been doing all summer, and it sort of hurt my feelings, but I totally tried not to show it. Then, after we ordered dessert (Have you ever eaten chocolate mousse? Damn!), Stan pulled a gift out of the canvas bag he'd carried in.

He handed it to me. "For your birthday."

I could tell it was a framed picture from the feel of it. Scared me a little. I immediately thought about the shot of Dad when he won the NCAA Championship—you know, the sad one? I peeled it open, feeling sort of nervous. Attached to the back of the frame was a check for a thousand dollars.

"*What the hell?*" I shouted.

"So you can visit that girlfriend of yours in Chicago," Stan said. "Take her out."

"Yeah, well, I don't know if she's interested in…"

"Have fun with it, okay?" Stan said.

I nodded.

So, I'm going to visit you and take you out for some fun, Aleah. You better figure out what you think is fun, though, because I don't really know how to spend that kind of money on fun. Maybe I'll spend it on groceries with Jerri. I eat so dang much I sometimes worry I'll drive her into total freaking poverty.

No, we can have fun, okay?

I paused before I turned over the photo. It seemed impossible that Tovi would let Stan give me that NCAA picture after it had bummed me out so much. Thankfully, it wasn't that shot. It was the picture of Dad in high school with a whole wad of friends.

"Your father loved every last kid on that team. Oh, they were good. The boy right next to him, Matthew Sedgewick? He's a doctor at the Mayo Clinic! Good kid."

"He could be a fellow working at Qwik Trip and he'd still be a good kid," Andrew said.

"He's also like forty-five now, so he's not really a kid," Tovi said.

"Good boy. Just like your dad." Stan nodded.

It's really a good picture too. I'm looking at it right now. Dad's hair is pretty long and Jewfroed out huge. He looks really, really happy. He's laughing in it, like somebody just made a great joke. I think I might let my 'fro fly, Aleah. What would you think about that? Can you picture me with big-ass hair? I'm serious!

Yeah, I love the picture. I'll show it to you tomorrow.

As soon as we finished dessert, people in the restaurant started flowing out to the beach. Apparently sunset is a huge deal at the Mucky Duck.

The four of us walked out there and parked it on the edge of a sandbank overlooking the gulf. The color in the sky, all blue and orange and purple and pink, really was beautiful. All the color just sort of melted into the ocean. (The water and sky were like one thing.) The sun seemed to hang just inches over the horizon for minutes.

While we waited, while people on the beach started clapping for the sun, cheering for it to go down, Andrew leaned over to me and said, "I'm going to stay here, Felton."

He caught me so off guard, Aleah, that I flinched like the squirrel I am.

"You're what?" I almost shouted.

"I want to stay in Fort Myers. This is where I'm supposed to be."

"Jesus Christ, Andrew. No!" I said. "You can't. Jerri will…"

"I've talked to Jerri a lot about this," he said.

"You have?"

"Yes."

"She's okay? She's hasn't said a word to me about…"

"I asked her not to. I wanted to…I wanted to be the one who told…Yes. She's okay. She's very happy, now. Much better than ever, don't you think?"

I nodded. She and Ronald are really together now, aren't they, Aleah? They're making their own plans.

I shook my head to try to get what he was saying into my brain. People around us stood up and clapped for the sun as its bottom edge dipped.

My next inclination was to say, *What about me?* I wanted to say, *I don't want to sit in the quiet house without you.*

No, Aleah. I couldn't say that.

Andrew had pulled off his glasses. He stared hard at me, sort of chewing so his jaw muscles popped in and out. I did worry, though. I worried he was running, which is what I do.

"You're not trying to get away from me?" I asked quietly. "Or from kids in your class who want you to be me?"

"No. I've thought about that. I'm not running away," Andrew said.

"Why, then? Why would you…"

"I enjoy the band very much. I like playing tennis with Stan, you know? And you're okay and Jerri's okay, but I'm not that okay. I don't think so. I'm sad a lot. I really don't think…I really think that Dad has messed me up. But I'm better here. And Stan and I have a lot in common and Tovi's leaving for school, and I know Stan's afraid of being alone, and he knows so much about music. There's a private high school nearby with a philosophy department and a chamber orchestra and Stan's our dad's dad, Felton. He's our grandpa. I think he can help me."

"And you can help him."

"Yes. That's true, I think."

The sun slid down. The colors changed. I nodded. "Jesus, Andrew, I'm going to miss you so much. You're such a good kid. You're so damn awesome."

"No, I'm not. Not at all," Andrew said.

And then the sun slid behind the earth. A flash of green light shot up into the sky. People cheered and danced, and a couple beat on drums and everybody clapped for the sun doing what it's supposed to do. Andrew and I stood up too. Tovi stood next to me.

She leaned into me and said, "I love you, man. You're pretty awesome."

"Nah," I said. "I'm nothing special." And I mean it. I'm just me, Aleah. Just a fast and jumpy dude. But you know I'm trying.

We all stayed at the White Shells that night. (Stan got his own room; we stayed in Andrew's, even though he'd only stayed there on Golden Rods gig nights since I left.) Tovi and Andrew wanted to walk out to the pier, but I was so wiped from the crazy days of travel that I showered, then fell asleep. I guess I had Greyhound bus lag.

In the morning, Tovi and I went into the gulf. Stingray season in Fort Myers lasts through October, but I wasn't afraid. I know how to deal. You just move slow, shuffle your feet when you walk in. The stingrays scatter then. We didn't say too much. Tovi goes back to Atlanta on Monday. I think she's kind of tired. I think she's ready to go home. I'm not sure I'd leave Fort Myers if I had a choice. I have responsibilities, though. I take them seriously.

Man, though, that water is really, really awesome. We floated around.

By the time we got back to the hotel, it was already time to get me to the airport.

Tovi drove the Beemer. Stan rode in the passenger seat. Andrew and I rode in back. Stan kept telling Tovi where to turn, and Tovi kept saying, "I know, Papa. I know. Stop. I know."

"Oh, you know everything, is that right?" Stan asked.

In the back, Andrew said, "Felton. There's something... Something else I wanted to say."

"Oh...Okay?" Made me nervous.

"When you first got to Florida, I was very mean and I changed rooms and threw your shoes in the ocean, you know?"

"Yes."

"That was bad behavior. Very reactionary and…I'm really sorry, okay? I didn't give you credit for your humanity."

"I was a narcissist. That's not human."

"No. You're pretty nice. You've always been basically nice, you know? Just sort of…"

"Squirrely?"

"Frantic. But you seem much calmer now."

"Yeah. I'm learning to think. I'm trying to be under control. I'm trying not to be such an idiot."

Then Stan turned around in his seat. He stared at me for a second, stared through his own plastic nerd glasses (old-man glasses that slid down his nose). "Tovi, pull over this car," he said.

"What?"

"Pull over the car, please."

"Okay?" Tovi pulled over on the side of the big road, next to a sign that seemed to indicate cougars or cheetahs or some other kind of large cat crossed the road there.

"Felton, get out of the car, please," Stan said.

"What?" I thought he was throwing me out. "I don't want to."

Stan opened his door. "Please. I need to talk to you." He climbed out.

I looked at Tovi in the rearview mirror. She shrugged. I looked at Andrew. He said, "Stan is weird." Then I climbed out.

Stan said, "Let's walk a moment."

"Here?"

"Yes."

He reached up and put his arm around my shoulder and pulled

me forward. We only walked ten steps before he stopped. The hot sun beat down on my head.

Stan turned and squinted at me. He said, "Your father had what would be called clinical depression. Real depression. That's a mental illness, you know?"

The air left my lungs. I nodded.

"He wouldn't treat it. He didn't believe that it existed. I didn't either, not until it was too late."

"Oh," I breathed.

"The first time I realized something was changing in him—now I know for the worse—he started calling himself an idiot. He would win a tennis match his senior year and come home and describe all of the things he'd done wrong. 'Idiot move,' he'd say. 'Stupid. Wasn't thinking.' And he took no pleasure in playing. All he did was remember how he'd failed. And because I wanted him to be the best, I took this to be a positive change. I encouraged him to be self-critical."

"Oh no," I said.

"Many things happened." Stan nodded. "Many things went wrong with your father and with me too. These things I can only begin to understand and forgive, especially my part in this…"

"Uh-huh." I was shaking, Aleah.

"But I am telling you something right now. I'm telling you right now. Are you listening?"

"Yes."

"I want you to love being on that field. Just love it, Felton. Play that game like it's the greatest thing you could be doing, okay?"

"Okay."

"Because it is, right? To play as well as you do is such a wonderful privilege. To be a great player is such a gift. Love that gift. Love that gift, Felton. You try hard and you love your gift. Can you do that?"

"I don't know."

"Remember. Think about it. Think how good it is to be able to run."

"Yes."

"I'll come see a game this fall. And when I do, I want to see you in love out there. Winning, losing, making mistakes. None of it matters. Be in love. Do you understand what I mean?"

And then I thought about how I'd wanted to make out with that Nashville ponytail girl who played Ultimate Frisbee (the one who was so fast and could chase down the Frisbee anywhere on that field) and how I really didn't want to make out with her at all, I just felt so damn happy being able to play and run that I felt love, Aleah. Really. So I said, "Okay, Stan. Okay. I know. I can do that."

Jesus, Aleah. I've never seen an old man smile so hard. He got big old-man tears in his eyes. He said, "That's good, kid. That'll help you. That's how Andrew tells me to play tennis."

We were both sort of bawling when we got back in the car.

"More Reinstein crazy," Tovi said.

Andrew just put his head on my shoulder.

Then I blinked (that's what it felt like) and I was on a plane high above the Gulf of Mexico, looking down at that big blue and the Dangling Sack dangling into it. And I thought: *This is good. Andrew's right. Andrew's right.* The only thing similar between this trip and the last? I wore my dad's Stan Smith tennis shoes. Otherwise, it was all different. I felt no regret. I didn't feel fear. I felt excited for Andrew.

Everything is different, Aleah.

And there were no delays! No cancellations!

Less than twenty-four hours after Tovi picked me up at that Shell gas station in Port Charlotte, I was back in Madison, standing outside the airport, getting picked up by Jerri.

The first thing Jerri said when we got in the car was, "Pretty strange, huh?"

We drove around Madison's east side to catch 151 home.

"I'm so sorry, Jerri," I said. I didn't know what Jerri thought about all of this, but I wanted to be nice to her.

"Why?" Jerri asked. "Andrew's on his adventure."

"Really. That's what you think?" I asked.

"He was made to do this. That's what I think."

"Yeah?"

"He's been trying to put things back together for years."

"Yeah," I said.

"Fourteen years old." She shook her head. "How did a weirdo like me make a kid like that?"

"You're okay, Jerri."

"I'm not exactly a traditional mom," Jerri said.

That made me laugh for some reason.

"What?" Jerri asked.

"I don't know," I said.

We drove the rest of the way to Bluffton talking about nothing much, the windows down, that awesome Wisconsin August air blowing in the Hyundai.

Oh my God, I have never been so happy to be at football practice as I was on Thursday afternoon. All the weird thought—all the worry I had about the future and recruiters and who I'm supposed to be—was gone. I ran. And the whole team just clicked. All I wanted to do was run with my friends. That's all my friends want from me, really. Nothing else matters.

This is what I'm beginning to figure out: if you act out of love (for the game, for friends, for your family), whatever you do is both perfect and right. It doesn't matter if you're a deep thinker or a squirrel nut if you act out of love. Crap starts getting seriously screwed if something else gets in the way, something like fear or revenge or even victory or being famous or some other dumb thing, I think. I think it's true. The only thing we need to do is figure out what we really love.

"Good trip, huh?" Coach Johnson asked after practice.

"Yeah. Yeah," was all I could say.

This afternoon, when you leapt out of Ronald's car on the driveway and ran up to me and hugged me and cried, I knew I loved you. When Tovi texted me when I was getting up to the high school to dress for the game, to tell me she was dying to be here and couldn't wait to hear what happened…I knew love. When Roy Ngelale came out on the field, those Bluffton stadium lights firing the green field, and said, "You're getting nothing tonight, nothing, man," I felt huge love for him because I knew something. I knew it. He's great. I'm great. I am a football player.

It was my third touchdown, a trap play I just totally dig, that made it clear.

We were on our own twenty-six-yard line. Kirk Johnson went into motion. Lakeside's linebackers called, "Watch end around, watch end around!" Cody took the snap and faked to Kirk as he passed by. Then he put the ball in my hands. Reese pulled from left tackle and crossed in front of me. Our center and right guard blocked down. I slowed to let the collision take place. Big-ass Reese cracked the crap out of the d-tackle, and I smiled and exploded. In a broken second I was past the linebackers, who flowed with the fake.

In a second it was only Lakeside's safety, Roy Ngelale, and me. He broke down to hit me. I dipped right then squirrel nut jumped to the left. He totally missed and had to turn to run with me. And we were off. The two fastest guys in the state. Oh, no…oh, no… There was nothing slow. I could hear the crowd screaming, roaring, sort of exploding…so good. And there was a great, buzzing fast forward. The green field dropped out. The stands turned to a rush of gray. I think I made Daffy Duck sounds. Ngelale roared, trying to catch me. I angled toward the sideline, then flew up the field. Ngelale's footsteps faded away behind me.

In the end zone, Roy grabbed me. He said, "You're too good, man. You're too good. This is your game."

I hugged him back. I said, "I love you, man. This is awesome. We're okay at this, huh, man?"

He'd already scored two long runs of his own. Ngelale laughed. "Yeah, man. Yeah. Let's play for the same team next year."

And we trotted back up the field to where my teammates jumped me.

After the game, in the good-game line, Ngelale just said, "Go Badgers."

I don't know. What about Gators? We'll see…

I'm not going to worry about college now. Right now I'm thinking of my little brother, Andrew. Tonight, right out there on the beach, he sang *Barbara Ann* like a beautiful canary while the old ladies screamed. Stan, my dad's dad, was there. Tovi, my cousin, cheered with the ladies.

I play football. Andrew sings songs.

Tovi plays tennis. Stan wants us all to be in love.

I think we'll do it. I think we can.

It's nothing special, Aleah.

It's just what we do.

We're just Reinsteins. That's all.

Welcome home.

I love you,

Felton

Acknowledgments

First, let me thank my agent, Jim McCarthy, for his help over what feels like decades. I would have no books without him. Second, Leah Hultenschmidt, my editor at Sourcebooks, is awesome. She is so smart and sweet and still capable of rattling my cage when I get stuck. Perfect! Thank you, Leah. Really, thanks to everybody at Sourcebooks. I love you all. Third, thanks, Sam Osterhout, for constant inspiration. Fourth, thanks to my pals at Minnesota State, Mankato, for providing the perfect climate. Fifth, thanks to my mom, Donna Herbach, for many (many!) decades of support. Sixth, thank you, Stephanie Wilbur Ash, the love of my life, for so much it makes me dizzy. Finally, thanks to teachers, librarians, and parents who care enough about the world that they get books into teens' hands. We all owe you so much.

About the Author

Geoff Herbach loves writing these books. He teaches creative writing at Minnesota State University, Mankato. He lives among excellent kids: Leo, Mira, Christian, and Charlie. He is married to the tall and otherwise fantastic Stephanie Wilbur Ash. Together they inhabit a log cabin on the side of a bluff.